PRAISE FOR DAVIS BUNN

"[A] page-turner reminiscent of *The Devil Wears Prada*, this novel is sure to please fans and increase Bunn's readership."
—*Publishers Weekly* (about *My Soul to Keep*)

"*My Soul to Keep* is a story of struggle, intrigue, and faith-in-action that will delight the author's fans and capture new ones. Bunn effectively weaves an insider's knowledge of the film business as the backdrop for this inspirational, suspenseful thriller. . . . The result is mesmerizing."
—*Christian Retailing*

"*My Soul to Keep* is an intriguing story. . . . Once again Davis Bunn demonstrates his keen ability to develop character portraits and breathe life into their experience in a way that touches the life of the reader."
—David H. McKinley, Teaching Pastor,
Prestonwood Baptist Church

". . . authentic, touching, and entertaining. *My Soul to Keep* opens up the world of filmmaking in a fascinating and believable way. . . . Characters came to life for me. . . ."
—Michele Winters, Reviewer

"The prolific inspirational novelist Bunn *(The Lazarus Trap)* is an able wordsmith, whether penning a historical romance series (HEIRS OF ACADIA) or a sweet seasonal novella *(Tidings of Comfort & Joy)*. But he's at his best in this absorbing faith-based suspense thriller. . . ."
—*Publishers Weekly* (about *The Imposter*)

All Through the Night

DAVIS BUNN

BETHANY HOUSE PUBLISHERS

Minneapolis, Minnesota

All Through the Night
Copyright © 2008
Davis Bunn

Cover design by Paul Higdon
Cover photography by Mike Kemp/Getty Images, and William Graf Illustration

Published by Bethany House Publishers
11400 Hampshire Avenue South
Bloomington, Minnesota 55438

Bethany House Publishers is a division of
Baker Publishing Group, Grand Rapids, Michigan.

Printed in the United States of America

Library of Congress Cataloging-in-Publication Data

Bunn, T. Davis, 1952–
    All through the night / Davis Bunn.
        p. cm.
    ISBN 978-0-7642-0541-5 (alk. paper) — ISBN 978-0-7642-0542-2 (pbk. : alk. paper)
1. Swindlers and swindling—Fiction. 2. Angels—Fiction. I. Title.

    PS3552.U4718A79   2008
    813'.54—dc22

                                                                            2008014107

DAVIS BUNN has been a professional novelist for twenty years. His books have sold in excess of six million copies in sixteen languages, appearing on numerous national bestseller lists.

Davis is known for the diversity of his writing talent, from gentle gift books like *The Quilt* to high-powered thrillers like *The Great Divide*. He has also enjoyed great success in his collaboration with Janette Oke, with whom he has coauthored a series of groundbreaking historical novels.

In developing his work, Davis draws on a rich background of international experience. Raised in North Carolina, he completed his undergraduate studies at Wake Forest University. He then traveled to London to earn a master's degree in international economics and finance, before embarking on a distinguished business career that took him to more than thirty countries in Europe, Africa, and the Middle East.

Davis has received numerous accolades, including three Christy Awards for excellence in fiction. He currently serves as writer-in-residence at Regent's Park College, Oxford University, and is a sought-after lecturer on the craft of writing.

All Through the Night

Weird as the job interview was, Wayne knew it was a whole lot better than he probably deserved.

Given the way he had shot holes in life itself, what Wayne should have been facing was a room lined with bars and razor wire. Three stone-faced officers should have been staring him down in a concrete room painted penitentiary green, with the sort of lighting that sucked out all hope and turned everybody into cadavers. Ordered to stand front and center and explain precisely why the officials shouldn't deny him parole and keep him locked away from the world for another six hundred years.

That was what he deserved.

What he got was a hard-back wooden chair before a large conference table. Two women and a man sat behind the table and studied him. The long room had three tall windows that looked out over an emerald paradise. He deserved a firing squad, and he got heaven. Which, until that very moment, he had never believed in. That would have been good for a smile, if he could only remember how.

The woman in the middle chair said, "Have a seat, Mr. Grusza."

Another guy was seated in the shadows at the room's far back corner. He was like guys Wayne had known in a different life. The kind of guy who always positioned himself where he could observe yet remain unseen. It was a sniper's sort of act. Only this guy was built more like an aged boxer. Wayne put him down as a detective. A thirty-year man with the patience of a somnolent bear.

Besides this man and the three people at the table, there were seven others in the room. Two young women, two elderly women, and three men over seventy. The room was large enough to swallow them all.

The woman in the center chair went on. "My name is Holly Reeves. I am president of the Hattie Blount Community. My fellow board members are Foster Oates and Victoria Ellis. Did I say your name correctly, 'Grusza'?"

One of the younger women, who was leaning against the wall by the window, corrected her. "It's pronounced 'Grusha.' "

Wayne fingered the knot in his tie. He had not worn either a tie or a shirt with a top button for nearly two years. He could feel the fabric rub against his skin when he swallowed. He also felt the puff of air-conditioning against his cheeks. He had shaved off his beard the night before at the request of the woman leaning against the wall.

The woman wearing a dark suit and pastor's collar.

The reason he was here at all.

"Mr. Grusza, your resume is incomplete." Holly Reeves revealed unsteady nerves as she lifted the single page. "Where it asks for your qualifications, all you state is that you obtained a degree in accounting from night school and then qualified as a CPA."

"That's right."

"But Mr. Grusza, you are—" she adjusted her glasses and calculated swiftly—"thirty?"

"Thirty-one."

"You have left the space for previous employment blank."

"Yes."

"Could you give us a bit more detail about your background and qualifications?"

"No."

Foster Oates, the lone guy at the table, was shrunk down to a pale prune. The man's collar was so large, he could scoot his head down on his scrawny neck, slip through the buttoned collar, and disappear like a tortoise in blue-striped camouflage.

Foster said, "You're expecting us to hire you based on an incomplete resume?"

Wayne gave the woman by the wall the kind of look that said, *Are we done yet?*

The female pastor aimed her gaze at the floor and gave a tiny headshake. As in, *The things I have to go through.*

She said, "Wayne Grusza is absolutely trustworthy."

Foster Oates said, "And you know this how?"

"Because," the woman pastor said, "he's my brother."

The woman seated closest to Wayne's sister most definitely did not belong in an old folks' community. It was not merely that the young lady was attractive. Which she was. Stunningly so. She held herself with a regal poise, and inspected Wayne with an intensity that threatened to peel back his armor. Why Wayne held such interest for a woman like that, he had no idea.

Foster said to Wayne's sister, "I've seen you around. What's your name?"

"Eilene Belote," the community president supplied. "If you'd ever come to one of our evening services, you wouldn't need to ask her name."

"Thank you for that update on the health of my soul." Foster kept his gaze on the woman pastor. "So what can you tell me about your brother?"

"He's made some wrong turns. But for what you want, you could not ask for a better man."

"Is that so."

"Yes," Eilene said. "It is."

The old woman seated at the conference table spoke for the first time. "That's good enough for me."

Holly Reeves asked, "Are you sure?"

"I trust Eilene and Eilene trusts him." She must have been pushing eighty, but even so Victoria Ellis had the rare ability to turn every word she spoke into music. "What more do you want?"

"A lot," Foster replied.

"That's because it's your nature to doubt."

The old guy smiled. "You say the sweetest things."

Victoria responded without taking her gaze off Wayne. The old woman had eyes the color of a desert sky and just as clear. "He's got my vote. I think we should hire him. Now. Today."

The way she shut her mouth left Wayne fairly certain she

would not speak again. Which he was a little sorry about. He liked her voice.

Foster said, "Well, I need more to decide."

Eilene shifted from her place against the wall. She said to those at the table, "You watched him enter the room. He marched straight in, sat down in that chair, and he hasn't turned around or looked back once."

Foster demanded, "This is going somewhere?"

"Wayne. Tell me about the man seated in the back corner."

He wasn't going to do it. Except she gave him that dark-eyed look from their childhood. The one that was half defiance and half plea. *Do this. One thing. For me.*

So he said, "Six one. African American. Two hundred thirty. Light on his feet. Seated at a slight angle because he's used to carrying."

Holly Reeves asked, "Carrying?"

Eilene answered for him. "He means Jerry is used to being armed. His holster would make him angle himself in his seat. Go on, Wayne."

"Pleated khakis, navy sports coat, yellow oxford shirt, frayed collar. . ."

"Shoe size?"

"Twelve and a half, maybe thirteen. Scar beneath his left eye. Nose broken at least twice."

The room was very quiet. Eilene gave him a tiny nod. Her way of saying thanks. "Wayne is the most observant man I have ever met. Which, it seems to me, is part of what you need."

The guy at the back of the room asked, "Have you ever done time?"

Holly Reeves started to say something, then subsided. So Wayne answered, "Never even been arrested." Which, given everything he had been through, was fairly remarkable.

"The reason I asked," the guy went on, "we were robbed."

"Jerry. Please."

Jerry had a voice to match his boxer's frame. Low and rough. "Just telling the man like it is."

Holly Reeves shook her head. "The police did not come to that conclusion. Besides, you're not even a member of the board."

"Don't need titles or letters after my name to have good sense. You want the man to help us, you got to tell him the problem."

"The board will decide what to say and when to say it."

"Oh. Wait. We're talking about the board that went and got us in this mess?"

Foster Oates rose from the table in stiff stages. He walked back and gripped the larger man's arm and tugged. "Let's go, Jerry."

"What, you're operating a gag order now?"

"You're all done here."

Jerry was large enough to have flicked the board member across the room. But he allowed the scrawny man to pull him toward the exit. "Might as well bring my gun next time. Give you folks a real reason for kicking me outta this cuckoo's nest."

The community president said, "We haven't reached a decision, Foster."

"With what we can afford, I doubt we'll do any better," Foster said. "You folks have to excuse my friend. He missed his morning meds."

The door closed on the bigger man saying, "Huh. Only meds I take are the vitamins I believe I'm gonna stick in your ear."

Holly Reeves sighed in the manner of having a lot of practice. "Mr. Grusza, given your reticence over certain elements in your past, the most we could offer you is a six-month trial arrangement."

The prospect of employment almost propelled him out the rear doors. The only thing that kept Wayne trapped in his chair was the strength of his sister's gaze.

"What Jerry Barnes said is unfortunately true. We have been robbed. The authorities are unable to help us. As a result, we are currently operating on a knife's edge." Saying the words pinched up the woman's features tight as pain. "We will not be able to pay you much at all. But the community can offer you a home on the property."

When Wayne remained silent, Eilene spoke for him. "If my brother helps recover your money, would he receive a commission?"

Holly Reeves stared down at the table and said tonelessly, "Naturally."

His sister's gaze was strong enough to squeeze the words from Wayne's throat. "Thank you. I accept."

Wayne had still not really decided about the job. He'd shaken hands with Holly Reeves. But so far it had all been for his sister. He was hooked but not landed. The ink wasn't on the page.

His sister hugged him in the community center's front foyer and left the building without him. Probably afraid he might feel the sunshine and bolt. He was standing in the doorway, staring at the front lawn and the palm trees and the sunlight, when the big former cop named Jerry stepped up behind him and said, "What were you, Special Forces?"

Wayne's attention remained clamped in a sunlit vise by the stranger walking out beside Eilene. The young woman who had sat near his sister during the interview.

Apparently Jerry was not troubled by Wayne's lack of response. He also shared Wayne's interest in the stranger. Jerry said, "I noticed your sister didn't ask you to describe the lady there."

From Wayne's other side, scrawny Foster Oates said, "A

corpse laid out in the refrigeration room would have noticed that one. What is that car she's heading for?"

"A Ferrari," Jerry said. "But it ain't no car. That's a bomb you strap on and ignite."

Foster stuck out his hand. "Guess you could call us your welcoming committee."

Wayne noted the interesting combination of callouses and strength, as though Foster's hand belonged to the man who had existed thirty years ago. A guy who liked doing guy things. "Thanks."

The community center building had a broad overhang where cars could pull in and drop off passengers. The Ferrari was a red missile parked in the first row of spaces beyond the overhang, two spaces over from Wayne's truck. The woman opened the driver's door, then glanced back toward the entrance.

Foster said, "My pacemaker is stuttering."

"News flash, Hoss," Jerry said. "The lady ain't looking at you."

Wayne had to agree. The woman gave Wayne yet another intent inspection. His sister the reverend glanced back, then said something across the car before disappearing through the passenger door. The woman finally turned away, opened her door, and did the woman thing with her skirt, hiking up the material another inch or so before bending low and sliding behind the wheel.

Jerry said, "She didn't need to do that. That dress is so short she could handle an obstacle course under full fire without raising it up like she just did."

"I'm sure not complaining," Foster said.

The woman cast a final glance back to where Wayne stood, the x-ray vision strong enough to scalpel through the shadows and sink deep into his ribs. Then she shut her door and started the motor.

"Houston, we have ignition." Jerry again.

The car did not pull away so much as vanish. They just stood there and watched the dust settle. The whining gradually dimmed into the distance. Foster said, "That's an interesting way for a pastor to get around."

Wayne felt a pat on his arm. Up close, octogenarian Victoria Ellis was as ethereal as smoke. She smiled up at him and said, "My, but they grow you big wherever you're from."

Jerry said, "I believe I recall Eilene saying she grew up in Dayton."

Foster harrumphed. "Leave it to Jerry to chat up all the cute gals."

The old woman had to twist her head slightly to make up for the slight hump in her spine and the inflexibility in her neck. She patted his arm again, as though judging the quality of flesh beneath Wayne's jacket. "I believe you are an answer to a prayer, Mr. Grusza."

The three men watched her totter away. Then Jerry pulled back the sleeve of his sports coat, revealing a very old tattoo on his forearm. The marine emblem was almost lost to time and curly black hair and the mahogany tint of his skin. Jerry said, "Semper fido, baby."

Wayne gave the answer he knew Jerry was after. "I was army. Did two tours with Special Ops."

Jerry asked, "Where'd you watch your life flash before your eyes—Iraq?"

"Afghanistan."

"And you don't ever want to say nothing more about what went down, am I right?"

Wayne turned his attention back to the outside. The portico roof cut a border with sunlight and freedom on the far side. Wayne knew all about borders. They were dangerous places. Safety on one side, mystery and peril on the other.

Foster said, "Why don't I go get the keys and we'll show you your new home."

Jerry clapped him on the shoulder. "You thought barracks life was bad, man, you just wait."

It was then that Wayne realized he'd been fooling himself all along. He had already crossed the border. Entered the zone.

He made a mental note to thank his sister properly.

But only after he got properly introduced to the lady with the ride.

THREE

For five days Wayne adjusted himself to life in a tie. Which was how he thought of the job—even though he wore nothing more than shorts and a golf shirt and slaps. It was the regular gig, getting up and making breakfast and sitting down in his bare front room to work as an accountant for eight hours. After he was done, he shopped at the local Publix and fixed dinner with the television in the background, worked a couple of hours on his new home, and went to bed. As normal as normal could be.

As though he ever belonged in a normal sort of life.

The cottage they gave him was within nodding distance of derelict. The former cop told Wayne it had been a cracker house, built by the Florida farmers who had planted the original orange grove. A few of the ancient trees survived, scrawny things with knobby limbs. Wayne's house had then been owned by a retired missionary couple, who had willed it to the community. It had since housed a trainload of temporary residents. Wayne spent his free time stripping off seven layers of awful wallpaper, ripping out rotten linoleum, basically working himself into a stupor.

Despite his best efforts to the contrary, the sixth night he had the dream.

The first thing that became clear was his breathing. Always his breathing. Loud and steady in his ears. Then the radio. His partner said something. He responded with, "Roger." Speaking the one word brought everything into dead-sharp focus. He walked a ridgeline, so high he was more a part of the sky than the earth. He was on point and scouting for danger. His attention was snagged by an eagle drifting in the updraft from a green valley to his right. Wayne looked down on the bird and the wings as broad as a jet's. It was the most beautiful sight he had ever known. Then they were hit. He never heard the incoming fire. Never felt a thing. Just bounced up and *bam* and gone.

When he jerked awake, the dream lingered so strong it was almost like he had left reality behind and entered the *real* dream.

Wayne rolled from his mattress. The floor smelled of raw wood and cleanser. He padded into the bathroom, the project he had planned to start that morning. Then he dressed and entered the kitchen and boiled water in a battered pot. He preferred his coffee black, but the instant was so bitter he added milk to smooth out the bite. He sat on his front porch and pretended to study the night. Doing what every addict did when coming off a dry spell. Drawing out the exquisite agony, pretending he had the strength to resist.

He finished his coffee and set the cup aside. He rose and stretched and looked around. Dawn was still at least a couple of hours away. He saw nothing but night. All the nearby houses were black. A pair of streetlights flickered off to his right, overlooking the parking lot fronting the community center. His truck was parked between them. Waiting. Beckoning.

Wayne reentered his house and went to the closet in his bedroom. He pried out the three central floorboards and reached down inside the crawl space. Pulled out the black canvas bag. It clanked softly as he settled it on the closet floor. He unzipped it and used his flashlight to sort through the contents. Sniper rifle, night scope, trio of serious blades, plastic explosive and a cluster of detonators, silenced assassin's pistol, lock picking set, wiretap system.

All the gear required for a high old time.

He pulled out the one item he was searching for. Rezipped the bag and settled it back in the hideaway. Fit the boards into place.

Wayne jogged to the truck, gunned the motor, and headed out.

Off to get himself a fix.

❧

Wayne hammered his way across the entire Florida peninsula. A hundred and sixty-three miles in two hours and a trace. Racing the dawn and winning. Almost regretting the absence of a cop to pull him over and keep him from his appointment with destiny.

Lantern Island was an enclave for the super rich located just south of Naples. Owning a property there was a declaration of financial superiority. A private bridge exactly one hundred and sixty-seven feet long separated the resort from reality. Even at a quarter past dawn the guardhouse was manned and the gates electronically locked. Wayne did not need to check this out. He knew from long experience.

He parked behind the strip mall a quarter mile away, on the highway linking the island to all the hourly wage peons who kept their myth neat and hedges trimmed. He jogged back to the bridge, slipped down the edge to the concrete embankment and did the hand-over-hand to the island. The pattern so familiar he could have done it in his sleep.

He ran the cobblestone path rimming the golf course, flitting from palm tree to hedge to live oak. Never in the clear for very long, and even if he was, the homeowners would just assume he was another health nut out for his morning dose. Which, truth be known, was exactly the case.

Lantern Island's residential compound had been one of the first of its kind, established back in the late forties when lawns were still measured in acreage instead of inches. The island was shaped like an elongated T, with the guard station at the base. The golf course formed the central aisle. All the residences were walled and ornate, and all fronted the water.

Wayne arrived at his destination and climbed a live oak so massive it probably pre-dated Florida's first white settlers. The middle branches formed a protective cover so that from his top perch he could not be spied by any passing security guards. He settled into place and waited.

An hour passed. Two. He checked his watch. A quarter past eight and the house was still silent. Maybe they had gone off somewhere. But that broke the pattern. The guy lived for his work and his family. And after more than two years of surveillance, Wayne knew basically everything. The guy was an oncology radiologist. He had a doctor's attitude, used to getting his way with everything. His lawn, his house, and his world were as clean and orderly as an operating room.

At 8:37 the front door opened. The guy stepped out. He grabbed the newspaper on his front porch and set it on the iron table between the two padded porch chairs. He wore a jacket and a knit shirt and pressed slacks. He glanced at his watch and called back into the house. He walked over and coded a number into the garage, which was connected to the main house by a covered walkway. The door swung up. He got in behind the wheel of his Lexus and started the motor. He drove to where the drive connected to the home's front walk of red brick.

Wayne took a deep breath. He was trembling. Like always. He breathed again and flexed the fingers of his right hand. When they steadied he slipped his hand into his pocket and came up with the scope. He fitted it to his eye, adjusted the sight, and waited. No longer breathing at all.

She came out first. Patricia wore her hair short, the new highlights burnished by the morning sun and his scope. She turned and smiled at the car. Said something lost to the distance. But the message was clear enough anyway.

This was one happy lady.

Then her son ran out. All youth and energy and laughter, so delighted with the day he could not bear to merely walk to the car. He wore a starched little shirt that was almost blue in the sunlight and navy shorts and white socks and little black shoes. He did a quick circuit around the front lawn, his arms out like wings. His three-year-old lungs shouted a joy Wayne did not need a scope to catch.

The lady scooped the air between them, calling the boy into the car's open door. Her hand held a black book.

Only then did Wayne realize it was Sunday.

He remained where he was until the car had driven away and the day was as empty as his spirit. He stared up at the sun, wishing it were a few degrees hotter, strong enough to melt him down.

❧

The more Jerry saw of this new kid, the more he liked him. Even now, when the kid was so deep into pain he crawled from his truck like the walking wounded.

Jerry and Foster were busy fishing. Or they would have been, if the lagoon held anything worth catching. They actually used their poles as an excuse to get under the skin of the retired pastors and missionaries who made up over half of the folks who lived in the community. Normally the sight of Foster and him standing by the lagoon casting their way through a late Sunday morning was enough to have the residents doing the stork walk, all stiff-legged and indignant. It had been like that ever since one of the do-good ladies had walked over and given them the saccharine invitation to come do something *worthwhile* with their Sabbath. And Foster had quoted a line from the Koran. To a *missionary.* The line went, "God does not count hours spent fishing against a man." It was doubtful the woman knew where the words came from, but she sure knew it wasn't the gospel. That was the last time the Sunday crowd had done anything more than lob stare-grenades at them.

Today was a little different, since the churchgoers were all shooting their blanks at Wayne. Only the kid was so internally wounded he didn't notice.

Victoria was seated in the fold-up aluminum chair Foster had brought down to the waterside. He always brought it down but never used it. Sometimes Victoria came and did needlepoint while they fished. Victoria and Foster had a thing going—or at least Foster wished they did, and they might have, except for the fact that Foster had deposited everything to do with religion in last year's compost heap.

Which sort of chopped off any chance he had with Victoria right at the knees.

Foster was fishing with his hands only. His attention was fully on the kid. "The boy Grusza looks in pain."

Victoria did not even look up from her needlepoint. "That's because he is."

"What is it, an old injury?"

Victoria pulled the thread up high, gave it a gentle tug, and dipped down again. Half of the houses in the community had pillows with her needlepoint. "In a manner of speaking."

"I'm not following you."

"That's because you insist on looking at the outside."

They were both watching Victoria now. Foster said, "The only reason you're talking like you are is because you got the scoop from his sister."

"Anybody with an open heart would see a lonely, troubled soul." Another stitch. "Jerry, why don't you call him over."

So he did. Which was only a little strange. He had been known on the force as having a problem with people ordering him around. Which was why he had never made it to the higher grades, even after he aced the lieutenant's exam. Jerry laid down his pole and headed off without a murmur. Because there was something to Victoria that he couldn't bring himself to argue with, a power strong enough to remain gentle.

Jerry angled his path so that he met Wayne up near his front door. Close enough so the kid could bug off if he so chose. Only he was not a kid at all. Jerry realized that as the *man* lifted his gaze from the pavement and the sun illuminated the caverns around his eyes. The guy might carry less than half Jerry's years. But whatever Wayne held inside had aged him so hard and so fast the number of days just didn't count anymore.

Jerry said, "Why don't you come down and help me hold my pole?"

Jerry knew the look Wayne gave him. He had seen it before. Officers involved in a shootout, especially one where a good guy took a hit. They carried that look. The one where the body might be intact, but the gaze was fractured. So Jerry didn't do what he had planned on, which was to slip in the invite and then walk away. Instead he gripped Wayne's arm and tugged. Gently, but with enough pressure for Wayne to know this was half an invitation and half a command. "I'd say come fish with us, only the biggest thing we've ever pulled out of the lagoon was a leech, and that was the day Foster slipped on the edge and we almost lost him to the quicksand. That may look like marsh, but it's really a bottomless pit. Consider yourself warned."

Wayne let himself be led forward, but it was doubtful he actually digested anything Jerry was saying. Victoria had turned in her chair and was watching their approach. Jerry switched verbal gears and gave it to Wayne straight. "You remind me of what I've seen coming into a house when the cordite is still thick enough to choke you. The place is quiet because the gunfire that just ended has blasted away all the air. That sound crazy to you?"

Wayne was listening to him now. "No."

"Yeah, I figured you for somebody who's tasted his share of dread. Me, I was the clean-up guy. You know how it is. The brass are outside singing for the cameras. I'm the one back in the cave of horrors, talking down a kid who's suddenly found himself about half an inch away from his last breath. He's shaking so hard his teeth rattle 'cause he's coming down from the most awful high on earth." Jerry pointed with his chin toward the water's edge. "The reason I'm saying this is because I want to make sure you hear what I'm about to tell you. That lady up there? She's the real deal."

Victoria smiled in that special way of hers, not so much sweetness and light as distilled wisdom. "Hello, son. I don't need to ask how you are. Why don't you come sit down beside me?"

Wayne hesitated only a moment before sitting on the ground beside her chair. Jerry didn't say anything more, just walked back over and picked up his pole and cast into the setting sun. Feeling for once like he'd done the right thing, getting the *man* to walk over and join them.

Victoria just started straight in. "Twenty-two years ago, my husband felt called to go work in regions under attack by the child soldiers of Sierra Leone. He was a doctor. The Foreign Mission Board refused to authorize it—they said it was too dangerous. We went anyway."

Foster cast Jerry a look. Jerry lifted his eyebrows in agreement. This was totally new.

"We spent four years in the war zone. It was an awful place. I saw things you can't imagine." She paused a moment, then, "Well, perhaps you can."

Wayne Grusza was a big man. Well over six feet. Panther lithe. His sister's dark hair. Features made for the stone carvings of a primitive race. A warrior's face. He said nothing, just drew up his legs and wrapped his arms around them, hiding half his face in the crevice between his knees. Trying to make himself small, but instead highlighting his muscular frame.

"I tell you this because I want you to understand where I am coming from. I can't say I have been where you are. But I've been close enough to speak as a kindred spirit." Victoria was no longer smiling. "I'd like you to take two things away with you. The first is this. The worst kinds of addiction, the very worst, are those of the heart. Anger and bitterness don't wound the body like drugs. They gnaw down deep, where the lie can be hidden from almost everyone. The addict even lies to himself and claims no one knows. Outsiders might not be able to name what they see. But the truth is visible just the same. And the truth is this: the addiction hollows out your soul."

Wayne raised his head and stared at her. The air around Wayne had become so compressed a cardinal's song sounded as ragged as a knife.

"And here is your second takeaway," Victoria went on. "No matter what you carry with you, no matter what dark night brought you to where you are, the Lord can make something good of this, if you let Him."

Wayne's voice carried the tattered quality of a man who had forgotten how to speak. "That's impossible."

Victoria gave her gentle smile. "Oh my, I do love a challenge."

Foster cast his lure with enough spite to wing it almost to the lagoon's other side. "Here we go."

Wayne said, "That's not a challenge. It's an absurdity."

"Is that a wager, young man?"

"Absolutely. I'd bet you anything on earth. Only I won't take an old lady's money."

"How gallant. But I'm not talking about money. I don't gamble."

"You want to make a bet but you don't gamble." Wayne looked at the two men. "Is this a joke?"

Foster reeled in so fast his lure scarcely touched the water. "Walk away from this while you still can. That's my advice."

Victoria said, "When I win, you pay me in kind."

"What's that supposed to mean?"

"You'll know at the time."

Foster flung his lure again, the line zinging from the reel. Wheeeeeee. "Now you've done it."

"Let's just be certain we're on the same page. I shall be asking God to reveal himself. I shall pray that God takes the worst, the very worst of what you carry, and makes it into a sign that lights up the heavens."

Jerry felt what he always did when Victoria started in that way. Like he'd been disenfranchised from reality. Like he'd lost half his body weight and was barely able to keep from floating away. Foster stopped hauling on his lure and stood staring at the lagoon. Limp. Defeated.

She carved a tiny hand across the air between her and Wayne. "I shall be praying that God illuminates your internal darkness. I will ask Him to quiet the storm that rages and tosses you and holds you in its dire grip. The storm that only He can still."

Only Wayne appeared untouched by the woman and her words. "What are you putting up for when you lose?"

Victoria gazed in sweet triumph at the young man. "Whatever you want."

"You'll let me name my own stakes?"

"Anything that's in my power to give. But I have to warn you, son. My God won't let me lose." Victoria offered Wayne a hand of parchment and spun glass. "Do we have a deal?"

FOUR

Wayne pushed hard through the work. Harder, in fact, than he pushed himself on the house. And he worked on the cracker cabin with more effort than he had ever worked on anything in his life.

Even so, it was another three weeks before he could see the situation with any sense of clarity.

His sister the reverend came around now and then. Eilene never pressed and seldom stayed more than a few minutes. Just long enough to let him know she was close at hand and thinking about him.

Eilene usually left around the time he was about to ask for the name of the lady driving the red rocket. Clearly the female intuition was working overtime.

The two guys, Foster and Jerry, had basically attached themselves to him. Jerry cut himself a key to the maintenance shed, borrowed what Wayne required without asking, and helped with the renovations. Even Foster helped out now and then. Puffing and groaning and not accomplishing a whole lot.

Foster spent most of his time reading the *Wall Street Journal*. When Jerry got tired he sat on the front porch with Foster and argued over things that didn't matter to anybody except a pair of old men.

One morning they arrived pushing wheelbarrows with two window AC units that now cooled Wayne's nights. Another day, they dragged over the community's lone maintenance man, a taciturn prune who scowled his way through the place, then returned with nine cans of paint for Wayne's walls. Wayne saw Jerry slip the guy a couple of bills but said nothing. Somewhere along the way, friendship of any kind had become alien territory.

Wayne was far more comfortable with how the others treated him. Which was, with watchful fear.

There were a hundred and seven houses in the community. All of them were of a similar age and saggy state. Foster supplied some terse details from behind the shelter of his newspaper. In the early fifties, an old farmer and his wife met a missionary couple returning home to a penniless retirement. The childless farming couple had built them a small home on the lagoon. One poor missionary family led to a second, and they to another dozen. By that point a number of the region's churches were involved. Two years later, soon after the farmer buried his wife of sixty-three years, he was approached by the foreign mission board. The Hattie Blount Retirement Community was born on a day perfumed by orange blossoms and a life well lived.

Most of the homes were still occupied by either missionaries or retired church workers. Then there were people like Jerry and Foster, tossed a raw deal by life's careless hand. The community also had a number of small separate facilities—Alzheimer's unit, a nursing home, assisted living unit, hospice. The community center served as a focal point for volunteer work. Almost everyone volunteered somewhere for something. Which was how the community continued to survive at all. North of the community center stood the activities house, the shuffleboard courts, pool, tennis court, and library. None of it was fancy, but all of it was well used. To the south of the center and connected by a covered walk was an interdenominational church. The community had so many retired pastors, the volunteers only preached once each year.

Eilene's Orlando church paid her to help one day each week. Her title was outreach coordinator. Basically she acted as a young pair of hands.

The community's president, Holly Reeves, did her best to stay out of Wayne's hair. She stopped in often enough to know he was working as hard as two men, far harder than the community deserved for the salary they paid. Wayne's front room held a makeshift desk in the form of a solid-wood door laid on two trestles and a growing number of fruit boxes—the community's filing system for the past year. As though they had given up and were waiting for the ship to sink. Holly took to arriving near sunset and studying him for as long as she could stand without shrieking her questions and her demands. When she left, they all breathed easier.

That entire three-week period, Wayne saw nothing more of Victoria. The old lady's cottage—a tiny place with an oversized screened-in front porch—was visible from his front doorway. Victoria's house was almost lost behind climbing bougainvillea and was framed by birds-of-paradise. Victoria's front door remained shut most of the time, the porch empty. Which was odd, since most of the folks there practically lived on their little screened-in havens. Several times Wayne started to ask Jerry and Foster about her. But something kept him back—fear over the answer, maybe. Something.

Friday afternoon of his fourth week in the community, Holly Reeves stopped by as usual. Only this time she planted herself front and center before his desk, crossed her arms, and declared, "Time's up, Mr. Grusza."

Wayne set down the ledger he was preparing, turned off the computer she'd given him, and waited.

"I've given you all the time I possibly can. Our tax statement is overdue."

"I've already filed for an extension."

"You . . ." Her mouth was already forming the next part of what she'd probably spent hours preparing before her brain caught up. "By whose authority?"

"I am your accountant. It's within my mandate."

"You should at least have notified the board."

Wayne said nothing because he figured there was nothing to be gained by arguing. Besides which, she was probably right.

"Really. I must insist upon your giving me a full report. Otherwise I will be forced to take action."

Jerry's bulk cut the light streaming through the front screen door. Holly raised her arm in the jerky stiffness of one working from a full head of steam. "Don't you even start."

Jerry remained where he was. Holly went on, "You must by now have some idea of the situation."

"Yes."

"Then you can understand how urgent our situation is."

Jerry said, "The man does nothing but work and work. Either the books or the house."

"Jerry, please."

"What you're paying, I figure he's making about sixty-five cents an hour. He wanted to make noise, we'd have a labor beef on our hands."

"Mr. Grusza, I really must insist."

"Tomorrow."

"If you don't . . . Excuse me?"

"I can give you my report tomorrow."

&

Wayne liked the fact that he never locked his door. A community so tight the prospect of theft was impossible. At least, that was the idea.

That next morning, he felt the eyes the whole way down the narrow oyster-shell lane leading between the houses. That was another thing, how nobody felt a need to drill open his skull and pour in a ton of rules. They basically governed by example. The cottages were all about the same double-wide trailer size, with screened porches either fore or aft. Cars crawled down the lanes, dropped off groceries and the ones too weak or old to make it from the front parking lot, then scrunched apologetically back. The community center ran a cafeteria for those who didn't want to cook. The prices were low, the food fresh, the choices basic. Wayne took his breakfast there, a yellow mountain of eggs and toast and sausage and three gallons of coffee. That morning, the maintenance guy was the only one who met his eye directly. The janitor leaned against the wall behind the cashier, giving Wayne a careful inspection. Any doubt Wayne had that the residents knew what was going down vanished then and there. If even the janitor knew, it was all over town.

No surprise, given what Wayne's inspection had uncovered.

The community center was essentially six big rooms with an equal number of offices. The cafeteria had three sliding glass doors that opened into an outdoor eating area. The grassy area's other side was rimmed by two massive oaks, several blooming fruit trees, and a dovecote. The lagoon was just visible between the trees. A marsh island decorated with swamp grape and wild azalea rose about seventy yards off shore. Beyond that sparkled the Intracoastal Waterway, known in these parts as the Indian River. The northernmost causeway leading to the Vero Beach barrier island rose like a concrete hill to Wayne's left. He ate his pile of eggs and watched the rising sun sparkle off the waters and the cars crossing the bridge.

He stayed where he was until the cleaning lady lowered the slat blinds against the rising sun. He took that as his cue and headed next door.

They were there waiting for him.

All the folks who had been avoiding him and then some were gathered in the room. The rear wall was a battery of walkers and electric wheelchairs. The chatter was mostly soft, except for those trying to communicate with the ones whose hearing was about gone. Even they shut up when Wayne walked up the central aisle.

The same three people were seated at the same conference table. The same chair waited for him. He had a little table of his own this time, as well as a glass and a water carafe. Otherwise the only difference was that his sister was seated in the front row, rather than standing against the wall. And the mystery lady. The one with the fire-engine-red Ferrari. She was seated beside Wayne's sister. Everybody was silent now and giving him the eye. Even his two pals, Foster and Jerry. Cautious and tight.

The hostile scrutiny reminded him of Kabul. Soft-spoken people whose natural hospitality had been cauterized. Wayne seated himself and waited. There might not be bullet holes in the walls. But the feeling was the same. Equal mix of helpless anger and outright fear.

Wayne decided there was nothing to be gained by waiting. So he settled his hands upon the table and declared, "You *were* robbed."

There was a quiet intake of breath. A hospital kind of sound. Folks fearing the worst and getting what they'd expected.

An old man said, "What?"

"Robbed, Harry."

"He said that?"

"Yes, Harry. Now turn up your earpiece. I'm not shouting at you for the rest of this meeting."

Holly Reeves said, "The police sent in a detective. He claimed differently."

"I can't answer for them. But your books tell a pretty clear story, far as I'm concerned."

Jerry said, "Explain it to us in words we can understand."

Holly glanced Jerry's way, but did not speak.

Wayne said, "The process was too systematic to be anything else. Sixteen months ago, you hired Zachary Dorsett as your accountant."

A woman seated behind him made a spitting noise. "Evil. The moment I set eyes on him, I knew."

A dozen people shushed her. Wayne continued, "He files your tax claims. Does the state and federal tax-exempt papers. Everything in order with both. Establishes his creds. Then he goes to work."

The woman behind Wayne said, "Just open the door and let evil sweep in. What do you expect, mutton? A nice cup of borscht maybe?"

The old man with the hearing problem called out, "Who is that muttering?"

"Hilda."

"Who?"

"Hilda!"

"Well, tell her to shut up! I'm trying to listen."

Wayne went on, "Up to that point, your assets were spread pretty thin. It made sense to reduce the number of commissions you were paying, which I suppose was how he convinced you to let him accumulate everything into one pile."

Jerry actually laughed out loud.

That gave Wayne reason enough to suppose, "Then he probably made a presentation to the whole group. Gave you a major song and dance about this great investment opportunity. I imagine he even had slides. Maybe a PowerPoint with music. Brought in a guy with fine teeth. The two of them ganged up on you and talked about some fabulous rate of return. Sign on the dotted line, wait six months, and everybody would be set up with new dentures and the latest Chevrolet."

Holly asked weakly, "How did you know?"

"I didn't," Wayne replied. "Until now."

"He actually promised us each a new Buick," Foster corrected. "But otherwise you've got everything else down pretty solid."

Holly waited until the chamber settled, then asked, "How much?"

"I won't know for certain unless I get access to the individual accounts."

"The community," Holly said. "How much did we lose?"

"I don't need a CPA degree to answer that one." Foster snorted. "Everything down to the nails and the plywood, is how much. We're stripped to the bone."

Wayne decided there was no need to answer with anything more than a look. Holly's somewhat green complexion said she already knew.

"Ask the man the question we brought him here for," Foster said. "How long do we have?"

It was bad to be the hangman. Even when the noose was tightened by somebody else's hand. Still it hurt to pull the handle. Wayne had never realized that more clearly than just then.

He said, "When I file this year's accounts, your community will officially be in receivership. I've applied for an extension, so you have another three and a half weeks to come up with another source of funds. Otherwise . . ."

The words punctured the room's air like a blade through a balloon. The old man's querulous voice rose above the hushed muttering. "What'd he say?"

"We're broke, Harry."

"I knew that already. That skunk in a suit stole every penny. Where are we supposed to live, that's what I want to know."

Hilda's voice broke slightly at that point. "He doesn't know the answer to that any more than we do, Harry."

"Then what good is he?"

The room filled with a wash of fractured talk. Holly and Foster's heads came together at the conference table. From the row behind him came the sound of weeping. His sister swiftly went around to offer her well-trained comfort. Wayne rose from his chair and headed for the rear door. It wouldn't be polite for an outsider to witness this private tragedy.

Two sets of eyes watched his progress. His sister's friend was actually wearing blue that day, but looked too hot for the color.

The other was Victoria. Seated there at the table like she hadn't played a vanishing act for the past three weeks. The only person in the room who was smiling.

Wayne pretended he didn't notice either one. Held to his

tight closed expression until he made the rear doors. Then he glanced back. Didn't want to, but he couldn't help himself. Almost like his head was drawn around of its own accord.

All but two heads in the room stayed together, talking and worried. For once, he did not mind the intensity of his sister's friend. And Victoria still watched him. Still smiling.

FIVE

Wayne sat in the shade of a live oak, a wild twisted sculpture of iron and bark. His bench formed a quarter ring around the tree, set where the branches offered the greatest shade. The bench was banded to the trunk with an iron rim, the woodwork pegged and grooved. The trunk had begun to flow over the band like wooden molasses. The bench was the work of a man who loved wood, someone who didn't need any more accolade than to have people come and rest and enjoy the tree as much as he did. The nearby dovecote was cone-shaped with screened walls. Another live oak formed the dovecote's central pillar. There must have been forty birds, chuckling and cooing and brushing the air with silken wings. Wayne sat and watched the old people totter from the community center, not actually clutching one another for support, but pretty close.

When Jerry sauntered over, Wayne greeted the former cop with, "It's not right."

"Glad to hear you say that." The black man settled himself on the bench next to Wayne. "I've had this thing caught in my craw for eight months. Doesn't make me feel a bit better that I didn't get burned. The only reason was, I couldn't get the money from my pension account fast enough. By the time I had the cash, the deal was done."

"So what happened?"

Jerry did a thing with his hands, gripping the bench's edge and trying to curl it, like he probably would've done to Zachary Dorsett's bones if he had the chance. "Man, that dude was *good*. Right to the end. Came in that last day, grey as old dust, laid it out in a voice from the tomb. How he'd lost his own shirt in the process."

"You're sure about that? The guy himself went bust?"

"Left all the papers laid out there in the hall leading to the cafeteria for us to inspect. Wanting us to understand he was as shot through by this as the rest of us. Last day he got hugged by every woman in the joint. Didn't even have a car to drive away in. His sister came and picked him up."

Wayne knew that sort of pause. "Tell me the rest."

"I called in a favor. Got a buddy with the state to go through their records. Found the man living large."

"Where?"

"Resort on the Gulf Coast, just outside Naples. Got himself a semi-palace on the water. Place called Lantern Island." Jerry's cop awareness must have caught Wayne's widening eyes and quick little intake of breath. "What?"

Wayne was still trying to shape a decent response when Victoria appeared. She tottered out the front door and waved cheerily at them with her free hand. Her other arm was gripped tightly by Foster, who appeared seriously concerned about keeping her upright. Wayne asked, "She been sick?"

"In a manner of speaking." Jerry gave the day a worried squint. "She's fasting. And she doesn't eat enough already."

Wayne caught the edge inside the growl. "That fasting, it's got something to do with me?"

"She's been praying for you around the clock. And don't you start on the worrying gig. I got enough going on with those two. Foster's stopped sleeping and she's not eating, I don't know which is worse."

But he wouldn't let go that easy. "She's praying for me?"

Jerry's face was mottled teak and umber in the shade. "What, you thought that bet of hers was some kind of joke?"

"I don't know what I thought." Despite the heat, Wayne shivered. Lantern Island.

"That lady, she sinks her teeth in, a viper don't have nothing on her." When he rubbed his face, the beard sounded like sandpaper. "Where were we?"

"Your former accountant is living the high life."

"My buddies at state, they say the house is leased from his new employer. They say as far as the law is concerned, his bankruptcy was legit and there's nothing we can do about it."

"Do you believe that?"

Jerry re-aimed his squint. "I look like a fool to you?"

❦

Wayne knew what he was going to do the instant he heard the words, "Lantern Island." But he waited to spring the news until after dinner. The old folks spent the afternoon acting like ants whose hill had been kicked up, rattling along the lanes in their chairs and their walkers, talking in those broken-tone voices of worried old folks. There was a lot of shaking of heads. A number of glances were cast at his empty porch. Like Wayne was the thief instead of just being the guy who told them what they already knew.

After dinner things wound down. The community had basically exhausted itself from worry and doing their thirty-yard dash up and down the lanes. Jerry sat on Wayne's porch reading a paperback and swatting at bugs. Wayne had hoped to get the former cop alone to spring his plan. But Foster had dragged himself over from the cafeteria and was now snoring quietly, the *Wall Street Journal* spread like a blanket over his lap. Wayne went into his closet, pried out the floorboards, and lifted out his carryall. He slipped into what he thought of as his professional gear, checked his watch, and decided he could not wait any longer.

Wayne's appearance raised the cop's eyebrows a notch. Jerry took in the outfit—black sweats, black sleeveless T-shirt, black Reeboks, black fingerless gloves—and said, "I'm thinking multiple felony."

"I need to do something, and I can't do it alone."

"This have anything to do with our pal the accountant?"

Wayne squatted down by the cop's chair. "I need some plastic. I've got to make a booking before the place shuts for the night."

Whatever Wayne might have been expecting, it wasn't what he got, which was a massive grin that puckered the uneven crevices of Jerry's broad face. "I wouldn't rate that the best explanation I've ever heard."

But before the cop could reach into his back pocket and come up with his wallet, a scrawny white hand reached across and offered Wayne a Visa. Foster did not sound the least bit sleepy as he said, "Use mine."

"I only need the help of one other person."

Jerry warned Foster, "I 'spect the man didn't dress up like this for an ice cream run."

"I signed my name right there beside Holly on that skunk's contract." Foster tossed his newspaper aside. "Go make your call."

They met again twenty minutes later. Jerry was dressed in dark shorts and top, no socks, and boat shoes. Foster's outfit was a bit more original—navy shirt buttoned to his neck, charcoal grey slacks, black socks, and wingtips. Jerry gave his friend a careful up-and-down, but all he said was, "Works for me."

Foster waited until they had piled into Wayne's truck to slip him a note. "Victoria asked me to give you this."

Jerry scowled. "You told the lady?"

"Didn't need to."

Wayne unfolded the paper and read, *"First Chronicles, chapter 20, verse 1: 'In the spring, at the time when kings go off to war . . .' "*

Jerry asked, "What's it say?"

Wayne refolded the note and stowed it away. "I have no idea."

Jerry leaned his head back. "Ain't that just like a dame."

They winged their way across the state. The truck followed two grooves, one in the asphalt and the other in Wayne's head. Jerry had the map unfolded in his lap. He glanced over a couple of times as Wayne swept the truck around tight turns on unmarked country roads, drilling through the night at a steady seventy per. Foster watched the proceedings for about fifteen minutes and then zoned out. Jerry, however, played like a creature of the night, just blinking and watching until he was certain enough to say the words, "You been this way before."

Wayne just punched down a trifle harder on the gas.

"Either that or you been planning this a lot longer than you been letting on."

Wayne kept his focus tight on the night and the road.

"Which would be a serious strangeness," Jerry went on, "seeing as how you didn't have a clue about the skunk living on Lantern Island till I told you."

That did it for polite conversation until they hit I-75, the north-south tourist artery flanking the Gulf Coast. Wayne skipped by the exit for Lantern, taking the next coastal route and easing back a trace when they entered civilization. Jerry didn't say anything more, just kept switching his gaze back and forth between the road and the driver. When they pulled into the marina and Wayne parked beside the boat moored at the dock, Jerry just shook his head and gave a soft little *hmmm-mmmm*.

Foster kept snoring as Wayne stowed his canvas carryall and started the boat's motor. Jerry poked his buddy in the ribs. "Come on, sailor. Rise and shine."

Foster snuffled and came awake in stages. "Where are we?"

Jerry turned and inspected the night. "Close enough to ground zero to smell it."

Foster rubbed his face. "I need a coffee."

Jerry's teeth shone in the streetlight. "My guess is, ten minutes from now you're gonna know an adrenaline rush that'll have Starbucks looking like baby food."

SIX

The boat skimmed over a water so slick it might as well have been oiled. The windless night was illuminated by a vast hunter's moon. The silver face just hung there in the sky, grinning down on them. The moon's reflection glinted every time Wayne scouted the waters. Like the entire universe was laughing at him. Wayne Grusza, thinking he had stuff under control. Like his own life.

Headed to Lantern Island.

The trip took almost two hours. They had to sweep out past a spit of mainland, then follow the channel buoys until they were straight west of the place. Wayne rolled the boat off its plane and threaded between a pair of marsh islands. When the lights along the shoreline came into view he cut the motor off. Sat there gripping the wheel with both hands, listening to the night birds and tasting the air.

Foster asked, "Where *are* we?"

"We're where we need to keep our voices down, is what," Jerry replied. "Water reflects noise worse than it does light."

Foster was obviously not impressed. "Who's going to hear us out here? Loons?"

Wayne asked, "You know his exact address?"

"The street was something like Palm."

"Palmetto," Wayne corrected. "What about the street number."

"I asked, but they didn't say. Probably figured I'd come out here and do something stupid." The boat rocked gently as Jerry moved to the seat across from Wayne. "Here's a question I bet you can answer if you try. How'd you know the street?"

Wayne unzipped the carryall. "Now you sound like a cop."

Something must have caught Jerry's eye—a glint of metal, or maybe just a hint of bygone days. He leaned over and inspected the contents. "Whoa, mama."

Foster's eyes went wide and round when Wayne fitted on the nylon-mesh belt and started filling up the pockets. "What *is* that stuff?"

Jerry's expression said he could name every item. Flashlight, pistol, silencer, flash-bang grenades, gutting knife, tape, nylon rope with grappling hook, plastique, detonator. "Ten to twenty, is what."

Wayne dipped back into the bag and came up with a knit cap. And two more. Not just backup. Overkill. Symbols of all the nights he had prepped his equipment and lusted after a deed he knew he would never commit. "Put these on."

Jerry unrolled his far enough to see the eyeholes and slit cut out for the mouth. "Somebody's done robbed the evidence locker."

"Don't roll them down till I tell you. It'll get too hot."

Wayne knew Jerry was searching for a comeback. Something cute that would also let them know he wasn't buying into the deal. The guy was, after all, a former cop. Sooner or later, Wayne would have to tell them. And once they started forward, the last thing Wayne wanted was chatter. So he leaned in tight enough for Jerry to stiffen. Not a lot, which was a good sign. Like, the big man knew he was in the presence of danger, but a danger not directed at him.

Wayne said, "My ex lives in the last house on the point down to your left."

Jerry huffed his surprise. "Now ain't that some kinda mess. So this sorta comes under the category of familiar territory."

"Yes."

"You've done this trip before."

"That's right."

"By boat. In the middle of the night. Threading your way through islands with gators for company." The former cop wasn't giving it much, though. Like he was already on Wayne's side, but still needing to know. "Your ex must've really stiffed you."

Wayne took a very, very hard breath. "That's right."

Something in the cop's eyes almost pushed open the door. The one he'd kept locked and hidden away for four long years.

But Jerry chose that moment to break off the inspection. He rocked the boat another time, craning forward and giving the carryall another hard look. Wayne made no move as Jerry reached into the case and came out with the sniper rifle.

Wayne knew the former cop was about to ask what a man

needed with a gun finished in nonreflective black, calibrated
to a thousand meters, with a clip of waxed bullets. And he had
no answer except the rifle had never been fired anywhere but
the range.

Which was the point when Foster started laughing.

The sound was totally out of place. Foster wasn't just grinning aloud either. He was lost to his hilarity. He gripped his belly
with one hand and pushed his spectacles up with thumb and
forefinger of the other, pressing against the tears Wayne could
see in the moonlight. Foster tried hard to choke off the noise,
emitting the laughs in tight little frames. Eh-eh-eh-eh-eh.

Jerry said, "You laugh like an old man."

Foster waved one hand. Wait. He wheezed a couple of times
but finally regained control. "I don't need a thermometer to
know this fellow's goose is cooked right through."

"This is serious business here," Jerry said.

"Victoria is gonna *love* this." Foster wiped his face. "We're
sitting in the middle of the Gulf, a thousand miles from any
reasonable explanation, and the nightmare that laid this fellow
out is right smack dab at the other end of hello. Talk about a
sign."

"Man does have a point." Jerry's hand scratched over his
beard. He said to Wayne, "Looks to me like you done lost
yourself a bet with Miss Victoria."

"Big time," Foster said. "Major league."

Wayne looked from one grin to the other, then decided
there wasn't a thing he could do about either.

"Okay," Foster said, settling back into his seat. "Let's go fry
us up some skunk."

Jerry said, "What, you think we're gonna just waltz in and take what we want?"

"I don't imagine our guide has brought us this far without something in mind."

Wayne took that as his cue and headed to the bow of the boat. As he unlocked the trolling motor and slipped it over the front, he could hear Foster there in the back, still chuckling quietly.

The electric motor was made for bringing fishermen close to prey in total silence. Jerry leaned across the transom and muttered, "Tell me what's going down."

"I've noticed this place before," Wayne whispered. He glanced back as Foster moved in closer, but did not complain. "The house is totally different from anything else on the island. The place is built like a fortress. The lawn is wired with motion sensors. It's rimmed by about six hundred lights waiting for the silent alarm to go off. Steel shutters, even over the front door. When the guy gets up, he hits a button, the whole deal just winds up and disappears. Suddenly it's just another waterfront palace in suburbia."

"So we're gonna sit out here until dawn, nab him when he comes out for the morning paper? And then what, spank him and let him go? I'm only asking, see, on account of how I'd just as soon not throw my thirty away on a totally futile gesture."

Wayne cut the motor back a notch. "I had a little something different in mind."

❧

Foster's mouth fell open when Wayne took the .30-.30 from the seat where Jerry had placed it and fit on the night scope and subsonic silencer. The scope was as long as the rifle barrel and a hand's breadth in width. He watched Wayne pull out the clip and select a second set of bullets, these individually encased in little plastic clips.

"Let me get this straight," Jerry said. "We're risking serious jail time by attacking a house in the middle of the night on a *hunch*?"

Wayne used the life vests to pad the bulkhead by the bow of the boat, then settled himself into a kneeling position. Legs about two feet apart. Entire barrel cushioned and stable. "Pretty much."

The two older men exchanged a glance. Foster gave Jerry back his own words, "Works for me."

"Hold the boat steady," Wayne said.

Most people thought a silencer worked by muffling the *bang* upon ignition. Which it did. But a professional silencer also slowed the bullet to subsonic speeds. Which eliminated the second major source of noise—passing the sound barrier.

Foster observed, "The house is over that way."

Jerry said, "Man ain't aiming at no house."

"Quiet now." Subsonic was still fast enough to do serious damage to an unarmored target. But Wayne was after taking out metal. Which meant he needed a bullet with a special kick.

The more modern resort islands had all their power and cable and phone systems buried. But Lantern Island was too old for that. Wayne sighted on the telephone pole closest to the house. The night scope lit up the home's transformer like a huge yellow target suspended at the top of a long grey pole. Wayne took a breath. A second. Then pulled the trigger.

The rifle *huffed*.

Wayne saw the streak of light through the scope and shut his eyes tight against what was to come.

The incendiary bullet hit the transformer dead on. There was a sharp *crack* and a palm tree of sparks.

From the azalea by the bulkhead, a bird chattered its protest over being awoken. A dog's muffled bark sounded inside a house somewhere along the road. The sparks littered the street, fizzled quietly, then went out.

Wayne waited and listened through a full five minutes. He turned to the wide-eyed pair and softly explained, "House alarms have a back-up battery. Not motion sensors in the yard."

He slipped over the side onto the sand, checked the night once more, then said, "When it happens, start the motor, untie the boat, and be ready. And don't speak more than you have to. The guy might recognize your voices."

Foster hissed, "When *what* happens?"

Wayne replied, "Now's a good time to pull down your masks."

SEVEN

Wayne loped across the yard. He was fairly certain nobody was going to bother him, especially not the guy inside that house, totally blinded as he was by steel shutters. The island estates were spaced well apart, a minimum two acres per, with all the extras any rich kid could come up with at Christmas. Stone walls. Borders of blooming trees. Wooden trellises rising ten feet above the walls, guaranteeing they would never have to glimpse another neighbor unless they hiked across their manicured lawns and rang the six-bong doorbell. High-impact glass and total soundproofing. As entombed as money could make them.

It was the high-impact glass that had him worried.

Up close the house looked fairly impregnable. Which was mostly bad and maybe a little good. Bad, because he was going to have just one chance to get this right. Even if blowing the transformer had also taken out the phone system as he hoped, the guy inside could not be given time to use his cell. Reach out and touch the local cops. Who would come swarming. With that one phone call, Wayne would become every security joe's dream come true, the reason most of them deluged the real cops with multiple applications. So they could blow away the bad guys.

If he didn't want to play one quick round of deer-in-the-headlights, he had to get it right the first time.

But it was also good. Maybe. A guy living inside a steel cell most likely lived alone. Wayne knew guys like that. These sorts of toys were definitely a guy thing.

The same sort of guy who trusted his own security more than a bank.

As in, the place to stow his illicit cash.

After all, this was the same guy who made a profession out of tweaking reality and taking money that basically wasn't his. A guy who lived to abuse other people's trust.

Of course, all this was assuming Wayne had the right house.

That line of thought kept him company as he danced his way across the moonlit lawn and inspected the corner of the house. Three stories, stone, high-pitched roof, sort of a pyramidal structure. The broad ground floor rose to a second story about half its width, and it to a third floor that was basically one large room wide.

Wayne was betting his life that top floor held the mother lode.

He unfurled his lanyard. The grappling hooks connected to the end were wrapped in foam rubber. Wayne began whirling, letting more rope slip through his hand until the circle reached almost the ground. Then on the upswing he lifted and tossed.

The hooks slid silently over the slate roof, then caught on something.

Wayne put his weight on the line, gripped hard, and put his foot on the stone wall. He pulled himself up hand over hand, and took another step. Walking straight up the wall.

That is, until the hooks came undone. Landing Wayne on his back. Blowing him hard.

He lay there for a minute, letting his ribs complain, reaching hard for breath. It was either tuck tail and retreat or try again. And Wayne had never been one for taking the wise course.

He rose to his feet, tested his spine, rubbed the spot where he was growing a pistol-shaped bruise over his right kidney, and recurled the lanyard. Swung and swung and swung and tossed. This time, when the hooks grabbed hold, he tested them carefully.

The climb was not hard and not easy. Wayne was in pretty good shape. His problem was the memories that came up as he climbed. Of other rock walls and cave mouths he had puffed his way around, hanging limpetlike and listening hard to all the sounds he was probably just imagining.

His muscles were doing a jelly dance by the time he made the fake balcony rimming the third floor's largest window. There was probably a set of French doors behind the roll-down shutters, with the balcony meant to keep the occupant from doing a face-first into the succulents Wayne had just mashed flat. Wayne propped himself on the balcony railing, gripped the wall where it connected to the metal shutter, and tugged. Harder.

The news was so good Wayne actually turned and mouthed a silent thanks to the smiling silver face in the sky. As in, this much good fortune had to be acknowledged.

Again, assuming Wayne had the right house.

He pulled once more, just to make sure it wasn't his imagination. The shutters accordioned through aluminum runners. Midway down, the right-hand runner was no longer firmly attached to the wall. It gave. Not a lot. But enough for Wayne's purposes.

Wayne got to work, all without touching the balcony floor. Which was probably overkill, but it would be just his luck to have the security freak put motion sensors there. So Wayne balanced on the railing as he molded little rings of plastique around the two middle stanchions and then along the shutter lid and down the sides of the top housing. He imbedded mini-detonators, connected the wires to the trigger, and looped the trigger through the front of his belt.

Wayne tested the lanyard hooks once more, just to make sure they hadn't slipped free while he did his dirty work. He rose to his full height and looped the lanyard around his back, making himself a sort of hammock. Then he rolled the lanyard once around his gloved right hand. With his left hand, the one closest to the shutters, he plucked another item from his ready-belt.

The proper name for a flash-bang was compression grenade. As in, a lot of sounds and light and no frags. The purpose of a flash-bang was to so stun a quarry they were left incapable of thought, much less attack.

What a flash-bang would do when slipped between a steel shutter and a set of impact-resistant French doors was anyone's guess.

But unless the doors were molded titanium, Wayne imagined he might earn himself a way inside.

Wayne pulled the safety clip with his teeth. Took a long breath, wondering if it was too much to make his first prayer in fifteen years be that he was actually aiming at the right room in the right house.

He pried the shutters out a trace and slipped in the grenade.

The canister rattled on the stone flooring. Which Wayne took as his signal to slip away.

He scrambled around the corner, unfurling the wires with his left hand. His heart raced fast enough to chop the seconds into billionths. He was in position and had the trigger out when the grenade went off.

He punched the trigger so fast the two booms, one from the grenade and one from the C-4, sounded as one. A great roar of sound. Then nothing.

This time round, there was no question which of the neighbors had dogs.

Wayne punched his legs out and leaned into the swing, such that he cleared the corner entirely. Just swept around the house and came flying over the balcony railings.

The shutters hung like an astonished metal tongue over the railing. The French doors were gone. There was no sign of them ever having existed. Instead, the entire room sparkled in the moonlight, like a truckload of fairy dust had been flung at the walls and ceiling and floor.

Thankfully, the bed was at the room's far end. Otherwise the lone occupant might have sparkled as well. Instead, the guy floundered around in his sheets. Clearly knowing he was supposed to do something right then. But his brain was so scrambled he couldn't be sure *what*. The guy made it to a seated position, sort of, just in time to watch Wayne come flying through what was supposed to have been an impregnable wall. Out of his nightmares and into his bedroom.

Wayne covered the distance from window to bed in three pounces. He gripped the guy with one hand and slipped the knife from his belt. Put the blade right up against the guy's cheek, directly beneath his left eye, letting him feel the cold threat. Then Wayne lifted the blade out far enough for the guy's moon-shaped eyes to get a glimpse of true terror.

"You've got one chance to save that eye," Wayne said. "Where's the upstairs security box?"

The guy stammered, swallowed, made the words come out. "Front hall."

Wayne carried such a load of adrenaline he one-handed the guy up off the bed and through the dressing area and into the foyer. He sped across from the gigantic curving stairway to where the security unit flashed its danger light. On this side of the house Wayne could hear the whooping siren attached to the home's street side.

Wayne refit the knife to the guy's face. "Shut it down."

The man did not hesitate. After all, why should he. The

siren was mostly cosmetics. There was little chance a neighbor was going to risk life and limb for him.

After the siren was silenced, Wayne forced the man hard against the wall. Waited.

The longest minute in Wayne's entire life passed. The only sound came from the emergency generator drumming softly in the garage. Nothing. No phone call. Which meant they had taken out the alarm in time and the emergency call had not been coded through to the security office.

Wayne flipped the guy onto the floor. Kneed him in the back. Pulled back his arms and taped his wrists together. Taped over his eyes and mouth. Pulled him to his feet. "Let's go."

The guy tumbled on the stairs and stayed upright only because Wayne was too busy tripping on adrenaline to notice. On the ground floor Wayne used the light of the motion sensors and one wall clock to find the rear doors. The switch for the shutters was beside the lights. He pushed it and waited as the shutters ground open in torturous fashion.

They basically flew across the rear lawn. The only sounds Wayne could hear were a pair of stubborn hounds. Wayne dumped the guy in the bow. Jumped in after. Jerry and Foster both wore their masks. Wayne hefted the man by his hair. "Is this him?"

The two men leaned forward. Foster whispered, playing for gruff, "Show me his eyes."

Wayne ripped off the tape. Their hostage whimpered.

Jerry shifted his bulk forward a notch, causing the guy to whimper again. Jerry had gone from a bulky man in shorts to a menace.

Foster said, "That's our boy."

Wayne made all his motions out where Dorsett could clearly watch. He took the pistol from his belt. Screwed in the silencer. As he did so, he talked. "Your security system is shorted out. You're almost two miles from the security station by the bridge. A passing guard might have heard the explosion. A neighbor might have called it in. They might run a check. But they'd have to go around to the rear of the house to see the problem. Otherwise it's just you and me, Dorsett. You understand the situation?"

Wayne stuck the gun's business end hard against the guy's nose. Pulled back the trigger.

When the prisoner started kicking, Jerry moved in and sat on his legs.

"You've got one chance," Wayne said. "Just one. Nod and tell me you understand."

He responded with more of a body tremble than a nod. But the moan was clear enough.

"I'm going to take off the tape over your mouth. You're going to tell me where your safe is and give me the combination. Nothing else. I'll go inside. Get what we came for. Then we'll leave. You haven't seen us and we were never here. Do we have a deal?"

This time the nod was for real.

Wayne ripped off the tape. "You cry, you die."

The guy chattered hard through the words. "You'll let me go?"

"You can trust us, Dorsett. More than we can say for you, right?"

"Don't have any choice, do I."

Wayne ground the pistol in harder. "Last chance."

"Ouch, wait!"

"The safe."

"In the wine cellar. Closet beside the pantry. Lift the middle bottle of champagne and hit the switch. The rear wall swings out. Combination is oh-four-six-two."

"Say the numbers backwards."

When the guy did so, Wayne handed the gun to Jerry. Or tried to. Foster stepped in between them. "Give me that."

"Can you shoot him?"

"You just go do your thing." The old man took a two-handed grip on the pistol and took careful aim. Foster's voice was raspy with banked-up rage. "I'll just sit here and pray this guy asks me to blow him away."

Jerry leaned over and mashed the tape back over Dorsett's mouth. "Naw. You watch. Our man is just *dying* to behave."

Wayne moved to his carryall and dumped the rest of his gear onto the boat. He balled up the empty bag and trotted back to the house.

The island made a few night-type noises. Otherwise it was totally quiet. Neither of the other two houses he could see even had a light burning.

Just another night among the isolated rich of Lantern Island.

EIGHT

They spent the rest of a ragged night driving and then counting. Foster was good at the latter, Wayne discovered. So good, in fact, that Wayne basically relegated himself to keeping the accounts. Foster's fingers lost about fifty years every time they took hold of another stack of bills. And there were a lot of those.

The safe had been jammed full. Wayne had stuffed with both hands, sweeping one shelf empty after another. The bills were all denominations, fives to hundreds. Wayne had crammed the sack until he could scarcely shut the zipper, so full he staggered trying to lift it. He had then returned to the kitchen, stripped the plastic garbage bag from the trash can, and filled that as well. Even so, he had left far more than he had taken. He was still roaring with his adrenaline high, still waiting with every breath for the lights to flash and the night to shrill and the voice from the dark to shout for him to drop it and spread. Which did not give his feet wings on the return journey but did keep him moving even beneath that double-armed load.

He had made it back to the boat with a couple of night birds sounding the only alarm. Wayne dropped the sacks into the boat, Foster pushed them off the bulkhead, and Jerry rammed the motor straight to full bore. The scam artist lay still, his eyes never leaving the sacks. They dumped him on the marsh island's sandbank, just out of shouting distance from his home. Their last image of Lantern Island was of Zachary Dorsett standing two hundred yards from the edge of his almost perfect world, watching a significant portion of his hard-earned cash drill through the calm Gulf waters.

❧

While Foster counted and Wayne made notes, Jerry kept order and brewed coffee. Wayne used the community records to list what was owed to whom. At his written instructions, Foster separated the cash into little piles, one for each of the homeowners who lost their stash to the scam artist. They didn't have envelopes, so Wayne wrote the names on slips of paper and fitted them under the rubber bands. A lot of the bills were old and greasy. Wayne doubted any of the group was going to object.

Jerry did not sit down until Foster shook his head to another coffee recharge and Wayne covered his own mug. Then Jerry dragged over a chair from Wayne's dining table. Foster looked up at the noise and frowned, but his fingers never stopped counting.

Jerry settled himself down and sipped from his cup, taking his time. Maybe giving Wayne a chance. Finally he stretched out his legs and asked his cup, "How come . . ."

Wayne just waited.

Jerry stared at his steaming mug for a while. "Never mind."

Wayne studied the big man. Jerry's refusal to cover more ground with his questions was about as big a gesture as Wayne had ever known. He wanted to thank the man, but all he could think to say was, "Ask me again and I'll tell you."

Jerry looked at him then. Really looked. Eyes of dark copper, steady and strong. "That works for me."

Foster slipped a rubber band around the pile he'd been counting, fitted Wayne's handwritten sheet on the top, and glanced over.

Jerry went on, "Some things that need telling don't need telling now. Wouldn't want to mess up how good we're all feeling."

"Speak for yourself," Foster said. "I wouldn't mind learning why you've got a pile of assassin's gear stowed in your closet."

"Sniper weapons," Jerry corrected. "And the man will tell us. Just not now."

Foster snorted. Wayne looked over. Offering him the same deal. Say it again, and Wayne would talk. But Foster dropped his focus back to the next slip of paper, shook his head once, and resumed counting.

Even so, for the first time since all the mess started, Wayne found silence was just not enough. When he was certain his voice wouldn't sound ragged, he said, "Last night is the first time I ever shot that rifle off a range."

Jerry said, "Let it go now."

From his place at the table, Foster said, "Don't see why you had to flap that big mouth of yours in the first place. Go and ruin everybody's morning."

Jerry turned around. "Yeah, like you weren't dying to know."

"Had to dump a heap of misery on my buddy."

"So he's your pal now. And what am I, chopped liver?"

Jerry sipped from his mug and said nothing more.

They stayed like that while the dawn took gradual hold. Wayne finished the last of the accounts and sat watching the light grow beyond his front porch. The only sounds were bird-song and the rattling air-conditioner and the flicker of Foster's hands.

Finally Foster scraped his chair back. He rubbed the small of his back with both hands. Stretched. Asked Wayne, "You want to know how much is left over for the community?"

But the strengthening day had revealed a house almost smothered in bougainvillea. "Later. First I've got to see a lady about a bet."

❧

Victoria was there waiting for him, an elfin hue inside the screened porch, painted in shadows and sunrise. Only her eyes were clearly visible. "Are you boys all safe?"

"Yes." He stopped on the front porch and found himself wishing he was back in uniform so he could sweep off his hat. The diminutive woman might have been dressed in a quilted housecoat, but her authority was unmistakable. "You were right. I lost and you won. I owe you."

76

She inspected him a long moment, then said, "Go ask your friends if they'd like pancakes for breakfast."

ॐ

The kitchen table was just a ledge off the back wall, proper for an intimate couple. They ate in the living room off fold-up trays. Foster hovered around Victoria as long as she was on her feet, sitting only when ordered. Jerry watched the two of them with the dark concern of a man who had learned not to say what he thought.

Victoria ate rations for a tiny bird. When Foster complained, she silenced him with, "Haven't we discussed this?"

"Well, if you won't look after your own health, somebody else needs to step to the plate."

"I'm healthy and I'm happy. That should be enough for anybody."

Two walls of her living room and one in the kitchen were filled with photographs attached to drawings and letters. Some of the pictures dated back to a monochrome era of crinkled edges. Tiny black children grew to have children of their own, who drew love messages on onion skin paper, many of them addressed to someone called *Maliaka*. Two Anglo girls grew up amidst the dark faces, smiling and laughing with them, and now held babies of their own, and soon these babies were laughing as well. All in villages of scrub and dust and a light so strong it shone across the years. Wayne asked, "Your daughters are missionaries?"

"One is. The other works in Cape Province. Her husband is with the UN."

"You miss them."

"They're where they should be." She sat as erect as a corporal on report. "Your sister Eileen tells me that your father was a pastor."

Wayne made a process of setting his tray to one side. "Yes."

"A stern man who lived in a state of perpetual disappointment, as far as you were concerned." She did not actually sing the words. And there was not really a hint of accent. Yet something in the way she spoke suggested she had spent years thinking and dreaming in a different tongue. "A man who never approved of his uniquely special children."

"You got that right." Wayne found himself so drained from the night he could speak without the old bitterness. "Eilene was the son he always wanted, only inside the wrong skin."

"There is absolutely nothing wrong with your sister," Victoria replied. "Or with you."

The two older men sat and watched the exchange like they would a good movie, silent and absorbed. Wayne said, "You're going to tell me to give God another chance, is that the wager?"

"No, son. I've spent my entire life witnessing the bitter legacy of people forcing others to believe." The morning light turned her features translucent. "But I will say this. God does not wear your father's face."

Victoria held him. Not with anything he had ever known before. Not with anger. Not with strength or authority or seniority. With *luminescence.* She said, "I know your father's ways all too well. Religion becomes another word for oppression and coercion. Religion specializes in shame and blame, a lot of energy and no inspiration."

"I probably deserved it."

"Son, listen to me. We all deserve it. Each and every one of us." She gave him a moment. When he did not speak, she went on. "You weren't allowed to live your own life, but instead were expected to conform to someone else's concept of order." She shook her head. "No wonder the old-time religion failed you."

Victoria leaned forward until he could see the sparks lifting from her eyes. Until he could *feel* them. "Jesus loves you, son. Deal with it."

Wayne said weakly, "You won the bet. I asked what I owed you."

Victoria leaned back in her chair. She did not show disapproval. Instead, the illumination dimmed somewhat. She said, "Go do whatever it is your sister asks."

Wayne felt as much heat as his weary frame could manage. "We didn't say anything about transferring debts."

"Your first mistake was not asking." Victoria used the arms of her chair to push herself erect. She waved away Foster's move to her aid. She was light on her feet, scarcely more than a sweep of quilted robe and eyes of diffused light. "Your second mistake, son, is thinking your sister brought you here only for your sake."

NINE

Three hours later Wayne woke from his drug-like stupor. He showered and dressed and walked over to Jerry's. He was very glad indeed to find the big man up and about. Jerry heard him out in silence as Wayne stumbled over the words, about how a bet was a bet and he needed to get this thing over and done.

Together they walked over and found Foster singing in the shower. Loud and off-key and happy enough to have them both smiling. Which, given the thing Wayne had staring him in the face, was quite an accomplishment.

Foster accompanied Wayne to Orlando while Jerry baby-sat their cash. It was unlikely anyone would come looking for a boatload of money in the middle of a low-rent retirement community. But Jerry was by nature a cautious man.

The afternoon was hot but the humidity low for springtime Florida. Foster kept his window down on I-95, his grey hair blowing everywhere and his eyes squinted almost shut. Wayne handed over his Oakleys. Foster slipped the bug-eyed sunglasses on his face. Wayne took one look and laughed out loud.

Foster said, "What?"

"You look like a roadie for the Grateful Dead."

"There you go again, fooling me with talk that sounds almost like English."

Wayne hooked onto the Beach Line Expressway and shot into the Orlando sprawl. His sister's church had recently moved to a campus near the John Young Parkway, sandwiched between the gleaming new convention center and a neighborhood straight out of a Tijuana barrio. Her outreach center was an old convenience store with a basketball court where the gas tanks had once stood. Next door was the main church building, with a free medical clinic on the first floor, where her husband the periodontist donated one day a week. The scarred asphalt parking lot sprouted a sign with doves and rainbows and a welcome in half a dozen languages.

They pulled into the lot and the first thing Wayne saw was his sister standing there with her hands on her hips, a look on her face he'd seen a billion times and more, her mouth going a mile a minute. Just handing it to a sullen kid holding a basketball, the kid a full head taller than the two dozen other kids standing and watching Wayne's sister dish it out. And from the big grins most of the other kids wore, Wayne figured they were just loving it, watching the big kid catch it from Eilene.

Which was why, when Wayne walked over, the first thing he said was, "Lighten up, why don't you."

Eilene rounded on him. Like she was eleven again and he nine, and their father was out saving the world, expecting his own kids to toe the line, put on the happy-sappy face and busting Wayne's chops because he refused to measure up. "Excuse me, did I ask for your help here?"

"The kid is sorry. Tell the lady you're sorry, kid."

The kid mouthed something behind Eilene's back that Wayne was fairly certain had nothing whatsoever to do with an apology. Which had him hiding his own grin, since it was basically an act pulled from his own life. "There, see? You've burned him so bad he'll never mess up again. He'll go through life staying totally clean. Right, kid?"

Eilene snapped, "Just like you."

"Sure thing."

"Mister Perfect."

"What can I say. If the shoe fits and all that."

She surprised him then. Because the one thing Eilene never did was what Wayne asked. He had bitter experience at that.

But this time she turned to the kid and said, "The ball is for bouncing on the ground, not on other kids' heads. Especially kids half your size. *Claro?*"

"*Sí, claro.*"

"*Vamanos.*"

Eilene surprised him again. Shocked was more like it. Had the pastor pulled a gun on her younger brother, the astonishment could hardly have been bigger.

She reached over and hugged him. Hard.

The kids clearly knew Wayne's sister well enough to know this lady was no hugger. The chatter stopped and even the tall kid with the ball turned and stared.

Wayne did the only thing his dumbfounded brain could

come up with, which was to wrap his arms around her in a feeble response.

Eilene said to his shirt, "I've been so worried."

"About what?"

"Victoria called. Said you were off doing something. In the middle of the night. With Jerry and Foster your only backup." She pushed herself out of his arms, the huggy-feely moment clearly gone. "All I could think to say was, 'That sounds just like Wayne.' "

He just stood there, a big hulking brute in worn jeans and T-shirt and slaps. His sister always left him feeling tongue-tied and too massive for his own good. Like having muscles and speed was a sin.

Eilene said to the pavement by her feet. "I'm so sorry."

The surprises just kept on coming. Wayne tried to recall the last time his sister gave him anything *resembling* an apology. And came up empty.

She went on, "I should never have gotten you involved in this."

"We got it all back, Eilene. The money."

She reached around and hugged herself. Not looking his way at all. "How many laws did you break last night?"

Now they were back on familiar territory. As in, nothing Wayne ever did was good enough. No choice ever the right one. "None they caught us at."

She started to respond, but broke it off before the words were formed and walked over to where Foster stood beside Wayne's truck. "You went with him?"

"Wouldn't have missed it for the world." Foster leaned

through the window, the bug-eyed shades mocking his age. "Your brother is one amazing guy. Leaps over tall buildings, takes on the world, saves the day, you name it."

"Jerry is all right too?"

"Thanks to the kid here. Did he tell you we got it all back?"

Eilene went back to hugging herself as tightly as she had Wayne. Like the news was something to worry over.

Foster's grin reflected a brilliant sunlit day. "Most amazing thing I ever did see. Just visited the local bank and made a substantial cash withdrawal."

Eilene's entire face was a frown. "My brother's always been good with numbers and guns. It's people he has problems with."

Foster's grin turned steely. "You might want to have a word with the folks whose homes your brother just saved before you give him any more heat."

Eilene kicked at a rough spot in the pavement. "Yeah, well, there's a first time for everything."

Wayne's comeback was halted by seeing new worry scars on his sister's face. He realized with a pang just how hard the last few years had been on her.

Wayne found himself recalling something he had spent a lot of time and energy stowing deep down inside himself. About what he now classed as his lost time.

Normally when the memories struck, Wayne knotted his insides into a fist. Just clamped down and forced the thoughts away. But not today. He had a vivid image of how, soon after leaving the armed forces, he had freaked out in a very serious manner. Just disappeared. Hit the road. Spent nearly two years sleeping rough. Working trench jobs when he needed. Until that morning in Santa Fe, waking up in the park under a pair of Joshua trees, when he'd been struck by two realities. Not thoughts, not imaginings, not insights. This was *real*.

The first was, if he didn't get off the road and fast, he would never make it back.

The second was, his sister was praying for him, right then. That very moment.

Which was why he had to clear his throat very hard before he could ask, "Did Victoria tell you about the bet?"

Eilene reached one hand toward Wayne and patted the air between them. "I've got to go make a call."

Wayne watched the kids playing their game and spinning the ball so it danced to either side of her. She just walked forward, her shoulders hunched slightly, too worried over what was coming next to pay the game any mind.

Foster asked, "We done here?"

Before Wayne could respond, the big kid got a bad toss, or maybe the other kid actually meant to slap him in the face with the ball. As in, Eilene was still within shouting distance, so the little kid was safe. But the big kid had about as much impulse control as Wayne, because he one-handed the ball hard enough to knock the little kid on his tokus.

Eilene veered off course so fast it might have seemed to everyone else like she wasn't just expecting it, but waiting for it to happen.

She gripped the big kid by the ear. A mean grip that had the kid howling. Walked him back to where Wayne was standing. "Julio, meet Wayne. Wayne, meet Julio."

"Ease up on the flesh there, sis."

"You pay off your bet in two parts."

Wayne was already backing away. "Hold on there. One bet, one pay."

Eilene thrust the ear forward and the kid followed. "The first part is, find some way to get through to Julio."

"Hang on . . ." Wayne stopped talking because his sister was doing her steam-driven shunt across the lot and toward the center. She slammed the door hard enough to punctuate everything that had gone unsaid.

Wayne glanced at the kid. Julio was doing a professional job of pretending he could not have cared less about anything.

Foster waited until Wayne turned back around to say, "I've got a favor to ask."

⟡

Foster went all silent after that. Just made his request and went so still Wayne assumed he was irritated. Probably over having to share the truck's seat with this barrio kid. Julio, though, he acted like this was totally in the realm of normal. Having a woman pastor dump him into the hands of two strange men, who take off in a pickup and don't speak a word.

Wayne put the kid down as a very strong fifteen. Julio was big-framed, muscular, and far too well padded for his own good. Not handsome, but he might have been if he could get his weight down by about a third. He was dressed in what probably passed for studly teen gear in the barrio—pants hanging low, baggy shirt, heavy silver chain on his neck. Semi-new Nikes, worn loose. Leather wristband with fake gemstone studs. And carrying a whole truckload of attitude.

Wayne did what Foster asked, which was to drive them to Orlando's international airport. The multi-story parking lot sported a different cartoon animal for each floor, as though the operators assumed a family overloaded on Disney would find it assuring. Julio gave the grinning camel a sideways look, as in, he hadn't expected this kind of twist to his day.

Foster didn't speak until they were inside the terminal. "Give me an hour, will you?"

"No problem. Long as you need."

"It used to be a sort of hobby, coming here. Back before they decided I was too old to drive."

"You don't have to explain." Only then did Wayne realize Foster had been silent out of shame. Wayne pointed at the giant departures board. "Rendezvous here in an hour."

He found Julio standing in a space all his own. The tide of pastel parents with their Snow White daughters and Darth Vader sons gave Julio a wide berth. These folks had traveled to Orlando for a break from reality, only to find themselves facing a kid who, if he wasn't packing, at least knew where to arm himself faster than they could find the Disney exit. For his part, Julio watched the crowds like he would a herd of wildebeests.

Wayne walked over and asked, "You ever been to Disney World?"

"You kidding? Man, just getting in that place costs sixty bucks. I look like I got sixty bucks to you?"

Wayne spotted signs for the food court. "You want something to eat?"

"I won't say no." Julio fell into step beside Wayne. "So you were in the army, right? I heard your sister say that once. Where you been, man?"

"Kabul, Kandahar, southwest frontier."

"That's like in Iraq?"

"Close enough. What do you want to eat?"

The Orlando airport was designed to swallow crowds. Every open space was huge and high ceilinged. The food hall was a two-acre dome encircled by takeouts. "Pizza and a smoothie."

"Go for it."

When they had their orders and were seated at a table, the kid asked, "So you ever been shot at, man?"

"That's a question you never ask a soldier."

"Sure, I hear that. Don't ask, don't tell. Just like the joint."

Wayne had to smile. "You know prison speech?"

"I oughtta. My old man's doing ten to twenty at Raiford."

"I'm sorry to hear that."

He took a massive bite of the pizza. "My brother. An uncle. Lessee, two aunts. And a cousin."

"They've all been in prison?"

"No, man. Doing time now."

"Get out."

"This is for real, man."

"I don't believe you."

Julio shrugged and went all quiet until he was licking the tomato sauce off his hands. "And my grandfather."

Wayne laughed out loud. "Now I know you're pulling my chain."

"You think I care what you believe?"

"Okay, where?"

"My old man's at Raiford, like I said. One aunt's in Perry. That's in Alabama. Brother and the other aunt are in county lockups, one on trial in Kansas City, the other in J-ville waiting for a space to open up. Granddad's doing life in the big Q."

Whether or not Julio was telling the truth, the geography lesson in the national penal system was impressive. "How old are you?"

"Thirteen."

"I figured you for older."

"Yeah, I get that a lot."

"So what are you doing at Eilene's center?"

Julio aged about fifty years. "Trying to stay clean, man. That's all. Just looking for a way out."

The kid looked so sad Wayne felt stripped down himself. "You want another pizza?"

"No, man. I'm good."

He slid from the booth. "Just stay here a second, okay? I need to go find my friend."

⁂

Wayne stood beneath the departures board, scoping the hordes. He was about to go have Foster paged when Wayne spotted him.

The old man was seated in the first row of chairs facing one terminal's wing and the light-rail station. The security line was a thousand strong. Older kids shouted off their sugar highs. Younger children wriggled and shrilled against being trapped in arms and this creeping line. Parents wore the weary expressions of having overdosed on fantasy. Foster did not appear to notice the surrounding bedlam at all.

The arriving passengers formed a tidal wave out of the light-rail terminal. They streamed between the security station and Foster's chair. He watched the reunions with a hunger Wayne could feel across the hall.

A college-aged girl rushed forward and danced out of her backpack so she could properly hug a tanned man and woman. A pair of young parents stopped, forcing the crowd to stream around them; the mother lowered her baby and urged her to walk toward an older woman trying hard not to cry. Kids raced through the gates and froze at the sight of the Disney store flanked by a giant Mickey and Snow White, and next door loomed a Universal Studios monster whose mouth framed the shop entrance; the kids took a giant breath and screamed over seeing their dreams come true.

Foster sat with his hands folded in his lap, just another elderly gentleman waiting for kin. Every now and then one unsteady hand rose and stroked the edges of his mouth.

Wayne returned to the food hall and slipped into his chair. He said to Julio, "My friend needs a little more time."

TEN

The neighborhood Julio directed them into was five miles and an entire dimension removed from tourist mania. Wayne drove down streets that looked recently imported from Kabul, right down to the graffiti he couldn't read and the bullet holes.

From Julio's other side, Foster muttered, "Who invaded us?"

"What, you think Orlando-town is all happy songs and marching bands?" Julio pointed at a trio of low-slung apartment buildings. "Here's good, man."

Wayne's tires scrunched over glass as he pulled to the curb. He faced an apartment building streaked with old smoke and graffiti. The ground floor windows were all boarded up. Two defunct bikes hung on rusting chains from a fence. "Who lives here?"

"My grandmother and me." He waited while Foster climbed down, then slid from the truck. He offered Foster a fist. "It was cool hanging with you guys."

Foster looked uncertainly at the fist. "Last time I checked, buddies were supposed to shake."

"Whatever. Later, man." Julio walked away without a backward glance.

Foster climbed back in the truck and waited until the kid had disappeared to ask, "What did your sister tell you?"

"Get through to him." Wayne waited until the kid had disappeared to pull away. "Some payback, huh."

They didn't actually plan that evening's action for drama's sake. But they didn't do much to stop it either.

The instant Wayne pulled into the community parking lot, he knew. The news was out, and the people were ready.

Maybe Victoria let it slip. Or Eilene. Or maybe just the oldfolks' ESP had been working overtime. However it happened, they didn't call a meeting, because they didn't need to. After dinner, Wayne, Foster, and Jerry started toward the community center, the cash split three ways so none of them had to stagger. The residents took that as their cue. They streamed out front doors and off porches and down stairs. They came out of lawn chairs and abandoned their favorite sunset benches. They hobbled on canes. They clanked on walkers. They rolled in wheelchairs. But they came.

"I feel like the Pied Piper of wrinkles," Jerry said.

"If anybody gets too close, swing hard," Foster said. "They bite."

"No telling what germs they got stewing in those dentures," Jerry agreed.

Holly Reeves was there to open the front door. She stood in one corner and watched them stack the cash on the front table. Then Foster and Jerry started taking a couple of stacks at a time, reading off the slips of paper Wayne had slipped into the rubber bands. Calling out the names, walking over, handing out the cash. Wayne just stood to one side, watching the pile on the table dwindle. When the last couple had received their share, he turned to Holly and said, "The rest is yours."

The community director trembled in a manner that sprinkled her cheeks with tears. "How . . ."

"Daughter."

To Wayne's surprise, it was Victoria who interrupted. "Perhaps it would be best if we focused on gratitude and not questions."

ELEVEN

The next morning was Florida perfect, a great day to kick back and pretend the world was free of bad news. Which was why Wayne left soon after dawn for a long country run. At least, it started that way.

Running used to be this beautiful thing, a time each day when his body could exult in being young and powerful. He would run until his legs simply gave way. Run and run, further and further, no idea how to get back. Not caring, really. Most days he just ran and wished he could just keep on down the road or track or beach, until a different reality rose up and swallowed him whole.

Then when his strength returned he'd stagger back. To a world that told him he didn't have a hope of measuring up.

Since leaving the army, runs had become times for the memory reel to spin out snippets of emotional junk. Technicolor spew was how he thought of it, wishing he could permanently delete the lot.

This particular morning, his memory did none of the

normal spinning. Instead, it focused down upon one particular memory. One he had not thought of in a very long while—so long it caught him totally by surprise. Today's selection was of the day Wayne joined his father's church.

He'd gone forward at age eleven. Wayne had been the last in his Sunday school class to do so. He had no idea whether he believed in God. But the previous Sunday, after dunking the next-to-last kid in Wayne's class, his dad had taken on a pressure cooker kind of frown. As in, do this or else. Wayne had been tempted to hold out, see if this might be the thing to actually unravel his father's pastoral cool, the mask he never took off for anybody. But Wayne caved. And walked forward. Doing it for the only possible reason that would actually have drawn him up there to the front. His big sister asked him to.

It had been one of those rare moments when Eilene's strength had given way. Even back then, Wayne had recognized his sister to have a power all her own. In some manner she was the stronger of the two. But that morning, while he sat avoiding his father's glare and Eilene prepared another silent breakfast, she had looked at him and mouthed one word. The hardest thing in her existence to say. *Please.*

At times like that, Wayne had never been able to deny her anything.

❦

This morning, Wayne made a seven-mile loop around a strip mall and a defunct waterfront park, then swung back by the community's newest neighbor. The new development was little more than raw earth and bulldozers clogging the early morning air. A huge sign proclaimed a Cloister development of championship golf course, deep harbor marina, competition pool, shopping center, and of course home lots available at preconstruction prices. Wayne stood and leaned against the fence until the earthmovers rumbled away the last of his recollections, then turned and jogged home.

The final half mile was a long sprint through old Florida, past the community gates and the final flock of orange trees, down the line of live oaks, his footsteps soft on the old lane of crushed rock and clamshells.

His regular crew was there to observe his sweaty return. Foster greeted him with, "You're late."

Wayne eased himself down in stages. "We finished the gig, remember?"

Jerry watched Wayne sprawl on the grass and start stretching. "Wonder what would've happened, I showed up for work only when we had a new crime."

Foster said, "You see the red rocket parked in front of the community center?"

"Hard to miss."

Jerry said, "Your sister's here too. They been in Holly's office for almost an hour."

Wayne showered and dressed and emerged to find the three of them standing in his front yard. Holly, his sister, and the mystery lady. He stepped onto the porch and wanted to say something cute like, The three horsewomen of the apocalypse. The ladies looked very serious. And seriously tense.

Jerry set aside his paperback novel and Foster stopped pretending to read the *Journal*. Wayne didn't say anything, but he wanted to, because right then it felt mighty good to have some backup.

Instead, he said to his sister, "This has got to be about the other half of my debt. As in, the debt that wasn't yours to begin with and nobody said nothing about splitting or doubling or whatever you want to call it. My wager was with Victoria."

"Yeah, well, you should've read the fine print."

Which, Wayne had to admit, wasn't a half-bad comeback for a pastor.

Eilene said to the community leader, "You first."

Holly had adopted his sister's stance, arms doing a tight body wrap and face seamed by a day that had dawned old. "We promised you a commission."

Foster said, "Thirty percent sounds good."

The community director absorbed the blow and refused to go down. "That's absurd."

"So is getting back enough cash to keep this place afloat."

"You can't possibly expect—"

Foster broke in, "Of what the community received. Not the families."

"No," Wayne said. "I don't want it."

Foster gave him angry. "As your agent, I would advise you to keep your trap shut."

Wayne told the community head, "Pay me what you paid the other accountant. Let me have this house."

He was about to say, *That's all.* Then he had a vision of two old guys smiling their way across moonlit waters and added, "And a boat."

"What?"

"Not a big one. A fishing skiff. For the community. Flat-bottomed, thirty horse kicker, trolling motor. And some decent fishing poles."

The three women exchanged a glance. One that suggested they had come over here with a lot more on their minds than Wayne's payday.

His sister asked, "You done?" Only her question was not directed at her brother and his comeback, but at Holly.

"Yes." The community director's voice was like the last puff of air from a busted balloon. "I suppose so."

Eilene glanced at the mystery lady. Who looked as fine close up as she had from an oblique distance. Maybe even better. Dark hair. Stunning features. Built. The mystery lady gave his sister a fraction of a nod. Eilene returned her sour gaze back to her brother leaning against the doorjamb. "We need to talk."

"What have we been doing so far?"

"Alone, Wayne." Turning his name into three syllables and a public scolding.

Wayne took genuine pleasure in a simple shake of his head. "This is my crew."

Foster said, "We're his background."

"The word," Jerry said, "is backup."

"Whatever." Foster waved it aside. "We're like family."

&

But once they were inside, all Eilene wanted to talk about was the kid. "Julio had a great time with you."

From his post where he was brewing coffee, Jerry asked, "Who is Julio?"

"Half the payback on the bet," Foster explained.

Holly asked, "What bet?"

"Never mind," Eilene said. She went on to Wayne, "The kid has nothing and no one. Then this guy shows up, a walking talking army man, and takes him for a drive, buys him pizza, asks him questions, treats him like he's somebody."

Jerry emerged from the kitchenette, his expression saying he didn't like being ignored. "Did Victoria okay this payment on her bet?"

Eilene rounded on him. "Hey. I'm talking here."

Jerry retreated into the kitchen. "I guess my questions can wait."

Eilene said to her brother, "You think maybe . . ."

"No," Wayne said. "No."

She sighed. Clearly wanted to argue. Instead she turned to the mystery lady and said, "He's all yours."

But before the lady could speak, Foster said, "I think introductions are in order here."

Eilene was still too worked up over being turned down. She gave Foster the sort of huff she normally reserved for her brother.

Wayne said, "Allow me. I'm—"

"I know who you are."

The voice was all burr and rough music, the words slanted at the edges like her eyes. Wayne thought it was silly getting a tingle in his gut, just hearing this woman finally speak. He saw in her gaze the message he had come to know all too well. The one that said, I'm not going to give you anything like what you want. Not now, not ever.

But there was nothing to be gained by letting her know he knew. So he leaned back in his chair, crossed his arms, and asked coolly, "And you are?"

"My name is my own. I will tell you only if you agree to help. Otherwise, I will leave here today and you will never see me again."

The longer she spoke, the more distinctive her accent became. A slight rolling of the *r*'s, a musical inflection to some vowels. Try as she might to give him nothing but serious chill, the woman tasted each word in a most exotic fashion.

She made a mistake then. That is, if she intended on holding this little gathering to a totally professional level. Nerves or a simple desire to dominate caused her to rise from her chair and begin to pace.

Jerry emerged from the kitchen. Foster settled back in his chair, deeply involved in the show. The woman transformed the bare boards into a catwalk rimmed with lights and cameras.

"I represent a very important businessman. He holds considerable power in central Florida. He . . ."

It was the woman's turn to take a two-armed grip upon herself. She wore a skirt of linen smoke and a matching jacket tight enough to make self-hugging a strain. But she did it anyway. She held on and she paced.

"You might as well tell him," Eilene said. "It won't get any easier."

The woman said, "He believes he has been visited by an angel."

She made two more circuits of Wayne's tiny front room before Jerry said, "Run that last bit by us again."

"You heard her," Eilene said.

"I heard the words, but I'm not putting them together well."

"An angel," the woman repeated.

"As in, guardian angel?"

"He doesn't believe in them."

Eilene said, "Guardian angel is a Catholic term. Or earlier. A lot of pagan sects hold to the concept. There's nothing in the Bible to suggest humans have individual . . ." She stopped because of the look her brother gave her. "What?"

Wayne said, "Skip the history lesson and get to the now."

The woman stopped by the rear window. She said to the outside world, "He believes he has been visited by an angel."

"God's holy messenger," Eilene said.

Jerry asked, "This guy, he's a religious nutcase as well as rich?"

The woman just stared out the window.

"I've known him for fifteen years," Eilene said. "He's a friend. Yes, he lives for his faith. And no, he's not insane."

"Delusional, then."

The woman said, "That's what I want you to find out."

Wayne asked, "Why me?"

The woman touched the glass by her face. As though wanting to assure herself of reality.

Eilene said, "Something the angel told him."

The woman corrected, "If it was an angel."

"Of course," Eilene said.

Wayne asked his sister, "You were there?"

"No."

"Then, if you don't mind, I'd like to hear it from her."

The woman said, "I was not there either."

"But this guy, he described it to you, right? So tell me what he said."

The woman's accent grew decidedly stronger. "The angel told this gentleman that he was in grave danger and must hide himself away—his life and the lives of his family depended on it. The angel also told him to find himself a warrior. Someone he can trust to act as his arms and legs. This warrior must be one who gives his strength to the weak. One who cares little for gold."

She was Russian, Wayne decided. Or one of the break-off states with *stan* at the end of its name. It went with the slanted eyes and the haughty demeanor. "I don't have anything against money."

"You refused your commission," Holly pointed out.

Foster asked, "That's what you three were doing in your office before you come marching over here. Talking about how you were going to set our buddy up, see if he'd go for the money?"

Eilene said, "We had to know."

"He's your *brother*."

"That's right. And this is a friend in a crisis situation." Eilene vented a trace of steam with her words. "Since the incident, her boss has refused to leave his estate. He's turned his entire empire over to associates. Some of whom she does not trust."

Wayne said, "So you think one of his people used this guy's religion against him—"

"His faith," Eilene corrected. "This has nothing to do with religion."

Wayne waited until he was sure she was done, then continued, "Used it against him so they could take control of his company?"

The woman did not respond.

Jerry said, "Man, that is *cold*."

"Tell me," Eilene said.

Wayne said, "So you want me to investigate this situation and discover who's behind the scam."

"No." The woman turned around and gave him a look of feline fear. "I want you to keep my friend alive."

TWELVE

Wayne found his sister seated by the dovecote. A stand of old pear trees formed a living canopy between the domed enclosure and the water. Eilene kept her gaze upon the birds as Wayne carried over an old plastic chair and seated himself. His sister was wrapped in a band of tension that just begged for a reason to spring.

He struggled to find a way to ask the obvious, which was, Is this for real?

Then Eilene said, "Mom dreamed about us sitting in a place just like this. Surrounded by a huge cage of birds. In the sunlight. As grown-ups. That was how she said it. Her two babies all grown up and sitting together while the birds flitted and sang. It made her so happy."

The surprise was great enough to push his own questions to the back. Eilene rarely spoke about their mother. "When was this?"

"In the hospital. One of the last times I saw her alone."

Eilene had been twelve when their mom died of cancer,

Wayne ten. Two little kids surrounded by people who thought the world of their father. "You never thought about mentioning this before now?"

He expected lip. If Eilene was tense and sad enough to be talking about their mother, Wayne figured she was a grenade with the pin in the dust. Instead, what he got was, "I totally forgot. You know how things were after she . . ."

"I know." Their father had refused to mourn. He was, after all, a pastor who dealt constantly with funerals and loss and a congregation's earthly woes. He had locked himself up tight and vented his despair in tight wisps of disapproval. Most of them directed at Wayne.

Eilene went on, "I sit here for a while almost every time I come. And I've never thought of that time with Mom until just now, when you walked over. I was standing by her bed. She stroked my cheek. She told me everything was going to be all right. God had given her a sign. She had dreamed of her two babies all grown up, sitting by a cage of birds as big as a house, and we were talking about her."

Eilene stopped then. Took a ragged breath. Put her hands together on the table in front of her and clenched them down upon the wood. Breathed again. "She was so happy."

He stared at her. Eilene did not do sad and resigned. "What is going on here?"

She did not look up. "The businessman she was talking about is a very good person. He helps a lot of people. Our church is built on land he donated. People hit on him constantly because they know he'll help if he can. He deserves better than this."

"So you think it's a scam." When his sister did not respond, Wayne said, "What else could it be?"

Eilene just stared at her hands.

"You want me to take this on?"

Eilene said to the hands gripping one another upon the table, "I don't know what I want."

❧

On the way back to the house, a very strange thing happened.

One moment, he was just Wayne Grusza, walking alongside his sister the pastor. A woman with whom, truth be told, he had a relationship that could only have been described as rocky. Eilene said to him, "Julio won't stop talking about you and the trip to the airport. The kid really connected with you."

Wayne was ready to give her back the sort of semi-argument that had made up about ninety percent of every conversation they had ever had. As in, was this still payback on a debt he didn't owe her?

When it happened.

A pair of ladies he could not have picked out of a lineup were walking from the bungalows to the parking lot. They spotted Wayne and Eilene emerging from the trees' shadows and veered off course, Wayne assumed to pass the time of day with Eilene.

Instead, the one using a cane said, "We were just going to the store. Do you need anything?"

Wayne did a double take at the realization they were talking to him. "I'm good, thanks."

"What's your favorite dessert?"

"Excuse me?"

Eilene answered, "Wayne takes a universal approach to sweets, but he's always been addicted to chocolate."

One woman said to the other, "Your chocolate mud pie recipe isn't too bad."

"It's better than yours, is what you mean."

"For chocolate mud pie," Eilene said, "my brother would become your willing slave."

"Oh, that won't be necessary." The ladies bestowed a twinned smile in Wayne's direction and tottered away.

It took him the rest of the way back to his home to identify the sensation. Until he spied Jerry and Foster seated on his front porch, talking softly to the mystery lady leaning against the side railing.

After all, Wayne had put a lot of years and miles between himself and the last time he had ever felt like he belonged.

Before Eilene started up the steps, Wayne halted her with a touch to the arm and asked, "About Julio. Tell me what you want."

She found it hard to plead. "School gets out tomorrow. By next week he'll be hanging. You know what that means, right?"

"I was Special Ops, remember? Most of my team were born to hang." One way or the other.

"Julio is ready game for the druggies cruising the streets. His brother and father are both made men. Julio's a known quantity. The dealers will pressure him to hustle their wares to the other kids. He's got nothing. How long is he going to say no?"

"I'll talk to him again if you want, Eilene."

Her silent thanks almost made him blush. As if he had finally managed to get the deal right in her eyes.

As Wayne climbed his front stairs, the mystery woman gave him a beautiful version of the stink eye, clearly expecting him to decline her offer. Instead, he leaned against the wall next to Jerry's chair and said, "I'll need to talk with your guy directly."

She looked first at Eilene, then said, "I can make that happen."

"Not just once. I need regular access."

"I will tell him."

"And his books. Corporate and personal. And somebody who'll walk me through the auditing process."

"He employs a battery of accountants."

"Just one. Somebody you trust. Better still, somebody who'll answer only to you. Someone you are certain won't blab to a soul about what we're doing."

"What I meant was, people keep a very close eye on his finances."

"Yeah, but how many are looking for an in-house scam?"

She nodded. "I will make this happen. Do you want to talk about your pay?"

"You strike me as somebody who came with a number you were going to argue over until you got it."

She gave a very European gesture, a slight forward thrust to her chin, a minimalist shrug.

"I'll take it. There. I saved us both a lot of trouble."

Jerry said, "You forgot to ask her name."

Wayne kept his gaze locked on target. "I didn't forget a thing."

"Tatyana," she replied. "Tatyana Kuchik."

Eilene said, "Tatyana is an attorney. She has just one client."

But Wayne could see Tatyana drawing back now, uncertain whether to speak this semi-famous guy's name in front of people she didn't know. So he said, "Where do you want this meeting to take place?"

"He lives near Vero Beach. First I'll need to go back to our Orlando offices and report in."

The idea struck him then. One that might draw a bit of sanity from a day that otherwise was totally off the wall. "When you come back, would you mind giving a kid a ride?"

THIRTEEN

Jerry wore his stone cop expression the next morning. Wayne came back from his run to find Foster sitting on his wide porch with the newspaper and Jerry in his kitchen making coffee. Wayne watched through the open window as Jerry lined things up on Wayne's new kitchen counter. The kitchen was to his right and the living room, with the door to the porch, was on his left. Wayne wiped his face with his T-shirt and then watched Jerry set the coffee utensils out, as neat as little soldiers. Wayne liked how the wood looked in the sunlight, liked the smell. He had found a pile of old boards behind the maintenance shed, probably roofing timbers and at least a half century old, thick as his calf. He had planed them and sawed them and laid out a new countertop to replace the peeling linoleum.

Jerry said through the window, "The thing kept me awake all night."

Wayne didn't need to ask what thing. He had not slept much either.

"We've got a crook working inside the guy's company."

Foster went through his folding routine with the paper, lining up the edges with a machinist's precision, getting it down to magazine size. "If he worked inside the company, the boss would've known him."

Wayne said, "We're not talking about the angel."

"Point one, it wasn't no angel."

Foster snorted. "Oh, and you're so well connected to the man upstairs you'd know one? I don't think so."

"Hey. My mama didn't raise no fool."

"And you think this guy got to be boss of some big company being a fool?"

"That's been bugging me too," Wayne agreed.

Jerry poured a mug, handed it through the window to Foster. "Let's say there's two of them for the moment. A crook in the company who wants to take charge. But he's a known quantity. So he comes up with this scheme, hire himself an outsider who's gonna play on the man's core weakness."

"Hold this." Foster handed Wayne his mug, set down his paper, and pushed himself erect. He took back his mug and said, "Who're you to call a man's religion a weakness?"

"Since when did you get big on the faith thing?"

"We're not talking about me. We're talking about a man who uses what he's earned to do good. That's got to count for something, even in this cockeyed old world."

Wayne accepted his own mug, hooked his T-shirt over the porch railing, and backed off a pace. Content to stand there on his partially redone porch, listening to two guys the world called losers argue over a man none of them had ever met. Wayne was flooded anew with the same strange sensation he had experienced the day before, walking back from the dove-cote with his sister. An elderly trio walked past on the lane, hard-of-hearing Harry and his wife and another lady. Harry hefted his cane in greeting. Harry's wife said something to Wayne about the weather. The other woman gave him a wave and kept going.

Jerry said, "You're taking this personal."

Foster said, "Doggone right. A man like this deserves better."

"You let your emotions cloud your judgment, you can't work a case clean."

"Yeah, well, that might work okay for Mister Ace Detective, but me, I do my best work when I'm good and hot."

Jerry refilled his mug and walked out of the kitchen and through the living room and joined them on the porch. "Let's get back to this scam."

Wayne said, "So we're assuming this was not an angel."

Jerry didn't even bother to respond to that one. "You notice any resemblance to what we just been through here?"

"You mean the accountant?"

"I'm not saying there's a connection. But it just hits me as strange, how we got two scams so close together. Big ones. Operated by pros." Jerry used his mug as a pointer. "Foster here is no dummy—he managed a whole string of dry cleaners."

"I did," Foster corrected, "until my stinko of a nephew robbed me blind."

"And I worked crime for thirty years. That accountant took us both in. Now we got another guy with some serious experience running people and managing money, who's been hit hard enough and low enough that he's holed up in his own house and letting other people run his company." Jerry tasted his mug. "Cops hate coincidences."

Wayne said, "We need to find out who leases the scam artist his Lantern Island house."

"Let me make a couple of calls," Jerry said.

A whining grew in the distance, the sound familiar enough now that they all turned as one. Foster said, "Here comes trouble."

The red Ferrari seemed impatient even when going slow. Particularly when the driver could not help but gun the motor once before cutting it off. The silence afterwards felt like a vacuum.

The two doors opened. Tatyana wore a business suit with a skirt so short, getting out of the Ferrari became a dance of the pinstriped veils.

Julio emerged from the car in a teenage daze. Big as he was, he scarcely seemed connected to the earth as he followed Tatyana over to the porch.

Jerry said, "Trouble is right."

Tatyana said something to Julio in rapid-fire Spanish. The kid responded with a goofy grin, clearly so in love with the woman and her ride he forgot all about the need for the street.

"Hope you made sure your radio is still where it belongs," Jerry said.

Tatyana spoke to Julio again in Spanish and his eyes congealed to black stone. The lady had obviously just revealed the black man's former profession.

"Nothing like a cop to kill a good high," Julio said.

"I'm retired, *ese.*"

"You know what they say. You can take a pig out of the pen—"

"Whoa. Enough." Wayne walked down the stairs. "We're all friends, okay?"

Jerry demanded, "What's Señor Drive-By doing here?"

"I invited him."

Foster said, "This is the kid I told you about."

"You spent a morning with this guy? You check your wallet?"

Tatyana found the exchange humorous. She asked Julio, "You'll be okay here for a while?"

The grin partly resurfaced. "If it means another ride with you, sure thing."

"I don't know how long we'll be."

"No problem."

Jerry said, "Guys that deal in stolen goods, they generally don't live by the clock."

Wayne snapped, "I said enough."

Jerry started into the house, then turned back to say, "I got your number, *ese.*"

Tatyana gave Wayne's sweaty form a swift up and down. "I was hoping for something a little more formal."

"I'll be right back."

Jerry was still banging around the kitchen when Wayne finished showering and dressing. He walked outside to find Julio in full slouch mode, sullenly determined to ignore the

117

glares Jerry was casting through the front window. Wayne said to Julio, "Let's take a walk."

He was aimed at the maintenance shed, hoping the caretaker might be open to a bribe, when Victoria pushed through her screen door and demanded, "Who do we have here?"

"This is Julio."

Victoria began pattering off in Spanish, even faster than Tatyana. The kid responded with a smile so huge his entire face was transformed. One minute a card-carrying member of the Crips, another and he was just a big-boned kid.

Victoria sighed with genuine pleasure. "I can't thank you enough, Wayne."

"Eilene asked if I could maybe . . ."

But the old lady was already waving him away and Julio inside, all in one grand gesture. "I missed this young man before we even met."

Something about the way Tatyana handled the car left Wayne wondering if she was showing off for his benefit. Which was more than a tad odd, since she had given him nothing except ice. But the longer he sat in the passenger seat with his tail almost dragging on the asphalt, the more certain he became. Maybe it was a female thing, wanting to show the jock she had what it took to handle the machine. Whatever the reason, he enjoyed it. The car was so low it made their speed seem even faster than it really was, which was already enough to stutter his heart. At the light leading to the causeway she was first in line. A lowrider with a pair of gardener's helpers drew up next to her and rattled the exhaust. A Hispanic teen leaned out his window and shouted something that was almost lost to the noise of two rumbling engines. Tatyana called back something that caused the other driver to rev his motor way past redline. Tatyana burned a quarter-moon of rubber onto the bridge and hit a hundred in second gear.

They headed north on A1A, flying through the two-lane traffic like the lanes and the double-yellow lines were laid out for mortals. She handled the road and the machine with the tight economy of a woman born to speed. The coastal highway opened up beyond the Vero city limits, rimmed by walls of well-tended green. Here and there Wayne spied fleeting images of seaside mansions and condos in wedding-cake pastels. Tatyana downshifted and took the turn to John's Island in a controlled four-wheel spin. And kept slowing when the gate arm blocking the entrance did not rise.

A grizzled veteran with worn tattoos and an expression to match Jerry's came out of the central guard house.

Wayne figured the beefy guard was going to give Tatyana as serious a warning as he could without drawing his gun. Instead, he leaned down, stripped off his aviator shades, and asked, "This the guy?"

"Wayne Grusza. This is Officer Coltrane, chief of John's Island security."

The cop was also seriously country. "He don't look like no pencil neck to me."

"He is—" Tatyana turned and gave him one of her patented slit-eyed inspections. "An investigative accountant."

The guard chewed on that for a moment, his belt creaking

as he shifted his weight. He said to Wayne, "Mr. Grey is a good man. Here on John's Island, we take care of our own. You hear what I'm saying, Mister Accountant?"

"Loud and clear."

He had watery blue eyes that floated in a web of red. "You tell Mr. Grey he needs anything, he's got my number."

FOURTEEN

A s far as Wayne was concerned, John's Island was seriously misnamed. The place should have been called Castle-by-the-Sea.

Two lanes ran side by side, one for cars and the other for golf carts. Wayne spotted a couple in matching togs and tans seated inside an electric surrey, right down to the fringed top. They were followed by a metallic silver cart with a fake Rolls Royce hood. Palms marched down both sides of both lanes in well-behaved rows. The orderliness defied anyone to speak an improper word or break rules that had no need of being posted. Even Tatyana lost her taste for speed.

"I hate this place already," Wayne declared.

Tatyana was too busy being tense to respond. She turned into a drive of pearl-white paving stones and rumbled up to a palace only slightly smaller than Disney's. Two peaked turrets sprouted from opposite ends, both sheathed in plates of polarized glass. The effect was like being inspected by a pair of frog eyes wearing Wayfarers.

She cut the motor but made no move to open her door. "There's one more thing I need to tell you."

"How did the cop know about the problem here?"

"He doesn't exactly ..." She waved that aside. "I need to tell you something. I fear I may have misspoken. The angel did not say my associate must find a warrior."

"I thought you didn't believe in angels."

The hand waved a second time. "What he said was, my associate's challenge was to find himself a hero."

≪

"Mr. Grusza, did I say that right? Easton Grey."

The man had a gaze to match his name, clear as winter smoke, biting and deep. There was nothing easy about this man—no wasted motion, no spare flesh. He was not small so much as economical. Wayne decided he would hate to sit across the poker table from this guy.

That is, if a guy who believed in angels played cards.

Mr. Grey might have been dressed for at-home casual. He might offer Wayne a buddy handshake and lead them through the living room into a small parlor by the kitchen. He might even pour coffee for them himself. But there was no question in Wayne's mind. Right from the get-go, he knew.

This guy was the real deal.

While on duty, he had met a couple of generals. Not on parade. In the field. Out where it counted. And both of those guys, they could take their medals off and pack away all the stars, and they would still be who they were. Leaders.

Just like this guy.

"How do you take your coffee, Mr. Grusza?"

"Black is fine."

"Take a seat anywhere. Tatyana, would you like any-thing?"

"I'm fine, thank you, Mr. Grey."

Wayne noted that. How even the frost queen was toned down in front of this guy. And no hint of lovey-dovey between them. Just a superior and his subordinate. Two pros.

Here to discuss a divine visitation.

"Do you believe in God, Mr. Grusza? I know your father was a pastor."

"And his sister," Tatyana added.

"Of course. But I still need to know. Are you a man of abiding faith?"

Wayne set his coffee on the table between them. "Proba-bly not."

Wayne took his time and scanned the place. The floors were patterned marble throughout all the rooms he had seen, including the kitchen. The coved ceilings were too high to measure, sixteen or maybe even eighteen feet. The kitchen had an open layout, with domed little false halls separating it from the living room on one side and the dining room on the other. The room where they now sat was an alcove that fronted onto the pool area and a long sloping lawn. A brown-haired girl in awkward adolescence tossed a Frisbee to a barking Lab. Beyond a border of blooming trees sparkled the blue-blue Indian River. And beyond that, over on the mainland, was a community of retirees in their little houses, three of which could fit into this guy's living room. Reality.

Grey asked, "Are you saved?"

The guy would just not let it go. "As a kid I walked the walk, but mostly for my dad. When I left home I pretty much left all the God stuff as well. So the answer is, I really have no idea."

They were seated in padded rattan chairs, with a glass-topped rattan table between them. The table was octagonal, like the room. The table was positioned precisely over an identical section of marble laid into the floor. The marble was as blue as the waters beyond the bay windows.

"Well, it wouldn't be the first time God uses a miracle to bring a nonbeliever home."

To either side of Grey's chair were smaller versions of the rattan table. On one rested an open Bible, a pad, and a pencil. The two pages of Scripture Wayne could see were heavily annotated, words underlined, passages highlighted, comments scrawled in the top and bottom and side margins.

Grey said, "Obviously my questions have made you uncomfortable, Mr. Grusza. I apologize. But you must understand that this is a very important issue to me."

A well-kept woman of middle years entered the kitchen. Wayne took her for Grey's wife. She paused by the central island, straightened a container on the granite top, and moved out of Wayne's field of vision. Something about the way she held herself, or how she glanced over and took them all in, the tight focus she pressed upon Wayne, left him certain. There was nothing offhand about her passage.

Wayne said, "Could you tell me about what happened?"

"I was at the dentist."

"When was it?"

"A week ago. Last Thursday afternoon. The dentist was running late. There was some kind of emergency. The receptionist asked if I'd like to reschedule, but it was so hard to find the time, I thought I might as well stay. I returned a couple of calls. Gradually the place emptied out until I was the only one left. That was when he appeared."

The young girl passed by their window. Up close she resembled her father a lot—the same spare frame, the same intelligent grey eyes, the same reserve. She gave Wayne a hard stare, then glanced at her father. Clearly very worried. The Lab kept tugging on the Frisbee she held in her right hand, trying to get her to play some more. But the girl knew what was going on inside that little room, and it worried all the play out of her.

Wayne asked, "Can you describe this person?"

"African-American. Hard to guess his age. Late twenties, possibly a bit older. I'd put him at about six feet. A handsome, strong-looking face, clearly defined angles, hair cropped very short. Not big. But he moved like an athlete."

"How was he dressed?"

"Florida standard—polo shirt, pressed khakis, loafers."

"Anything about him that caught your eye?"

"Nothing except a sense of power."

"What did he say?"

"That he was a messenger sent by the Most High God."

The way Grey spoke the words, calm and straight ahead, made the angel almost real. "You didn't think to question this?"

"At first I thought he was a pastor. I meet so many of them. Perhaps I had donated to his cause, or maybe he was going to ask me for help. I had a thousand thoughts running through my head. But one thought stood out above all the others. This man was for real."

Wayne glanced over. Tatyana had extracted a notepad and silver pen. But she wrote nothing. And she saw only her boss. Her expression was unreadable. But her features had gone very pale. Wayne asked, "What else did he say?"

"The exchange lasted a grand total of ninety seconds. He told me that he had been sent to warn me. That I and my family and my charges were in grave danger."

"That was the word he used, 'charges'?"

The skin around his eyes tightened. "You know, that was an interesting thing. When he said the word, he hesitated. Like he was searching for the right term, the way a foreigner might."

Tatyana said, "You didn't mention this before."

"It just struck me."

Wayne asked, "Did he have an accent?"

"None at all. What I mean is, I couldn't say if he was American or not. He spoke English. His voice was very deep, very strong. He told me that we were in real and immediate danger. He said that for the sake of my family and my future, I needed to take refuge in my home. I should remove myself from my work. I should watch and pray. I should seek out a hero. A man with a warrior's past, who had learned to set aside his weapons and who gave no importance to money. A man who was strong when others were weak."

Easton Grey stared not at the sunlight-dappled waters beyond his lawn, but at the past. "The angel walked to the door. Then it was almost like he read my mind, because I hadn't said a word, I was too shocked. He said, 'If you identify the right hero, he will know what needs doing.' Then he left."

Tatyana gave him a minute, then said, "Tell him what happened next."

Grey directed his words at his aide. "I walked over to the receptionist. She was busy on the phone and it took a while. When she hung up I asked her who the man was that had just left. She asked, 'What man?' I described him. She said there was no African-American patient scheduled that day, and no new patient that week. She had no idea who I was talking about."

Wayne said, "Somebody got to her."

Grey nodded slowly. "That's certainly a possibility."

Wayne studied the man. This corporate general. "But you don't think so."

"Well." Grey almost managed a smile. "I'd hate to think I've spent a week in hiding for no reason."

FIFTEEN

W hen they drove back down the retirement compound's central avenue, they noticed a police car in front of the community center and another parked over by the lane leading to the waterfront homes.

Tatyana said, "Something's happened to one of the seniors."

"Or Julio's done something really special," Wayne replied. Thanks a lot, Eilene.

Before they had emerged from the car, Jerry came hustling over. "You ain't gonna believe this."

"Tell me it's not Julio."

"What? No. The kid's . . . Tell the truth, I been so busy I have no idea where the kid is." The man revealed a side Wayne had never seen before. A cop in high gear.

Tatyana remained by the car. "I need to get back to the office."

Jerry said, "You got a minute, you might want to tag along."

Wayne said, "I need to speak with you."

"First you are coming with me," Jerry insisted.

Tatyana looked genuinely worried. She had a two-fisted grip on the car's roof and door, intent on not going anywhere. "I will wait here."

Jerry studied her, reading the woman at below skin level. "Come on, let's go." He waited until they had crossed the lot to say, "That lady's got a thing about bad news."

"Or cops."

"Nah. I told her what I did, or used to do, she didn't bat an eye. A lady who drives a car like that ain't afraid of the odd run-in with the law." They hooked a left on the oyster-shell lane and headed down toward the bay. "I seen that before. Some folks get spooked on account of how things've gone down before."

As Jerry's house came into view, he lowered his voice and said, "Might be a good idea not to go into a lot of detail about the other night."

The two cops were waiting in Jerry's minuscule front yard. Each house had patches of private ground before and behind. Some grew flowers. Others set up borders and laid out Japanese-style gardens of stones and miniature trees. Jerry had a cluster of indoor-outdoor chairs set at an angle where the occupants could see the water. A young cop leaned against the side of Jerry's screened-in porch. Holly was seated between Foster and a heavy-set cop. His jacket was tossed over the back of his chair, revealing a badge and pistol clipped to his belt. He asked, "This the guy?"

"Wayne Grusza, Detective Mehan, Naples Police."

The detective was built like a cinder block and had a grip

to match. "Grab a chair, Grusza. You don't mind answering a few questions, right?"

"That depends."

"Now, that's not the sort of answer I'd expect from an innocent man."

"Innocent of what?"

Mehan's smile was a rubbery stretch of face and lips, there and gone. "Where's the lady I been hearing about?"

"She elected to stay by her car," Jerry said.

Mehan said to his young associate, "Why don't you go have a word, see if she'll join us."

Jerry warned, "She's a little skittish."

"Make sure she understands how important this is."

When the other cop had left, Mehan said, "I did a little checking around before I came over." He lifted his chin toward Jerry. "It seems your friend here has buddies right up to the governor's office. Five times decorated for bravery. Taught rookies at our own state school for five years, then decided he'd rather go back on the streets."

Foster said, "I live next door to you for six years, and I gotta learn these things from a stranger?"

Mehan slipped off his sunglasses and polished them with his tie. "Me, they gave me a chance to sit in a classroom all day, I'd be off duty in a heartbeat."

Wayne looked to where Jerry stood by the side of the house, his attention suddenly focused on the trees and the sparkling water. "He never mentioned any of that."

Mehan turned to Wayne. "And I guess you never thought to tell him about your bronze star or the purple heart."

Jerry looked up. "You took a hit?"

"What do you know. Something else you guys got in common. Besides breaking the law." Mehan slipped a notebook from his pocket. "What I'd like to hear about is, how come two stand-up citizens got involved in a felonious B&E that apparently went totally wrong."

Jerry said, "I never said anything about whatever you just mentioned."

"And I wasn't asking you." Mehan's sunglasses remained fixed on Wayne. "Well?"

"I was brought in to straighten out the community's books. I discovered they had been victims of a scam. One operated by their former accountant, Zachary Dorsett."

"You were sure about that. I'm asking, see, on account of how the experts I talked with at the state level said it was all supposition and conjecture."

"They're wrong."

"Well, that sure works for me."

"I can lay it out for you, but it took me weeks to work it out. Time your investigators at state weren't willing to give to a group of no-count retirees. People living on tiny pensions and Social Security in a patchwork of cottages the size of double-wides. People without a shred of clout. People easy to ignore."

"Hey, what do you know. Heat. I like that." Mehan made a note. "We can call it motive."

Jerry said to the waters, "Dorsett's been murdered."

Wayne felt a bitterness clogging his throat. A step or two ahead, just around the bend in a smelly concrete corridor, was a tiny room with bars. He heard the door give a foreboding clang. "That's why you're here?"

"What else could it possibly be, Mr. Grusza? Don't tell me you're responsible."

Jerry said, "I called you and asked where the guy was located. I called back and asked who the guy worked for. You want to connect the dots from a couple of innocent questions to where we're at?"

"Right now I'm just looking for a little help from a retired colleague. You want to make this official, say the word."

Jerry gave Wayne a tight look. But his words were directed at Mehan. "Can you tell us what happened?"

Mehan looked like he was tempted not to respond. But he gave in. "Victim was shot twice. In his front doorway. Either bullet would have done the trick. Spaced maybe two inches apart, both through the heart. ME puts the time of death at approximately five this morning."

"A professional hit."

"Sure," the detective agreed. "Just like some highly trained former military joe might do, right?"

Holly rose unsteadily from her chair and staggered away. Jerry watched her go, then asked, "You got anything else?"

"The attackers totally trashed the house. They're calling it a burglary." Mehan turned to Wayne. "I'm still waiting."

Wayne said carefully, "We went to see him. But not last night. Two nights before."

"That's real interesting. On account of how the guard

station has no record of any visitors to the Dorsett residence for the entire week leading up to the day in question."

"We confronted him over what he had done," Wayne went on. "We left. He was alive and well when we departed."

Mehan looked from one to the other. "I assume you both got somebody to account for your whereabouts last night."

"That is correct, Officer."

The unexpected voice turned them all around. Victoria was there, and she was not alone. From where Wayne sat, she appeared to lead an army. Grey haired and tottering on a variety of canes and walkers. But there. It looked to Wayne like almost the entire community had turned out.

If Mehan was impressed, he did not show it. "Oh look. An alibi."

"As many as you need," Victoria replied.

"Doggone right." Harry, the semi-deaf guy, shouted from somewhere at the back, "We take care of our own."

"Make way, there. Coming through." The other cop led Tatyana forward. The woman looked shrunk down within herself. "The lady's got something she wants to report, Lieutenant."

"About Dorsett?"

"No. About this guy Jerry mentioned. The rich dude."

"Easton Grey." This from Tatyana. "He's the victim of another scam."

Mehan was not pleased. "We're not here to talk about some scam that might or might not have taken place."

Victoria replied, "Well, you should be."

Wayne said, "Dorsett basically confessed to fleecing these people."

"Which was just prior to you shooting him, right?"

"We didn't shoot anybody. Try and look beyond that for just a second," Jerry said. "There's something seriously devious about two professional scams happening so close together."

"Let's get this straight." Mehan wrestled himself out of the plastic chair. "You got old folks who let some rip-off pro in a CPA suit waltz in here and steal their dough."

"So you're accepting there was a scam."

"What I'm saying is, let me finish." He waved his hand vaguely in the direction of the barrier island. "And you got one of the richest guys in the state who's been scared out of his corporate suit, and you're telling me they're connected?"

Jerry shrugged. "It's too much of a coincidence, is all I'm saying."

"Well, hey, I'd say that's enough for us to take straight to the DA."

Jerry was untouched by the man's bitter sarcasm. "You don't mind, I'd like a copy of Dorsett's photo. Show it to Grey, see if he recognizes him."

Mehan worked on that for a while, but couldn't find anything wrong with the request. "I'll lift the picture from the guy's driver's license."

Jerry said, "Back to the scam. Dorsett declared bankruptcy before taking off with our money. Claimed he got ripped off the same as everybody else."

"Are you going somewhere with that?"

"Think about it. The guy makes such a bad move he goes

bust along with his client. Next thing you know, he's got himself another job, one that gives him a castle on the water."

"So somebody decides to give him a second chance." But Mehan put no force behind his words.

"I'd like the name of his employer, and whoever owned that fortress he was living in. Pass the names by Grey, see if they ring a bell."

"I'll think about it." Mehan motioned to the other cop, then said to Wayne, "We'll be back."

Wayne did not wait for the others to disperse. He figured the afternoon would run true to form, the people doing the old folks routine of standing around and talking the thing to death. He was suddenly too tired to care. The previous few days had released an entire lifetime of fatigue. He slipped through the crowd and took aim for the house.

But when he arrived back, he thought he had gone to the wrong place.

It was full of people. Old people. People he knew vaguely or not at all. And they were *doing* things. Scrubbing at the stubborn chips of paint he had not managed to scrape off the doorframes. Washing dishes. Going over his new countertops. Sweeping out the piles of sawdust and debris he'd managed to ignore. Even the maintenance guy was there, putting a coat of paint on the living room walls.

Hilda was on her hands and knees, scrubbing the porch floor. She glared at him and snapped, "Who lives like this? I'll tell you who. A nincompoop lives like this. A rat lives like this. You call this healthy?"

That was when Foster caught up with Wayne. "You're not supposed to be here yet."

Hilda exclaimed, "Look at what I'm finding here. Germs I'm finding. Accidents waiting to happen. You're going to bring that nice young lady back to *this*?"

"That's enough, Hilda."

Wayne asked, "What are they doing?"

"Saying thanks," Foster replied.

"And just what will that nice young lady think of you, she sees this mess of a house?" Hilda shook her wire brush at him. "What will she think of us, letting you live like a rat in his hole?"

Wayne made a mess of expressing his gratitude. He finally slipped into the back room, shut the door, sat down on the bed, pried off his shoes, lay down, and fell asleep to the sound of others working on his home.

SIXTEEN

I n the dark predawn hour, the dream came to Wayne, striking for the first time since he had last traveled to Lantern Island alone. He awoke in the standard manner, clawing for air, heart hammering, sweat pouring from his skin. Only the hour was different. By the time he toweled dry and dressed and emerged on his front porch, the eastern sky was tinted grey. Normally the dream struck in the dead of night. If he left now it would be full daylight by the time he made it across the state. Full daylight meant danger and the risk that the family would already be off doing whatever rich families did.

He was going anyway. He knew that before he stepped through the door. His gut was gripped like always, a raging vacuum that went way beyond hunger, even further than lust. More like rage with the destructive force all focused on himself. He had never thought of it so clearly before. Not that it mattered. He was still going.

Until he turned to go back inside and spotted the figure

hulking on the steps of the house down the lane. He whispered, "Julio?"

The kid unwrapped his arms from his legs and stood, a lumpish creature rising from its chrysalis. He crossed the lane, stopped by Wayne's bottom stair, and whispered, "It's so quiet here, man."

"Why didn't you go back with Tatyana?"

"Miss Victoria, she said I could stay."

"Victoria let you spend the night?"

"No, man, the summer." But Julio was scarcely paying attention to his own words. He was scouting the low-lying mist, the trees scarcely separated from the dawn, the ghostly structures. "I never thought quiet could be like this. It's spooky."

"I don't get it. Victoria is letting you spend the summer with her?"

"She made me a cot on the porch. Fixed me dinner and everything. Said she'd try and find me a job."

"What about your grandmother?"

"Miss Victoria, she made me call. But my grandma, she doesn't care. She comes and goes." Julio glanced not at him, but at the porch to his right. "You gonna make me leave?"

Wayne felt the tense craving collapse into a fume of burnt cinders. Whatever else came from this, he was not making the trip to Lantern Island that day. "No."

"So what are you doing up, man? The quiet get you too?"

Wayne slipped back inside. "I'm going for a run. You too. Go find some shoes."

❧

Wayne had to take it very easy for the kid. Julio fought the road. Before they reached the end of the drive, his feet had started splaying slightly. He lumbered and he sweated and he groaned. But he kept on. Wayne let Julio set the pace, something between a walk and a slow trot, and stopped when they had gone a little over a mile. "You did good."

Julio propped his hands on his thighs and puffed.

"I know you like basketball. I bet you can shoot. Are you a shooter, Julio?"

Julio gulped enough air to reply, "The best."

"On the court, a big guy like you, he can just stand and wait until somebody hits him with the ball." Wayne heard himself talking, like he was prepping a green recruit. "But even the biggest guys in the pros, they've still got to run. Look at the Shaq. Big as he is, that guy floats up and down the court, light as a feather."

Julio pushed himself back upright. The front of his T-shirt was black with sweat. "Okay, man. I'm ready."

"No, that's enough for day one. You wait until you're cooled off, then jog back home. Don't sprint even if you feel like it. Hold it steady and give your muscles time to get used to this new routine."

"I can go farther."

"I know you can." No question, this kid had grit. Wayne patted his drenched shoulder. "Jog on back, and hang loose till I return. I'll show you some stretches. We'll go again tomorrow."

But Julio was still waiting there on the side of the road when Wayne returned an hour later. Wayne usually raced the final half mile or so, using the straight avenue running through the last orange trees as a perfumed wind sprint. But today he slowed to a foot-dragging trot, letting Julio set the pace and the footwork. Entering the community together, both of them on their last leg.

Tatyana was seated on the porch next to Foster when they came into view of Wayne's cottage. He pulled up early, not wanting to have Jerry come down on the kid while Julio was still winded. If Jerry was there. They plopped onto the grass together and took their time stretching, until Foster and the lady stepped down off the porch and approached.

Wayne said to Tatyana, "You could have given me directions and let me come meet you."

Today's outfit was a midnight blue so dark it appeared only a half shade off black. Matching silk camisole. No jewelry except for a lady's gold Rolex. Hair pulled back. Severe and reserved and dressed for big game. "Not this morning."

He said to Julio, "Try to keep your shoulders level when you bend. Don't jerk toward your toe. Lean until you feel your hamstrings go tight, then release. Easy motions. You've got weeks to get it right. Years." He said to Tatyana, "I'm not ready to speak with Mr. Grey again."

"You want to see the company books and you need to speak to an accountant." Even when speaking in the precise manner of reading off a sheet, Tatyana's voice stirred a shiver in his gut. "I need to be with you the first go."

Foster said worriedly, "Jerry's in with Holly."

Wayne was instantly on his feet. "Since when?"

"She came and got him while we were making coffee. The lady's upset. The way she looked, I'm thinking she spent the night distilling yesterday into another major league worry."

Tatyana said, "We need to—"

But Wayne was already running for the community center. "Five minutes."

❧

Holly's stone expression matched Jerry's when Wayne knocked and pushed open the door. Jerry said, "Oh, look. Formal wear."

Wayne brushed off the grass clinging to his legs and shorts. "Everything okay?"

Jerry returned his attention to the woman behind the desk. "Everything is just swell."

"I want to know," Holly said.

Wayne did not risk a look at Jerry. "We weren't there. We had nothing to do with anything—"

She gripped the air between them, the cords in her arm as taut as her expression. "My work here might seem small to a lot of people. Insignificant. Petty. But it is my *life*. It is *my* life. This is all I have."

Jerry's voice went soft. "I don't class your work as insignificant, Holly. Not at all. And neither does Wayne."

"I have given twelve and a half years trying to make this community run smoothly. Keeping it alive. Fostering an environment where people with very little can make a true home.

We are a village. We *care* for one another." She glared at Wayne. "Do you have *any* idea what I'm talking about?"

He nodded slowly. "Belonging."

Jerry said, "Holly, the man risked his life to bring back the money to keep this place going. What more do you want from him?"

She wavered, but held on to Wayne's gaze. "I need to ask you something."

"Holly, please. This isn't—"

She raised her voice. "Are you a threat to this community? Will you put my people and this place at risk?"

"I don't want to."

"You don't want." She huffed, thoroughly dissatisfied. "You don't *want.*"

Jerry said, "The guy has given you everything he can, Holly. He's asked for nothing in return."

Wayne had a jerking sensation, like the community chief's stare had the force to pull the earth out from under him. And she was tempted. Wayne could see the words shaped in her head. Telling him to leave. But what she said was, "You have absolutely nothing in common with us or this community."

There was one thing. Wayne added in a voice he did not recognize, "This is the only home I have."

"He cares for us, Holly," Jerry added. Soft as Wayne. "He's one of our own."

❧

Wayne left the community center and made his way back to the cottage. He had been wounded before, and not just the one time he caught the edge of the blast that took out his two best friends. Every soldier wore armor down deep, protecting the core of their being from all the stuff nobody should ever have to face. Even when they knew the armor was a lie and they were still vulnerable, such as after his ex had stabbed through the invisible chink, and now Holly. A soldier wore his armor. Sometimes it was all he had.

Wayne listened to two strains in his head, like his antennae had become tuned to two different sound tracks. One spewed out the tirade he had heard voiced by other guys trying to rebuild their armor after an attack. How these women weren't to be trusted, how they were enemies, and if they didn't consider themselves that, it was their problem. An enemy by any other name was nothing but a target. He didn't need them and he didn't need this rat hole of a place. He could be packed and out the front gates in three heartbeats, and he would never look back.

Like that.

The other internal voice just wept.

One mistake piled on another, that was how he felt. A lifetime of getting things wrong. Holly's face floated in the harsh sunlight, wavering like heat rising from the oyster shells scrunching beneath his feet. She had not been angry with him. She had been afraid. Afraid *of* him and afraid *for* her community. Afraid he would be responsible for bringing them down.

Victoria stood where the bougainvillea was so thick it formed a natural wall reaching from her home to the lane. Julio stood beside her. The maintenance guy switched his focus from her to Julio and back again. Victoria's natural stoop made the two men seem like giants, behemoths from another world. The maintenance guy was smiling. As was Julio. And not from mirth. They shared a taste of whatever it was that emanated from Victoria.

Victoria gave him a little wave as he passed. "Come join us."

Wayne pointed with his chin to where Tatyana and Foster stood on his porch. "I think I'm wanted."

"A man with great responsibilities." She turned the words into the finest of compliments.

Tatyana came down the steps. "Can we get started now?"

"Fine. Sure."

Foster asked, "What's keeping Jerry?"

"He's still talking with Holly."

Tatyana said, "I am assuming you do not own a proper corporate outfit."

Wayne looked up at his house. Somebody had applied a new coat of varnish to his front door. It gleamed like congealed honey. Hilda had scraped the front porch down to the nubs. He could smell the disinfectant from where he stood.

Tatyana said, "I am talking to you."

"No. No monkey suit."

Foster said, "Two of the ladies came by and left you dinner. Pot roast and potatoes and vegetables. I put the dishes in your fridge."

Wayne reached up and massaged the area above his aching heart.

SEVENTEEN

Pulling up in front of Vero Beach's most exclusive men's store with a beautiful woman at the wheel of a Ferrari caused no more uproar than a Brazilian soccer riot. The manager himself bustled out to bow and scrape them into the shop.

Tatyana said, "I need a full makeover."

The manager's double-breasted jacket bore gold buttons with crests. A sky-blue handkerchief peeked from his pocket. He wore a thin gold chain over his tie, and another around the wrist that also bore an oversized gold watch. "Is madame seeking to go butch or is she referring to her gentleman gardener?"

"I want him ready for the boardroom."

The manager's hair was shellacked into a helmet that shivered with the rest of him. "Who did your hair, sir. Lawn-mower man?"

"The army."

"Oh, this really is too much. Derek, phone next door and tell Mimi she has to cancel whatever comes next." To Tatyana, "Your

147

Samson has the shoulders of an ox and no waist at all. We can either fit him with suspenders or do some serious tailoring."

Wayne said, "No suspenders."

"Excuse me. Who is the payee here?"

"That would be me," Tatyana said.

"Then the gentleman will kindly permit his betters to sort out his future. Pretend you're Eliza and dream in silence."

"Who?"

Derek hung up the phone. "Mimi says for you, she's ready."

"Excellent." The manager plied his tape measure. "Did madame have anything special in mind? Navy serge, pinstripe, desert camouflage?"

"Expensive. Something with a label that will flash across the conference table."

The manager sighed with genuine pleasure. "I do so love a customer who knows why they invented the platinum card."

❧

By the time they reached downtown Orlando, the sky had gone leaden, the day's humidity so great it coalesced overhead. Wayne redirected the Ferrari's AC away from his face and down where the suit jacket and tie and fancy striped shirt congealed around his chest. Tatyana pulled into a multistory parking garage, ignoring the bearded attendant who stepped from his guardhouse to grin and wave her through. She rumbled into a slot with her name, the engine a thunderous roar in the concrete cave.

Tatyana cut off the motor and said, "I can trust you to act like a true professional inside the company."

"Sure."

"No comments about anything we have discussed." Tatyana spoke like she already knew the answer, but being a lawyer, she needed to say it anyway. "Everything must remain totally confidential."

Wayne asked, "How many others are there?"

"Others?"

"If I was in your position, I'd have a couple of in-house dudes set up to run the same check. Allies who might know at least a part of what's happened. Not the bit about an angel. But that the boss might be under attack from within or without."

She just turned and looked at him, her cat's eyes unblinking and unreadable.

"I assume that means they don't know about me."

In response, Tatyana opened her door and climbed out.

Wayne followed her across the lot to the elevators. "I need to know anything they discover."

"Clip this to your jacket pocket." She handed him a guest badge, then used a mini-card attached to her key ring to signal the elevator. When the doors shut she said, "From now on, you must assume everything you say can be overheard."

The garage elevator opened in the corner of the main lobby. The lobby was marble and five stories tall. The building was full of tense people rushing around on self-absorbing duties. A crystal sign the size of an SUV hung above the guard station. The sign was etched with one word, *Grey*. They joined the polite push into the next elevator that opened. Tatyana said, "Twenty-seven, please."

When Tatyana's floor pinged, Wayne followed her through an open-plan office of ringing phones and quiet urgency. She led him into a corner conference room. A laptop was open by the front chair. Bound computer-generated ledgers were stacked along the sides like two leather-bound arms. Yellow legal pads and pens sat before three of the empty chairs.

Tatyana scouted the empty room, checked her watch, and said, "I told him twelve o'clock."

"Looks like I've got enough here to make a start."

"Do you want me to walk you through it?"

"Let me have a look."

She watched him settle into the chair at the head of the table. Tatyana stood in the doorway as he turned on the laptop. Wayne saw that the user had already logged in and thus opened the door to the company's books. He slid the computer to one side and opened the closest ledger. As expected, it contained the latest overview and summary of everything to be found stacked on either side. Wayne looked up then and said, "I'm good to go. Why don't you go find your guy, I'll try and make myself useful."

She remained where she was for a moment, then said, "That is what I like about you, Wayne Grusza. You speak to me only about what is required, and do so with a respect for our time and the value of words."

Wayne sat as he was for a while after she had left and shut the door. Tasting the aftereffects of a compliment from the ice queen.

Numbers had a language all their own. Rules of grammar and speech and strength and resonance. These rules had to be mastered before the language could be understood. A student needed to learn how to tell lies from truth and the makers of both. Wayne's sister had said it all that day in his cottage. He had always had a gift with numbers and guns. It was people who gave him an itch.

An hour later, he rose from his chair and stretched. Beyond the inward facing glass wall, life swept past him but he remained utterly isolated. The place was so soundproofed he might as well have been inside an air-conditioned crypt. He returned to the table, took a deep breath, and dove back in.

The next time he rose, his watch read half past four. The numbers he had been examining swarmed before his eyes. Wayne took a slow turn around the table, gradually digesting what he had found, wondering what had happened to Tatyana. But not sorry she had left him alone. The hunger pangs he had been sensing for the past couple of hours were stronger now. But Wayne had years of experience pushing discomfort to one side. In fact, moments like now he could use the internal friction to hunker down, focus more tightly, almost like using anger as a fuel. Staring out at the afternoon vista and seeing numbers race by in a crystal-clear stream.

"What's going on here?"

Wayne turned in stages. His body moved slowly so as to give his brain time to let it all go and return to the glass-walled room. "Excuse me?"

A stranger with a wisp of dark hair encircling a bald bullet of a head stood in the doorway. He stared at the ledgers and the legal pad now full of Wayne's notes. "Who authorized this?"

"Obviously somebody who didn't feel any need to tell you about it."

The top of the stranger's skull was the first portion to go red. "I asked you a question, mister."

The office beyond the interior glass wall had entered the afternoon wind-down. People were watching without actually turning in their direction. Wayne said, "I'm here on a specific brief and I don't recall any mention of a need to answer your questions."

"We'll see about that." He was a bull in a suit, tall and big-boned. He had twenty years and fifty pounds on Wayne. He was also used to shoving his way forward. He stalked around the table and made a grab for Wayne's arm. "You're coming with me."

Wayne moved without conscious thought. A quick slap of the hand, a slight turn of the body. "That's where you're wrong."

The guy had a boxer's attitude, short punchy actions, the voice to match. "I said let's go!"

Wayne slapped the hand harder this time. "Last warning."

"I'm executive vice-president!"

"Go execute somewhere else."

The bullish man might have backed off then. But he made the mistake of glancing back to where a crowd now clustered beyond the window.

The guy had never known the dance routine, never been

warned about reaching into a sniper's space. When he reached out, Wayne's response was automatic. He gripped the man's wrist just where it connected to the palm. He hit the pressure point, saw the red-hot pain register, heard the grunt. He should have stopped then. But he had never had time for bullies.

Impulse control. A serious drawback, Sergeant Grusza. Somebody short-circuited that breaker switch. Get it repaired or you'll never advance.

Wayne thought the words loud enough to have almost said them out loud. Just breaking my heart, sir.

He flipped the guy's arm around, carrying the body along with it, using the man's own anger and force to slip him about to where the other pressure point was exposed. The one between his shoulder blade and his armpit. Wayne knuckled him a lot harder than was required.

"Ow!"

Wayne just kept pushing the point, driving the guy over until his face met the table. Smack.

"Ow!"

"Name?"

"Let *go!*"

"I asked you a question. Give me your name."

"Jim."

"We're halfway there. Jim what?"

"Jim Berkind. Let me up!"

"Okay, Jim. What are you going to do when I release you?" When the guy responded by heaving back, Wayne applied a trace more pressure to the knuckle. The guy grunted and went limp. "We're a long way from max here, Jim. Answer the question. What are you gonna do?"

His mashed face muffled the word. "Leave."

"Right answer." Wayne let go and stepped back.

The guy huffed his way up, massaged his wrist, made it to the door in record time, then turned back and said, "I'm calling security."

"Whatever." Wayne went back to his ledgers. "Shut the door on your way out, Jim."

The pneumatic hinge kept him from slamming the door. But he punched the glass wall and shouted at Wayne as he stomped down the hall. Wayne didn't look up until the bull had departed. When he did, two young ladies gave him discreet applause.

He walked around and opened the door. "You know him?"

"Sure. Berkind," one said. "He's awful."

"He said he was a VP. Is that true?"

"I have no idea. Probably." This from the other lady.

"In this department?"

They both made a face. "Not a chance. I'd move to Nome before I worked for that man."

"Do you know where his office is?"

"Far away," one lady said.

"Not far enough," the other said.

Wayne nodded. "Do either of you know Tatyana Kuchik?"

"Sure. In legal."

"Could you call her and say the guy she left down here in the conference room is done?"

"No problem." The lady reached for her phone. "What name should I give her?"

"Ask Tatyana."

"Oh. It's like that."

"Afraid so." Wayne let the door sigh shut and returned to his chair.

But the numbers did not come together again. They just lay there on the page, a text without a voice. He had enough experience with the aftereffects of wrongdoing to know he would make no more progress that day.

Then he looked up. And froze.

A man stood by the door.

Wayne was supposed to be a hotshot at noticing things, so how come the guy had made it inside the room and Wayne had not heard a thing?

This was one seriously black man. He stood where the door blocked him from view of anyone passing the conference room. He was as tall as Wayne and had him by maybe twenty pounds. All muscle. The guy was wearing a dark suit, white shirt, dark monochrome tie. But there was no masking his warrior's build. He emanated a force—not a danger, just a raw power. Standing there and staring at Wayne, filling the room with his presence.

Wayne could come up with absolutely nothing to say.

The guy said, "James Berkind's question was right. His motive was wrong. Who are you, Wayne Grusza?"

Wayne remained silent.

"Who do you serve? The question is hard only if you wish to make it so."

Wayne could not speak.

"You must find this answer for yourself before the real issue can be addressed. You are being called, Wayne Grusza. A hero is required. A hero for the Most High God." The guy opened the door, took a half step out, then said, "You are not responsible for the deaths of your two friends."

Fifteen minutes or six hours later, Tatyana opened the same door and found him seated in the same position, staring at the same point of empty space. "What is wrong?"

EIGHTEEN

W ho do you think it was?"

"I have no idea." Wayne knew Tatyana didn't want to believe him. Which wasn't comfortable, but there was nothing he could do about it. If she had come to him and told him she'd been confronted by a man who *might* be the same guy as hit on Grey . . .

No. Scratch that and rewind.

Might as well say it, at least in his head.

The same *angel*.

If she had done that, he would have been suggesting she switch her ride for something both stationary and padded.

Tatyana shut the conference room door and stood there, as far from him as the room's confines would permit. He had not actually said the word. He had not needed to. The thought hung there in the space between them.

She used the phone on the side table to call downstairs and ask security if they had passed in a man by the description Wayne supplied. Security took her seriously enough to check and phone back. No, no one. Tatyana reported it as a possible security breach, asked them to report back to her on her cell phone, and gave them the number.

Tatyana said nothing more until they were downstairs in the garage and she was firing up the car. "Are you hungry?"

"I missed lunch."

"I thought about that. But something happened after I left you."

"You got sidetracked."

She did not race out of the garage so much as ignore her speed. "I got pulled before the disciplinary board that questioned my *ability* and my *record*." She stopped for a light, jammed in the clutch, and pressed the gas pedal hard enough for her next words to be lost. When the engine whined down, what Wayne heard was, "—questioned my handling of a case two *years* ago. They said there had been a complaint brought against me that potentially tarnished the entire corporation. Then they wouldn't tell me what it was!"

"Green," Wayne said.

"What?"

"The light. It's gone green."

Somebody beeped from the left-turn lane behind them. Tatyana slapped the lever into first. Gunned the motor. Eased off the clutch. The engine roared, jerked the car forward, and died.

Tatyana sat there as the light went red again. "I *hate* this car."

It was only then Wayne realized the woman was close to tears.

"Easy does it," he said. "Deep breath. Okay. Start the car. Good. Ready now, the light's about to go green again." Walking her through like a new grunt on the firing range. "Is your blinker on? It's important to breathe. Okay, green light. Steady on the gas. Ease off the clutch."

"I'm okay now."

"I know you are." But he remained poised to reach over and take control as she navigated the turn. "Okay, there's a bus stop coming up. Why don't you slip over into the right-hand lane. Good. Might be a good idea to stop here and sort through things."

He thought she would probably snap at him. Instead, she pulled over, braked, cut the motor, and said, "Would you drive?"

"No problem." Calm as ice. Like he was asked to drive a beautiful woman's Ferrari every day of the week.

Before she could take it back, Wayne sprang from the car. He hurried around and was there to offer a hand as she rose in unsteady stages. He didn't need to ask if she was okay. A woman who made a profession of being in total control did not ask a guy to drive unless the day was seriously fractured.

The seat was so far forward he had to wrestle himself behind the wheel, then thought he might become asphyxiated before he found the seat controls, which were on the door. Even with the seat all the way back, he could feel his hair graze the roof, and testing the clutch brought his knee in contact with the steering wheel.

Not that he was complaining the least tiny bit.

The clutch resembled that of an aging Humvee, one eaten

159

up by highland desert driving and guys who treated military equipment as toys they were paid to destroy. He had to bunch his entire leg to get the thing down to the floor. He started the engine. Punched the gas. Just sat there a second and listened to the lady sing.

He knew it was an awfully macho act. Even before he gunned the motor and checked his mirror and slapped the gearshift into first. Long before he spun the wheel, he knew he was acting like a fourteen-year-old in a stolen vehicle.

He laid a smoking track down the entire block. Had a trio of youths shout a warning or a cheer or maybe just a shout in time to the engine. Redlined it through the caution light and slapped it into second. Burned a second streak of smoking tires.

Hit ninety-three miles an hour. In second gear. In downtown Orlando. In rush hour traffic.

Impulse control, Sergeant Grusza. It will kill you one of these days.

He caught a glimpse of his idiotic grin in the rearview mirror and silently replied, So sue me.

"Take the next right." Tatyana had to almost shout the words over the engine's bellow.

The Ferrari was the most perfectly balanced machine he had ever experienced. All he had to do was *think*, and the car was already halfway through the turn. He wasn't suspended upon tires, but claws.

He *owned* this road.

He let the traffic slow him. A miniature airspace invited him to slip over two lanes and cannonball through the intersection. But just as he was preparing to downshift, he glanced to his right.

Tatyana looked so utterly unhappy.

He resisted the car's rumbling urge to let go and release the power and fly. He sat there. Idled between an SUV and a pickup. Ignored the stares flung at him from all sides. And said, "Sorry."

She shook her head. "Take a left through the stone gates."

He did as he was told, calm and slow. Which was easier said than done. The Ferrari resisted his hand upon the reins. It lived to buck and roar and leap. The tiniest punch upon the gas, and he would be ten miles beyond sheer abandon.

Ten feet beyond the open gates, Wayne left behind all the weary stress and entered a world of gentility and old wealth. Trees that had been planted long before the first white footsteps graced a perfect lawn. A manor of peaked corners and Victorian foppery rose in the distance. "Where are we?"

"Easton's club."

Wayne parked in what was probably the guest lot, given its distance from the clubhouse. He cut the motor and sorted through a number of things to say before settling upon a simple repetition of what she had said. "You hate this car."

"I have to fight it all the time." The ice woman sounded about six inches from tears. "I can't go slow. I can't take it easy. I don't . . ."

He twisted in his seat as much as the car's confines allowed. And waited. Either she would tell him or she wouldn't.

She looked at him then. For the first time since they had left the company. Her eyes matched the sky overhead, a grey so dark it could be mistaken for sheer night. "It was my husband's."

Wayne nodded. Like he understood.

Which, in a very strange way, he probably did.

She seemed to want to speak, but couldn't.

So he said the words. "You drive it around his town for revenge."

He did not notice the tear until she wiped it away. "I caught him with . . ."

He did not let the laugh out, except for the tight punching of his chest and the quick breaths through his nostrils. It did not matter who she had caught the guy with. "Your husband," he said, "is a loon."

"My ex," she corrected.

"How long?"

"Nineteen months."

He gave a slow nod, as though the number required deep thought. Gave her time to come up with the next thought herself. "But you hate the car."

"Yes, but he loved it. Sometimes I think . . ."

"Nineteen months, Tatyana." He gave it another moment. "I'm assuming you didn't marry a guy dumb as an oil stain. Which means the guy has definitely gotten the message."

She took an easier breath. And nodded to the gathering gloom. "You're saying I should sell it and move on."

"I'd be the wrong fellow to offer you advice. Seeing as how I've got all the experience in the world at not being able to let go. But I can tell you this." A shard of his own pain sliced at his voice. "That knife you're carrying stabs you a hundred times worse than it ever will him."

NINETEEN

They were halfway to the clubhouse when Tatyana stopped in her tracks. She reached into the pocket of her pinstriped jacket and came up with her phone, which buzzed quietly. "Kuchik." She listened a moment, then said, "You're certain? No, Chief. I did not mean to question either you or your men. But the information I had was very specific. Yes. My source is valid. Yes. I vouch for the description I gave you. No. I can't explain it either. Thank you for checking. Good night."

She snapped the phone shut and said, "There was no visitor's pass issued to a tall African-American in a dark suit. And yours was the only board-level pass today."

"What does that mean?"

"A board-level pass is granted in exceptional circumstances only. A senior executive is required to personally explain why the visitor does not need to go through the normal screening process."

Wayne signaled his understanding with a nod. "You photograph all normal visitors."

"We go much further. First-time salesmen are vetted. Passes are coded to certain areas within the building. Visitors are required to be accompanied by their host. Failure to monitor a visitor is a firing offense. Two of our divisions handle matters related to Homeland Security. We are extremely careful."

The remnants of daylight mingled with the city's lights, granting the sky a dour glow. "I'm telling you the truth, Tatyana."

"I believe you."

In the gloaming, her hair was a dark veil parted precisely in the middle and falling in soft waves on either side of perhaps the most beautiful face he had ever seen. The gathering night was oppressive with a growing need for rain. Wayne tasted the air, savoring the calm certainty with which she had spoken. He said, "I might have received a nicer compliment. But right now I can't remember when."

The club entrance had a broad three-story portico designed to keep arriving guests dry in the worst of gales. They were just outside the perimeter when Tatyana drew up a second time.

"What's the matter?"

"That's my ex-husband."

Three limos had pulled up in a line, the drivers scurrying to open the rear doors. A bevy of people disembarked. One man stood out. An older gentleman, probably in his early fifties. Sleek as a desert cat, king of the corporate maze. Everything about him, from his coiffed silver hair to his alligator shoes, was perfectly groomed. He spotted them, took a pair of steps away from his entourage, and said in a voice as well modulated as a professional announcer, "Good evening, Tatyana."

"Eric."

He dismissed Wayne with one tiny flicker of a glance, a fractional raising of his chin. He then snubbed his former wife with a smile. "You're working late."

When Tatyana did not respond, the man smirked once, then turned back to his waiting guests.

Wayne noted the hesitant way Tatyana followed the group into the club and said, "We can go somewhere else if you want."

"He is not chasing me away from here or anyplace else," Tatyana said. "Not ever again."

"I like that."

Even though her cat's eyes were tightened in cautious inspection, even though the gaze was directed down the chandeliered hall, Wayne sensed she was really thinking about him. So he said what came next to his brain. Knowing it was a risk.

What he said was, "I've got my own stories, Tatyana. The kind that leave me feeling like I've gargled acid after I've told them. However you want to make this play out. Just say the word."

The lady stopped a third time. And inspected him very carefully.

Wayne kept his eyes focused steady upon hers. Which, given the way this lady looked, was about a billion miles away from punishment detail.

Tatyana reached some internal decision. She nodded once, to herself. She took a half step toward him. Close enough he could hear her breathing. Feel the occasional brush of her shoulder upon his arm. She kept tight hold of his gaze as she reached over, her hand searching out his own.

The instant her fingers touched his, Wayne felt the charge. Like he was standing not in the foyer of some fancy club but a power station. And himself straight into the main grid.

Her fingers were surprisingly long. Her touch amazingly soft for a woman with so many barbed edges. She spoke in a voice Wayne had not heard before. "All right."

"You ready?" He did not need to say it. But the moment and this side of her took some getting used to. Not to mention the fact that his body practically *hummed*.

"I think . . . No. Yes." She actually moved in closer still. Reached over with her *other* hand. And took a grip of his arm. Just *molded* to him. So tight he could feel the hem of her skirt, the press of her calf upon his, the bone of her hip. She said, "I'm ready."

Wayne took it very slow. Not really walking. More like floating down a cloud carpeted by Persia's best and lit by crystal. A couple of the old guys with their wives dripping jewels as big as life's mistakes paused to watch them. Wayne resisted the urge to look down, see if his feet were actually connected to the earth. He'd just let the lawyer lady take care of such details. As in, the lady who matched her stride to his, who breathed as slow as their tread, who made the walk into a dance that went *way* beyond cheek to cheek. Yes *sir.*

They passed through a bar filled with people who had boardroom training in gawking without showing it. But they were watching. Wayne was certain of that.

The headwaiter stood like a dislocated prince behind the

little wooden station. He gave them a professional smile and asked, "Do you have a reservation?"

Wayne did not realize Tatyana was leaving it up to him until her head leaned against his arm. His voice actually shook a little when he said, "Afraid not."

"Are you members?"

"The name is Kuchik. We're here as guests of Easton Grey."

"Ah. Of course. We're very busy tonight but I'm sure . . . Yes. Table fourteen. Right this way."

They continued their weightless waltz across the oval restaurant, with tinkling silverware and soft conversation for music. Wayne knew he was taking everything in. Knew also he'd lay in bed that night and relive it and see things he was missing right now. But for the moment, his attention, his entire *being*, was focused on the lady walking next to him.

The headwaiter led them to a table by the outer wall. To his left, cream drapes framed twenty-foot windows. When the headwaiter reached for the back of Tatyana's chair, Wayne said, "I'll handle that."

"Of course, sir."

He selected the chair so that Tatyana's back would be to her ex. Tatyana released him with a dancer's grace, her lingering touch the finest thank-you he had ever known. When he was seated, the head guy offered Tatyana a menu only slightly smaller than the table. She waved it away. "The gentleman will decide."

The gentleman agreed to basically everything the

headwaiter suggested, which was Wayne's only choice, since he couldn't understand most of what was on the menu anyway.

They were seated at an angle to each other. Not touching, but within groping range. That is, if the lady in question had ever in her entire life done anything like grope. If Tatyana had looked over her right shoulder, she would have been able to return the glare her ex was speeding across the room. But she didn't. Wayne knew, because he did not turn from her, not even to *blink*.

She said, "We need to talk business for a moment."

"Sure." He started to draw away, move back into a professional distance. But she made no move herself. So he remained close enough to taste her perfume with every sense, every pore. "Fire away."

"Can I ask you what you found?"

"You can ask me anything you want."

A waiter came and poured something and stood by Wayne's chair, clearly expecting him to do something. Tatyana looked up and said, "That's fine."

"Thank you, madame."

She had tiny flecks of golden in her dark grey eyes. Or perhaps it was merely that her gaze was made for crystal and candlelight and silver. "I trust you, Wayne Grusza."

He had no response to that one.

"You asked me who else I had working on the inside, inspecting the company's books. There are two others. An accountant and an aide to the board."

"They didn't find a thing."

"What makes you so sure?"

"Your company's books are totally clear, Tatyana. If people

wanted to hide something, they'd start by shutting off some segments. Tangling up fragments of real stuff with myth. Weaving in knots and convolutions. There's nothing. The data couldn't be any more well laid out if it had been carved into the crystal block over the security desk."

This time, she leaned back. "That is what Easton wanted. A company without financial secrets. Books that would say to anyone who looked, This is who we are."

"You like him."

"More than that. He gave . . ." She breathed hard. "Easton gave me my life."

"Can I ask something that isn't business?"

She nodded slowly. "I don't want to talk business anymore. I haven't had a night away from work since . . ."

"Since Easton met the man, whoever he is."

Laughter boomed from the long table running by the side wall. Tatyana's gaze started to shift over. She held herself back with a strength of will that turned her rigid. "Longer than that."

Wayne closed the distance between them. "I haven't had a date since my wife divorced me."

That turned her focus back to the table and to them. Which was the only reason Wayne had said what he did. She asked, "How long ago was that?"

"Almost four years."

She did not respond, unless a blink was communication. But her silence was as nice as a caress. "What did you want to ask me?"

"Where are you from?"

"I was born in Kamchatka. Do you know where that is?"

"Yes." Matter of fact, he had actually touched down at an air base on the peninsula once. He had a fleeting image of ochre hills with razor edges, so high and sharp they threatened to shred the sky. Or shatter the dreams and hopes of small girls.

"I came to America when I was eleven. Easton had set up a charity for adopting . . ."

The laughter sounded like a barrage. Artillery fired by human throats, intended to break the moment apart. Wayne heard a voice rise above the others, and knew who it belonged to by the way Tatyana winced.

She kept her focus on him, though. And she waited. Her expression was open enough to reveal two things. First, she would tell him whatever he asked. Second, to speak about it would hurt her badly.

So Wayne leaned a fraction closer still. Even though it hurt him to do so. Even though he knew he would wake up in the middle of the night now and remember not the good times, but how he had opened the raw boiling pit and showed it to another. For no good reason. Because no reason was good enough, no matter how nice the moment might be.

What he said was, "When I got out of the service, all I had was a pocketful of back pay and a kit bag full of stolen munitions. I had some crazy idea of heading to Florida and doing the job on my wife's new guy. Instead, I spent two years minus two weeks avoiding the place. Bumming rides and sleeping rough."

"You were a hobo?"

"Nowadays the word is homeless. But the answer is yes."

Her gaze knitted back together. Almost as though he had

actually come up with the right thing to say. No matter that it left his chest feeling like he'd used a power mower on his heart. The way she leaned forward, forgetting the questions he was not going to ask her was enough.

Almost.

"What was it like?"

"Good in some ways, bad in most. The worst thing is how you start to believe what people say or don't say with their eyes. How you're not worth anything. How you'll never . . ."

Wayne stopped because her hand reached over and settled upon his. Then the other. Even though the waiter chose that moment to approach with their dinner. She did not move, did not even shift her focus. She just held him with her hands and her eyes and made the waiter work around them. When they were alone again, she said, "Tell me you no longer believe those lies."

For some reason, he felt his eyes burning. As in, if they had not been surrounded by a roomful of money and power and witnesses, he would have broken down. He clenched down. Just gritted everything.

Tatyana must have noticed. Which would have shamed him terribly. Except for the fact that she reached across the impossible distance. And kissed the point where his lips joined his cheek. A soft gesture of a caring friend. He told himself that in a mental shout, a quick reality check. Her gift worked, because when he lifted his gaze he was able to see her without the burning sheen.

She saw he was okay, and gave him a very peculiar smile. One that did not touch her lips, and scarcely showed in her eyes. But one he knew was there.

She said, "Let's eat."

TWENTY

As luck would have it, they left the clubhouse the same moment as Tatyana's ex did. Which, truth be told, Wayne did not mind at all. Because Tatyana kept a double-handed grip on his arm as they stepped into the night.

Which was when the idea came to him.

Tatyana started down the stairs, taking aim for the distant lot. But Wayne stayed immobile upon the bottom step. Tatyana halted in the process of walking away and gave him a questioning glance.

The valet chose that moment to appear.

Wayne took in the white jacket with the ridiculous gold braid and the shorts and the running shoes, just the sort of getup some rich lady would design because she liked the idea of handsome youths doing a cabaret. He drew the key from his pocket and said, "It's the red one in the far lot."

The guy's eyes went round at the sight of the prancing horse upon the gold-plated seal. "For real?"

"Tell me you can handle a stick."

The kid beamed. "I'm a fast learner, sir." He did not run. He vanished.

Tatyana rewarded him with a chuckle so low and throaty Wayne felt it in his gut. He had never heard her laugh before.

A man's voice rose from the group to Wayne's left. It was the voice of someone who never asked twice, never waited for anything. "Where are my limos?"

In response, a motor whined into life. One moment the Ferrari was out beyond the light's perimeter. The next the valet was popping out the door and springing out and racing around to open the passenger door.

The door into which Wayne helped Tatyana settle.

Wayne reached into his pocket and handed the kid a bill he did not bother to look at. The kid pocketed it without taking his eyes off the car or the lady. "My dad's always telling me to find a goal in life."

As Wayne settled behind the wheel, a petulant voice behind them yelled, "Can we have some *service* here?"

He revved the motor a little more than was required, then eased away at a crawl. Tatyana rewarded him with another of those laughs. One drawn from Siberian honey and dust the color of unrefined gold.

TWENTY-ONE

The magic remained with them on the ride back to her town house. Tatyana rode with her head resting on the seat back, so relaxed her eyes glittered half shut in the streetlights. She spoke only to give directions. The security guard at the entrance must have recognized the sound of her car, because the gate swung open before Wayne turned off the highway. She did not stir until Wayne pulled into the parking space and cut the motor. "You don't mind driving yourself home?"

"That has to be a joke, right?"

She kept hold of her little smile as he rose and went around to open her door. As they walked the path of pale bricks, she asked, "Any thoughts about what happened today?"

"Tell the truth, it's been nice to step away from it for a while."

She did not disagree. "I'm supposed to speak with Easton tomorrow. I just wish I had something to tell him."

"You do. Just no answers."

Wayne assumed she spoke about business to re-orient herself

away from what had just happened at the club. He minded, but he knew it was futile to object.

Which made what happened next doubly surprising.

She stepped up on the broad stair that made the front-door landing, bringing her to almost eye level. "I'd forgotten how nice it was to walk close to someone taller and stronger than me."

For once, Wayne had the right words there at the ready. Perhaps on account of how his heart had suddenly leapt into hyperdrive. "Taller, maybe. But definitely not stronger."

He knew he had done well when she leaned forward and kissed him. Then touched his lips as she drew back, sealing inside both the kiss and anything he might have said to spoil the moment.

He stood there a long moment after she had vanished inside the house. Waiting until his world stopped rocking.

❧

Wayne made his own coffee the next morning. Which was good, as it gave him time alone to get his head around the dream.

The vile apparition had come again. Only this time with differences.

Wayne was still a little too rocked by the images rattling inside his brain to be certain, but standing on his front porch with a steaming mug in his right hand, it seemed that any change was good. Even one this extraordinary.

The dream had started in normal fashion. He'd been walking the ridgeline, up above the eagles. Almost able to touch the sun. A place so alien it was hard to call it Earth. Only this time, he had been *aware* that he had been dreaming. *Aware* that this was a memory twisted by pain and regret and guilt. *Aware* that in the next moment his squad would be hit by two incoming RPGs. One of which would take out his best buddies. The other fragging him in the thigh and shoulder. *Aware* that he'd wake up in a sweat, heaving for breath, almost sick to his stomach with remorse.

Then the strangeness had intensified.

He looked to his left. The side from which the shoulder-fired missile had been launched. And instead of the streaking trail and the rushing dot of death, he had seen only sky. Then a figure had appeared. One walking in line with him. Only it had not been the other guy on left point. Oh no.

The guy walking there on the ridgeline's far side had been the stranger. Tall, dark as onyx. Hard as a major calling his troops out on review. The stranger had looked at him.

And Wayne had woken up.

No heaving chest. No sweats. No guilt. Nothing.

Except for the whisper of a voice, the final tendril of a dream that had already weirded him out. The voice said one word. *"Choose."*

⁂

The rain had started while he was asleep. The morning was made timeless by its wet grey sheath. Wayne returned inside to recharge his mug. The AC purred softly, drying out the cottage's air. The clock above the stove read half past eight. Which was strange for two reasons. First, it meant the nightmare had come long after dawn. And second, the boys were late. But the dream impacted him so hard, Wayne was midway through his second mug before he realized the four-wheeled reason why he was still alone.

He wore stone-washed jeans and a sweatshirt with the sleeves cut out. He slipped his bare feet into a pair of rubber-soled boat shoes and padded down the rain-washed lane. The wind blew off the eastern water and carried a strong flavor of sea salt. He saw Julio standing on Victoria's porch and slowed enough to ask, "You doing okay?"

The kid did not have his arms crossed so much as clutched across his chest. "Quiet."

"Why don't you come over, I'll fix us some breakfast."

Victoria chose that moment to appear. "Julio has kindly offered to walk me to the Saturday chapel service. I can't hold the umbrella against this wind. Why don't you join us?"

Wayne had a number of reasons not to. And seeing that it was Victoria doing the asking, he also knew no excuse was required.

Maybe it was the dream. Maybe the sight of the kid rocking back and forth slightly and clutching his upper body. Maybe the reason didn't matter.

What he said was, "I'd like that."

Her smile conflicted with the grey day. "You'd best hurry. We're already late."

"Be right with you." He strode over to where Foster and Jerry sat on Jerry's front porch. Wayne said, "It's okay, guys. You can go on over."

Foster spoke to him but was watching Wayne's cottage. "We're just fine where we are."

"Tatyana isn't here."

Jerry asked, "The lady gave you her wheels?"

"She didn't feel like making the drive."

"She gave you a hundred-thousand-dollar car because she was wore out?"

Wayne turned to where the car sat in the corner space, just visible between the cottages. "That pretty much sums it up."

Jerry pushed open his screen door. "All I got to say is, she must see something in you that I don't."

"It's not like that."

"I don't know what you two are talking about and I don't care." Foster didn't actually creak as he entered the wet. But he moved like he should have. "What I want to hear is, when are you taking me for a ride?"

"Later." Wayne turned toward the community center. "I've got to do something first."

Wayne caught up with Victoria and Julio when they were approaching the parking lot. "Can I have a minute?"

"For a handsome man like you, I can certainly spare longer than that. I've been late for chapel before." Victoria's gaze was as penetrating as it was sweet. Julio, however, took the time out to gape at the Ferrari. Then back at Wayne. From the car to the guy and back and then over to the cottage. Wayne refrained from telling the kid Tatyana was not there. Julio probably wouldn't have believed him, and he didn't want to go down that road just then anyway.

Wayne had mentally worked through a couple of scenarios.

As in, how to lead around to the topic without sounding totally bogus. But the day was damp and the wind splattered stray raindrops on Victoria's dress. Wayne decided this was no time to tango partway. "I was wondering what you could tell me about angels."

At that point, Julio's eyes came off the car and the cottage to fasten intently upon him.

"Ah. Is this about the incident with that very nice gentleman, what is his name?"

"Easton Grey. And no, or . . . well, partly."

"Partly yes and partly no. Does this mean you have something of a more personal nature that has you wondering about angels?"

The way she said it, the calm nature of her voice, left him able to say, "I sure wish I knew."

"How remarkable." Victoria used a gentle nudge on Julio's arm to start them moving toward the center. "Well, the answer is as simple or as complicated as anything else about the universe of faith."

"That sounds like the kind of answer I'd get from my sister."

"Then she is wise beyond her years. Understanding what I have to say about heavenly hosts will depend upon sharing a faith in our Lord. Do you see where I am going with this?"

"If I don't believe in God, your answers won't mean a lot." Wayne felt the dream's final whisper fall with the rain. *Choose.*

Victoria's smile cut through the wet. "Why don't you start seeking answers from the only One who can give them?"

CR

Wayne left the church alone. Victoria and Julio remained seated in the pew. Julio looked miserable, but something in the way he sat hunched slightly toward the old woman gave Wayne the impression Julio did not want to leave just yet. Wayne exchanged greetings with a number of people, then felt eyes on him. He scouted around until he spotted Holly Reeves watching him. The community director's expression matched the rain and the grim sky.

The wind had picked up while he was inside. Wayne took the umbrella from an old man's hands and did his best to shelter the couple, she on the walker and he not much steadier on his pins. Wayne liked how they thanked him quietly and just let him go. Not that he was being taken for granted. Rather, like he was a part of their community. He was a friend. Of course he helped where he could.

When he returned back down the lane he saw Julio holding the umbrella as Victoria used the rail and the doorjamb to climb her own front steps. Julio nodded at something she said and headed back to the center. Wayne followed behind him. Julio used his umbrella to shelter Harry and his wife. Wayne took aim at a pair of ladies, one in a wheelchair and the other on two canes, both of them in dime-store ponchos. He knew they had stood there waiting for him, hoping without saying anything that he would come back again. Holly was at her desk but with the office door open. She watched him come and go that second time without speaking or nodding.

The ladies lived at the community's far corner. He refused their offer of coffee and a towel, and started back to find Julio waiting for him. The kid held the umbrella shut on one shoulder, ignoring the rain. Wayne agreed. Trying to keep the old people dry had left him too drenched to care.

Julio fell into step beside him but did not speak. Their footsteps squished across the puddles. The rain whooshed through the palms and the live oaks, rustling branches and granting them a stormy isolation. Where the lane ran between the cottages fronting the water and the bay, Julio said, "*No temer*. You know what that means?"

"No fear."

"I hear that all the time. Like, you want to be respected, you gotta be hard. Never show no fear. Not to nobody. But inside . . ."

"Every time I saw action," Wayne said to the wind and the rain, "I was scared. Sick to my guts scared."

Julio walked with his head so far forward his dripping hair hid his face. "That old lady, she don't weigh nothing. You know? She's so tiny, I could throw her through the wall with one hand. But she ain't scared of *nothing*, man. I tell her something, and all she does is . . ." Julio lifted thick hands and shrugged.

"She's been through some dark times," Wayne agreed. "She knows what it can be like."

"No man, it's more. A lot more. She, I don't know . . ."

Wayne nodded, and when he realized Julio could not see the gesture, said, "I understand."

Wayne's kitchen window squeaked. Jerry poked his head out. He gave Julio the cop's stare, but said to Wayne, "Lunch is on the table."

Wayne waved acknowledgment. No doubt Julio noticed

the exchange but gave no sign. Wayne said, "Why don't you get into some dry clothes and join us."

"The cop don't want me around, man."

"He's probably got reasons that he calls good." Wayne regretted the words before they were completely out. But Julio made no response, and the words fell onto the ground with the rain and washed away. Wayne tried again. "You're going to be here a while. Jerry is a friend. I'd like you two to make peace."

Julio stood there staring at the puddle by his shoes, then turned and went into the house. Wayne climbed the stairs and said through the open window, "I've asked Julio to join us."

Jerry snorted. "Right now everything is cool. But there'll come a time when the lady will run screaming into the yard, saying either her jewelry is gone or he's after her with a knife. One or the other. You watch."

"Maybe not."

"Yeah. Sure. I've only arrested that kid about seven hundred times."

Wayne waited until Jerry had slammed the window shut to say the words, speaking them to the rain, tasting them and hoping they might be true. "People change."

TWENTY-TWO

The lunch started poorly. They were seated at the old linoleum-topped table in Wayne's living room. He cut off the AC and opened the front door so they could listen to the sounds of wind and rain. They were cramped seated at Wayne's table, three grown men and an oversized boy. Jerry filled the place with silent tension. Julio responded with a barrio kid's professional sullenness. Foster looked from one to the other, and revealed a side to him Wayne had never seen before, that of a confused old man. Wayne decided he didn't have to take it, and he wouldn't.

"All right, enough."

His meal half finished, Wayne pushed back from the table and stood with a military stiffness. He paced and he talked. He started with the eccentric manager of the men's shop, even bringing out his suit for them to admire since they'd all been in bed when he'd finally made it back the previous evening. Talked them through the Grey headquarters building, how Tatyana went in search of her colleague and vanished for the day. He described his confrontations with the bullish VP and the dark stranger. He left out the drive and Tatyana's past and the club and the dinner. Just saying they'd ended the day with a meal and a conversation that resolved nothing.

When he finished, Wayne stood in the middle of his bare-plank living room. Waiting with a hair-trigger to shoot Jerry down if he started back on Julio.

Instead, the former cop said, "You spent six hours inspecting the company books."

"About that."

"And?"

"Forget hunting for a scam or an enemy in those accounts. The answer is not there."

Foster said, "You're sure about that?"

"I could spend months in there and come up with nothing."

Julio said, "That dude who showed up, you think he was an angel?"

"I have no idea."

Julio looked at the two older men, just to see if they found that as mind-blowing as he did. "Man, that is some serious craziness."

Jerry said, "I'd say amen."

Which was enough of a good sign for Wayne to return to the table and his meal. "This food is great."

Foster said, "Harry's wife, she fixed the roast. You like, I could heat it up again."

"It's fine as it is."

Julio said, "I heard them talking with Miss Victoria. They're lining up your meals from now to next year. Man, you got it made."

"It's the least they can do," Foster said, "seeing as how he's the only reason they've still got homes."

Julio rose from the table and started gathering plates. Jerry said, "I'm gonna count the silverware when you're done in there."

"Hard to do, old man, when I done already stole your spectacles."

Jerry waited until Julio returned for the next load to ask, "Who you calling old?"

"You prefer fat, it's no problem."

Jerry raised his voice a notch. "Like you got room to talk."

"Miss Victoria, she says a growing boy like me needs extra padding. What's your excuse?"

Foster told Jerry, "You'd best quit while you've still got fingers and toes."

Jerry stared at the kitchen doorway. But when he spoke again, it was to tell Wayne, "I'm still trying to get my head around the idea that you think you spoke to an angel."

Wayne started to deny it, then decided there was no need. "All I can say for certain is, he was identical to the guy Easton Grey described. Something about him spooked me so bad I couldn't talk."

Julio poked his head through the doorway. "You didn't say nothing?"

"Not even good-bye."

"What about, you know, the brave soldier in Iraq and everything?"

"You were in Iraq?" Foster asked.

Wayne shook his head, said to Julio, "I'd almost prefer another firefight. Least I'd know what was coming at me."

"Not me," Jerry said. "Give me a fake angel any day."

Foster said, "You don't know the guy was faking it."

Jerry gave his friend a look. "Are you even listening to what you just said?"

Foster carefully folded his napkin. "It's something to consider."

"No it's not," Jerry said. "Julio."

"Yo."

"Punch the button on the coffee machine." He noticed how Wayne was watching him. "What."

"Nice to hear you talk civil with the kid."

"Hey. I'm nice to prisoners too. Don't mean nothing."

Foster said, "I expect you stand in front of the mirror every morning, practicing how to be a misery."

From inside the kitchen, Julio said, "Talking about angels, you got company."

Footsteps climbed the stairs and crossed the front porch. Wayne found it necessary to drop his gaze to the table. He did his best not to allow his peripheral vision to take her in. He had been waiting for her arrival since before he had climbed out of bed. Even so, he wasn't ready.

He studied a pair of hands that knew years of gun oil and fierce living. The table stood on a floor older than anybody in the room, streaked where the sander had not taken up all the old paint. The air tasted of reheated food and brewing coffee and sawdust and age.

There was nothing, not in the house or in his person, that made for a natural fit with the woman standing in the doorway.

Foster and Jerry vied for the pleasure of playing host. Wayne had no choice but to rise with them and force his gaze to meet hers.

Gone was the lady in pinstriped armor. Gone were the spike heels and the expression carved from Siberian ice. Instead, she wore linen trousers of a grey to match the sky and a sweater one shade darker. Gold watch. Single strand of small pearls. Diamond stud earrings. He knew that because she snagged the right-hand side of her hair and slipped it behind her ear. The gesture was new as well. As easy and natural as the look she gave him.

Wayne tried to tell himself that it was only a matter of time before the lady returned to a world where guys arrived in Ferraris to sweep her away. But all he could think to say was, "You look great."

"They are clothes from . . ."

"Before."

She nodded, grateful for his gift of understanding. "A different time, a different me."

"You're still who you are, Tatyana."

"Am I?"

"He didn't own you, he didn't shape you, he didn't steal who you are."

Wayne had never been good with either words or women.

He had no idea where that came from, and right then he didn't care. All he knew was, the words fit, especially because of the look she gave him.

Jerry asked, "How about a coffee, Tatyana?"

"I would like it, but we must be going. Easton Grey wishes to speak with you."

Wayne said, "I'll go change."

"Easton doesn't care what you wear."

But he wasn't going anywhere in cutoffs, slaps, and a knit shirt so worn not even he could remember its original color. He kept the door to his bedroom ajar as he slipped into the same outfit he had worn the day before, minus the tie. Which was why he heard Jerry say, "Mind if I ask you a professional question?"

"No."

"I understand if you don't want to discuss this problem of yours with a stranger."

"You're not a stranger, Mr. Barnes."

"Call me Jerry."

"You're a retired police officer. Being retired doesn't make you suddenly become ignorant."

Foster said, "That's right, honey. It sure doesn't."

"Don't call her honey," Jerry said.

"I didn't mean anything by it."

"We're trying to talk on a professional level here."

"I took no offense," Tatyana said.

"There, see?"

Tatyana went on, "You are both friends of Eilene. She has

only good things to say about you. She trusts you. Wayne trusts you. How could I do otherwise?"

Wayne stopped in the process of buttoning his shirt. He just stood there in his bare feet and fancy slacks that the lady had bought for him. Staring at his fingers. Wondering why those calmly spoken words made it necessary for him to clench his gut up so tight.

There was the sound of a chair scraping across the floor. Jerry said, "Have a seat, why don't you. Yo, Julio. *Café negro.*"

"What am I, your butler?" But there was the sound of a kitchen cupboard squeaking open, then footsteps crossed the plank floor.

"Gracias." Jerry took a noisy sip. "Wayne told us about him studying the company books and about meeting the guy."

Tatyana said, "The angel."

"Now you're sounding like Foster. Let's say for the moment that we're looking at a scam. An inside-outside job. With a real pro. Just for argument's sake, you understand. Not that I'd ever question your ability to class the dude as an angel, even without anybody laying eyes on him."

Wayne said loud enough to carry, "I saw him."

"And have you called him that? No, you have not. What you said was, you don't know who he was. Which is all I'm saying. So let's keep our feet on the earth here. For this scam to work, somebody on the inside has got to be hooked in solid."

Foster said, "If it was a scam."

"Man, you are about to get me seriously worried."

Tatyana repeated, "You are suggesting the man was hooked into our company."

"Men, plural," Jerry said. "One, you got either security or somebody watching the front doors, knowing when you entered."

"We came in through the garage."

"Same thing. You got security cameras, you got a watchman on the garage gates, somebody." There was a slight pause. "Two, there's the man who confronted Wayne. Three, there's the exec high enough in the food chain to tie you up with this bogus threat to your job."

Wayne added, "What about the assistant you intended to walk me through the accounts?"

"He's in Iowa," Tatyana said. "At a training course. Last-minute shift. His director was supposed to go, then decided it would do him more good."

Jerry asked, "You believe that?"

Wayne slipped into his jacket and rejoined his friends. Tatyana stood in the middle of the room, staring out at the rain. Yet even now she carried none of her customary tension.

"That's what I thought." Jerry glanced over, gave Wayne a pair of raised eyebrows. "Looking good, my man."

Wayne said, "You forgot to count the angel."

Jerry sipped from his cup. "Now don't you start."

The rain stopped by the time they crossed the Intracoastal Waterway and turned north. The barrier island was as wet as the mainland, but held up far better. The shoulder along both sides of A1A was as wide as the road itself and bordered with carefully tended banks of flowers and other indigenous plants. Wayne said, "Did you know palms don't grow straight up?"

Tatyana drove a pearl-white PT Cruiser with a caramel convertible top. A plastic Hertz tag dangled from the keys. She had appeared almost shy as she had beeped open the doors and watched him slip into the passenger seat, clearly waiting for his response. But Wayne had not spoken until now. She looked over and said, "Excuse me?"

"Palms. Go for a walk down a hammock line. Hammock, by the way, is Seminole for dry land surrounded by marshes. There are more than twenty-six hundred types of palms. Most grow long and low, like rail ties. They only rise at the end, where the leaves search for sunlight. The palms you see here have to be trained to grow straight. Sometimes for years."

She slowed enough to give him a longer look. "Is everything all right?"

"Fine." Which was the first lie he had ever told her, but still better than the truth. He kept staring out his rain-streaked side window. "Everything's fine."

She put on her blinker and turned into the John's Island entrance. She rolled down her window, waved to the guard, drove through the raised barrier, and turned west on the avenue fronting the golf course. There she pulled to one side and stopped. "Tell me what's wrong."

"Nothing."

"Please." She was not a woman who said the word easily.

Wayne had no choice. He looked at her. Long enough to acknowledge the truth that splintered his heart.

Not even the iron-hard day could extinguish the golden

flecks in her dark grey eyes. He could talk or he could look at her. But he couldn't do both. Because when he was looking at her, all he wanted to do was say the words he knew he could not utter. Because to say them was to force her to say what he already knew.

He saw so much. He saw how she was still so wounded by that polished beast of an ex-husband that Wayne's silence both frightened and hurt her. He saw how she yearned for someone to be strong, not *for* her, but *with* her. He saw . . .

Wayne forced his gaze away, made a process of brushing off the knee of his spotless trousers. "Last night was one of the nicest times I've ever had."

There was a whole world of past misery in her sigh, volumes of lies that had started with sweet words. "And?"

He could not make her carry more sadness. So he turned and he said the hardest words he had spoken in four years. Speaking what he knew was the raw hand of fate, the closeness and the distance. "I will always be your friend, Tatyana."

She studied him long enough to be certain nothing more was coming. Then she rewarded him with the mystery of an almost hidden smile.

TWENTY-THREE

T he enclave of John's Island held the special silence of the rich. The wind was still strong enough to push the palms around. Raindrops rattled off the leaves and sparkled in the emerging sunlight. The lawn was the shade of liquid emeralds. A chickadee sang from around the side of the house. A car whished by on wet tires. Otherwise the world was orderly, calm, restrained.

Tatyana rang the front doorbell and said, "I hate going to Easton with just more questions and no answers."

"He's the one who asked for this meeting, right?"

"Even so, I feel that I am letting him down. My job is to identify solutions. That is why we are close. Most attorneys specialize in finding problems. I look for answers as well."

"That's one reason you're close, not the only." He heard footsteps tapping across the interior. "You're close because he trusts you."

The door was opened by the same girl they had seen on

their previous visit. Tatyana said, "Hello, Clara. Your father is expecting us."

She did not look at either of them directly. "He's on the phone."

"Can we come inside?"

Wayne had the clear sense that the girl really wanted to shut the door in their faces. Just slam out all the impossible terrors. Her face was pinched tight as she stepped back. The Labrador retriever kept so close she bumped him with her leg. The Lab moved forward and nudged Wayne's hand with his wet nose. Wayne stroked the dog between the ears and felt the Lab's tail thump against his knee.

"Come here, Jody."

The Lab returned to his position behind the girl. She directed her words to the door as she shut and locked it. "Dad's in the kitchen."

"Then maybe we should go wait in his study."

The girl gave a teenage shrug and walked away. As if she didn't care. As if she could block them out. Then the Lab nudged her leg, just a little, and she almost tumbled. The slightest force was enough to wreck her fragile equilibrium.

Tatyana pointed Wayne toward the stairs. Midway up the girl spoke from the bottom of the stairs, "Do you know who's doing this?"

Tatyana leaned over the railing. "No. I'm sorry. I wish I could say it was all behind us. But no."

The pinched features almost hid the tight quiver to the girl's mouth. Almost. "He won't go out. Not even to the store. Not even to play golf. It's like he's sick or something."

"We're working on this just as hard as we can."

She looked at the panting dog without seeing him. "Daddy is scared. He says he's not. He says he likes the time at home with us. But I know."

"Would you like me to call you from time to time? I could do that." Tatyana hesitated, then added, "I know what it's like to be scared."

"Mom's scared too." Her voice broke then. She turned away.

"I'll call you, Clara."

The girl padded in her bare feet across the marble-tiled foyer and disappeared.

The room at the top of the stairs was everything a rich man's study should be, paneled in some wood that glowed, a matching desk, big leather chair, fireplace, oil paintings, awards, books. The smell was like a man's cologne, or a musk. If money had a scent, Wayne decided, it would be this. "Nice."

Tatyana walked to the window, or started to. But her attention was snagged by something on Grey's desk. She picked up the two sheets of paper and studied them. Wayne could almost feel her intensity. She was still looking at them when Easton Grey entered the room and said, "Thank you for coming, Mr. Grusza."

"Call me Wayne."

"Have a seat. I understand you have something to tell me." He saw how Tatyana remained absorbed by the sheets of paper, and told her, "Names and times of every call I've received, just as you asked."

Her face had returned to its customary lines of singular

focus. Wayne felt a sudden stab of loss, which he knew was absurd. But he couldn't help himself. She asked in the voice of old, "Trace Neally called you at two fifteen yesterday afternoon?"

"That's right. Take a seat, Tatyana."

She remained where she was. "Can I ask what you talked about?"

Grey waved Wayne into one of the leather chairs and chose the sofa for himself. "We talked about you."

"Those charges the disciplinary board brought against me are utterly false."

"Tatyana, think of who you're talking to. I know they're false. Now come sit down. Please."

She moved with the stiffness of repressed anger. She selected a high-backed chair next to the fireplace. The pages dangled from her hand. Wayne asked her, "This guy was one of those who accused you?"

"Trace Neally was the last member of the disciplinary board to arrive." Her face now resembled Easton's daughter. Same pinched features, same small mouth, same tremble so tight it appeared almost a tic.

"Who is he?"

"A property developer. One of the biggest in Florida."

"And a friend," Easton added. "We've known each other for almost twenty years."

"So why would your friend level charges you know are false against your company's legal counsel?"

Easton nodded approval. "Exactly what I asked him.

He replied that he was there because he had been asked to come."

"We need to know who brought up this issue against Tatyana with the disciplinary board," Wayne said. "The timing is too perfect for this to be chance."

"Trace promised to check into it and come back to me."

Wayne gave Tatyana a chance to take charge. But her attention had returned to the sheets in her hand. So Wayne said, "Did this Trace guy say who asked him to come?"

"His secretary made the appointment. After I got off the phone with Trace, I checked with her. She arrived that morning to find a board-level memo waiting for her. The signature was illegible." Easton turned his attention to the lady seated by the fireplace and said, "You look very nice today, Tatyana."

Her eyes returned to the page. "My ex-husband called you three times?"

"Just as I recorded there on the page." Easton kept his voice intentionally mild.

"Was that about me too?"

"To some degree. Eric Stroud is now representing Teledyne." Easton added for Wayne's benefit, "Teledyne is a company we are seeking to acquire."

Tatyana said, "I've been responsible for those negotiations. Eric's name has never come up before."

"Eric's firm is Teledyne's outside counsel. You know that. Their board specifically requested that Eric take personal charge. He would not say why. He approached me because, well, he feared there might be some difficulty dealing with you."

She directed her words to the page in her hand. "So he's going behind my back."

"He tried. I told him if he could not handle the matter with you, Teledyne would either need to find new counsel or the deal was finished."

Tatyana blinked once. A second time. The tension gradually drained away. She moved her lips back and forth, as though trying to massage blood back into them again. She said in a very small voice, "Thank you, Easton."

"You are my chief in-house counsel. How else could I possibly respond?" He dismissed the issue by turning to Wayne and saying, "I understand you have met the gentleman in question."

"Hold that thought." Wayne turned to Tatyana. "We need to follow up on this Trace guy."

Drawing the room back into focus clearly required serious effort on Tatyana's part. "He is Easton's friend."

"Think about it. You were tackled by this disciplinary group. How many were there?"

"The same as always. Four. Two company executives, two board members."

"And it's a very serious matter to be brought before them on charges, right?"

Easton asked, "Where are you going with this?"

"I have a friend who's a former cop. Since this thing broke, he's kept saying how he hates coincidences."

Wayne expected the company boss to object to his sharing of confidential information with an unknown. Instead, Easton said, "You think someone on the board is involved in this scam, if that's what it was."

"Maybe." He directed his words to Tatyana. "Does your ex handle a lot of corporate buyouts?"

Easton replied, "Eric Stroud is partner in Orlando's largest firm. They handle whatever comes their way."

Wayne had assumed that already. His question, however, had the desired effect. Tatyana was back fully with them. She said, "The takeover."

"I'm thinking that's what Jerry would say. After you're pulled away I'm confronted by an exec from a completely different department. Your husband pops up like a rabbit out of a magician's hat." He shrugged. "So we follow the coincidences and see where they lead. We need to talk with this Trace guy, see if he can give us a feel for what happened when you weren't in the room."

Tatyana nodded. "I'll set that up."

Easton leaned back in the sofa, his gaze moving back and forth between the two of them. "Well, well."

Tatyana glanced at her boss. "What?"

"It sounds to me like you two have become a team."

She made that gesture from her distant past, the raising of her chin, the noncommittal full-body shrug. "Is that bad?"

He said to Wayne, "In a matter of a few days, you have moved from arm's length to trusted ally. Tatyana does not trust easily. I hope her confidence in you is justified."

"I hope so too," Wayne replied.

"Back to my earlier question. You spoke with the gentleman who claimed to be God's messenger?"

"More like, he spoke to me."

"Describe it, please. In as much detail as you can."

Wayne did so. When he finished, he watched Easton pull at his lip for a moment, then added, "I dreamed about him last night."

Easton Grey revealed neither shock nor derision. Just a return of that absorbed concentration. "Was it just a dream, Mr. Grusza?"

"Excuse me?"

"I think you know what I'm referring to."

He licked his lips. He wished he had not brought it up now. "I don't know how to answer that."

"Did he speak?"

"I don't know. Maybe."

The leather squeaked as Easton Grey leaned forward. "What did he say?"

"Choose."

The corporate chieftain surprised him. He smiled. The invisible strain he had carried with him both times they had met suddenly lifted. "He told you to choose."

"Maybe. I sort of heard the word after I had woken up."

"Choose," he repeated, and rose from the sofa. "The same word he spoke to you in the conference room."

"That's right."

"The same conference room where he could not possibly have appeared."

"So I'm told."

Easton Grey was slender in the manner of a long-distance runner, lean and taut. He moved across the room and tapped his hand thoughtfully upon the oiled wood of his desk. He spoke to the polished surface. "And still you insist that he must be part of a scam."

Wayne found the breath hard to come by. "I don't . . . No. I'm not insisting."

Easton Grey's smile was both gentle and as taut as the rest of him. "So what are you going to do about it?"

"I think we should track down this possibility of a scam. See if there's a connection between anybody on the disciplinary board and Eric Stroud and Teledyne."

Easton Grey kept smiling. "The *possibility* of a scam."

"Yes."

"And what about the *other* possibility? What about that?"

Wayne swallowed. "I'm going to check that out too."

TWENTY-FOUR

As Easton Grey opened his office door, a figure as lithe as a seaside sprite scurried down the upstairs hallway. He stared at where her bedroom door clicked shut. "Clara is worried about me."

Tatyana replied, "Of course she is."

"She is also very angry. She feels like her world is slipping from her control. Control is as important to her as it is to me. Maybe more. I try to talk to her about faith's testing times. . . ." He stared at the door. "She's thirteen. She loves me and she's angry at me and she feels guilty about her anger."

Tatyana walked down the carpeted hallway and knocked softly on the door. "Clara?" When there was no reply, she said, "I meant what I said about us talking."

Tatyana fished in her pocket for one of her cards and wrote on the back. "This is my card. I'm putting my home phone and my cell on the back." She bent down and slipped it under the door. "I'll call you tonight. Is that all right?"

Easton led them down the stairs and across the front foyer.

He unlocked the front door but did not draw it open. "That was very nice of you."

Tatyana shook her head. "She's a wonderful girl."

"Yes. She is."

"I understand what she is feeling. If I can, I would like to help."

Easton opened the door. "I wish—"

Wayne slipped between them. "Hold it there a second."

The two corporate professionals stared at him. He kept his voice very calm, his manner as nonchalant as he could manage. "Tatyana, take a step back into the foyer. Like you've just realized you've forgotten something. Easton, go with her."

"What is it?"

"Just go." It was the only answer he could give because he had no idea what exactly had triggered his alarm. Sometimes it was like that. A shadow glimpse, a fractional image that did not fit with normal. Staying alive meant responding before the conscious brain formed the final structure.

Wayne stepped outside and raised his arms, as though stretching out a kink. He rolled his head from side to side, scouting the perimeter. He stayed on the top step, as the elevation gave him a bit more scope.

There.

Two men. They were across the street and one house north of the Grey residence. A gardening truck, all the normal gear. The men looked normal as well. One of them up a ladder, working the line of Imperial palms. Call it seventy yards from where Wayne stood. He checked his watch and shook his head. He turned as though calling into the house for Tatyana to hurry, but said, "Stay where you are and don't come out."

He inspected the clearing sky as he took the steps and started down the front walk. Looking everywhere but directly at the men.

They wore normal gardening clothes, dirty and old. The truck was battered and draped with gear.

Wayne had worked for several gardening services in his time on the road. Gardeners everywhere had one thing in common: they got paid by the job. Which meant they *ran*. One of these men was up on a ladder. The other used a curved saw attached to a long pole for trimming off the dead palm fronds. Only the men were not racing. As Wayne crossed the street the guy not on the ladder switched to the next palm. But he moved slow.

Wayne patted his pockets as he crossed the street. "One of you guys got a match?"

Even this close he could not see their faces. Both wore floppy hats with the brims down low and streaks of dirt on their faces like camouflage. As he approached, the guy on the ladder started coming down. The other guy kept on with his sawing. His face remained turned up toward the branches.

Which was how Wayne spotted the pistol.

The gun was jammed far down inside the guy's belt, with his shirttail out and draped over his waist. But the way he lifted his arms and sawed at the branch drew the sweat-stained shirt into sharp definition over the pistol's handle. Wayne's mind automatically sorted the data even as his feet turned him about and started back. A shooter's pistol, was what he was thinking. A nine mil, fourteen in the dock and one in the chamber. Fourteen more than they would need on him at that range.

"You know what? Forget it. I left my cigs in the car."

He meandered back, taking it slow, not really aiming for anywhere. Still glancing at the sky and his watch. Calling out for good effect, "You folks found it yet?"

The lady, bless her cautious heart, did not show.

It took him about seventeen years to cross that street. He forced himself not to scratch the hollow itch between his shoulder blades. There was nothing he could do about the growing stain of sweat. The one shaped like a target at the center of his back.

He was midway down the Greys' front walk when he heard the rattle of a ladder being stowed and the truck cranking up.

In the distance, a siren wailed.

The driver gunned the motor and pulled out fast enough to burn rubber. Wayne kept moving up the steps, slow and easy. Only when the motor disappeared in the emerald distance did he turn around and take his first full breath.

"Tell me again about those men."

Wayne had been through it twice before. But he did as the John's Island security chief ordered. "One was six feet one or two, two-twenty, mid-forties. Couldn't see his hair, and he wore a long-sleeved shirt. Hair on his hands might have been dark or it could have been dirt. He wore sunglasses. His features were thick—might have been either Anglo or Hispanic. The other guy was up a ladder and the perspective wasn't good. I'd put him at an inch or so shorter than the other guy and much lighter."

"In other words," the chief said, "you didn't see a thing that'll do us any good."

"I guess that sums it up."

"That is, if they weren't just a couple of guys on the job."

"They weren't gardeners," Wayne replied.

The chief's radio crackled. He thumbed the mike on his shoulder lapel. "Coltrane."

The voice on the radio said, "Maintenance reports no crews were scheduled for tree work today."

Officer Coltrane had eyes of muddy marble. He blinked twice, examining Wayne, then clicked the mike and said, "Swing by the front gate. Find out which gardening crews were checked in."

"Roger that."

"Chief out." He was a thick man, with forearms like beefy clubs below his short-sleeved shirt. "I think we'd all be better having this discussion inside."

Easton Grey said, "Wayne wants us to stay here on the porch until your men are done."

Easton Grey's wife had arrived back about five seconds behind the first security car, whining down the lane like she was on the Daytona track. She stood behind her husband now, clutching her daughter. Easton kept one hand resting lightly upon his wife's arm. Connected.

The chief did not argue. He glanced across the street to where another of his officers was up a ladder, inspecting the palm where the men had been working. Wayne was not going anywhere until he saw if his hunch was right.

"You say one of them was packing."

"A pistol under his shirt. Nine mil is my guess."

"You know enough about small-arms weaponry to identify a pistol by its butt through a shirt?"

Wayne did not shift his focus from the tree. "That's right. I do."

The officer up the tree hefted something and called, "Chief!"

The chief moved remarkably fast for such a heavy man. His belt squeaked audibly as he trotted across the street. Wayne was one step behind.

The security officer was a woman with copper skin and the solid look of someone who spent a lot of time fighting off excess poundage. She leaned over and handed the chief a black box about twice the size of his hand. "This was fastened to a branch."

He turned the box around in his hands. Other than a thumb-sized on-off switch, there was nothing to see. "You know what this is?"

"My guess is, a radio-frequency amplifier." Wayne gestured back toward where Tatyana and the Greys stood on the front porch. "They've bugged the house. The mikes have a limited transmission range. This catches the signals and boosts the power enough for them to catch it outside your perimeter."

Officer Coltrane touched the switch, but did not turn it off. "I can probably tell you how it went. The gardeners, they're hired by the individual houses and a lot of them don't speak much English. So if my guy at the front gate don't know Spanish, he'll make a note of their tags. If he's doing his job proper."

"And if they haven't got so much dirt on the tags they can't be read."

The chief sighed his agreement. "We're our own township. Most of the time, we operate without outside help. But I can call on just about anybody I like."

"Somebody needs to sweep the house for bugs."

"I know that. What I'm asking is, who else do I need to make contact with?" He lowered the box and took aim at Wayne. "That is, assuming there are other police involved in this thing."

"Right now I don't know for certain what it is we're facing. But there's a homicide detective in the Naples area, Mehan."

"Homicide."

"Yes."

"Clear on the other side of the state."

"A scam artist operating as a tax accountant bilked a senior community across the bay out of its entire operating budget. Did the same to a lot of the individual families. The guy turned up dead."

"Did you have anything to do with that?"

"With discovering he was scamming the old folks, yes. With him winding up dead, no."

The chief returned his gaze to the box. "This Detective Mehan, he'll vouch for you?"

Wayne hesitated. "I wish I knew."

TWENTY-FIVE

S unday morning, Wayne joined Julio and Victoria for another dose of church. He spent the afternoon and early evening working on the new computer Tatyana had left with him. The laptop had a high-speed remote linkup, which he used to troll the Web for everything he could find about Eric Stroud and Teledyne.

Toward sunset, Jerry arrived at Wayne's cottage with Foster and Julio in tow. They prepared and ate a shepherd's pie and reheated biscuits like they'd been dining together for years. Wayne took a call from Tatyana after dinner, walking the cell phone she'd left him out into the trees for privacy. Not that it was needed. Tatyana was in a breathless hurry. She asked about his day, reported that she had to fly off that night for an all-day conference, asked if he'd meet her at the airport the next evening, and hung up.

Wayne remained outside with the sunset's last glimmer for company. He walked down to the bayside. Wind briefly touched the palms lining the waterfront. They dimpled the water with remnants of the day's storm. Two dolphins appeared, their fins rising and falling in musical cadence. They were close enough for Wayne to hear the sigh from their blowholes. He stood there until the darkness erased his ability to follow them, then returned home.

Home.

The guys were gone but had left the lights on for him. A natural gesture among men comfortable enough with each other not to need farewells. He saw Julio on Victoria's porch, the kid's face glowing in the light of a single lamp. He was hunched over a book in his lap. The lady was nowhere to be seen. Wayne entered his cottage and closed the door, wishing he could shut out his questions and his fears so easily.

He slept well and did not dream. He awoke the hour after dawn—a long night for him. When he descended his front stairs, he saw Julio on Victoria's porch, waiting for him.

Together they jogged through veils of mist, the damp air a mere myth of morning coolness. The palms and live oaks were half-formed sentinels who measured their passage in stately silence. Wayne let Julio set the pace. When they arrived at the massive new housing development, the young man stopped and huffed over his shoes. Wayne patted his shoulder and ran on. When he returned forty-five minutes later, Julio turned from his inspection of bulldozers scarring the earth. Wayne pushed them a little harder down the community's front lane, challenging by example. Julio kept up with him. Huffing hard, sweating harder, but determined.

They found Foster and Jerry casting lures off the bank. Wayne and Julio stretched under the loblolly pines for almost twenty minutes. The air was scented with sap and the ground cushioned by years of needles. Cardinals sang the only words the morning required.

Julio's first words of the day were, "Miss Victoria, she wants to fix us all breakfast."

Jerry was reeling in his line before Julio was finished. "I smelled something mighty fine on the way down here."

Foster kept his back to the others, staring out over the water. "I'll pass."

"Say that again."

"What, a man can't want a little peace and quiet for a while?"

Jerry shook his head, then turned and walked away, gesturing for Wayne and Julio to follow.

Wayne waited until Julio had peeled off to go shower to ask, "What's going on between Foster and Victoria?"

"All I know is his side, which has got a lot less to do with Victoria than with what the man left behind in Philly." Jerry followed Wayne up his front stairs and into Wayne's cottage. "Foster and his wife ran a half-dozen dry cleaners they'd bought using money they raised from all the family. He lost his wife to something awful and pretty much fell apart. His nephew went from managing one shop to top dog. When Foster was ready to come back, his nephew wasn't ready to let go. The family backed the nephew."

Wayne stepped into his bedroom and kicked his shoes into the closet. "What does this have to do with Victoria?"

Jerry replied through the open door, "Foster never got that far, and the lady ain't saying."

Wayne showered and dressed and returned to the living room. He was on the verge of asking what had landed Jerry in the retirement center, until he saw the man's face. Dark and stolid and unblinking. Stiff as the man's big body. Ready to deflect with a cop's expertise. So all Wayne said was, "Ready?"

On the way over to Victoria's, however, Wayne had an idea. "I'll be right with you."

Wayne headed back down to the water alone. Foster was where they had left him, throwing his lure toward the green island he would never reach. Wayne stood behind him for a time, giving the older man a chance to send him away. When Foster said nothing, he offered, "When Tatyana called last night, she asked me to take the Ferrari to the Orlando dealer."

The hand reeling in the lure hesitated, then kept winding.

Wayne said, "I'm thinking we should make a day of it. Drop you off at the airport on the way. Come back after I see about the car, you and me take Julio to Disney."

Another cast. "How do we get home?"

"We could ask Jerry to follow us in the truck. Or Tatyana said she'd rent us a car."

The frenetic rewind slowed. "That could work."

"Maybe you ought to join us at Victoria's, tank up before we take off." Wayne let that hang for a moment, then patted the bony shoulder and turned away.

Victoria was there on her little front porch when he returned down the path. But her eyes were fastened upon the empty path behind him. "He's not coming?"

"I guess not." The door squeaked softly as he entered her porch. "What's between you two?"

A look he had never seen before came and went in that softly seamed face. "All people have walls between them and God. Same wall, different reasons."

"We were talking about you and Foster."

"That's right. We were." She seemed to teeter slightly as she reentered her little home. "Your breakfast is getting cold."

But Wayne was halted in the doorway by the sight of his sister seated on Victoria's sofa next to Julio. "What are you doing here?"

"Same as you. Having breakfast."

"Sorry. Dumb question." He leaned over and kissed her cheek. "I was planning on coming by later."

"Saved you a trip." The hand holding her fork rose and touched the spot on her cheek. "Wow. An apology and a smooch on the same day. Somebody must be doing some heavy lifting in your life."

Julio's plate was piled to the brim. His fork made a continual arc between the dish and his mouth. "Don't look at me."

Her thoughtful expression refocused upon the young man. "You're doing good too, you know."

Julio's fork paused in midair. "You talking nice to me?"

"Yeah. I guess I am."

"Wow. A miracle." He beamed at Victoria. "Guess what you been telling me is right after all."

Victoria handed Wayne a plate, utensils, and a paper napkin. "You bet your life, son."

Wayne took the seat next to his sister. "How you been?"

"Never better. The kids are fine, the hubby's happy, Julio is down here behaving himself, my brother kisses me hello. God is good."

Victoria said, "Amen."

Eilene asked, "Where's Tatyana?"

"She called me last night from the airport. She had to go somewhere and do some work."

Eilene smiled. "Good old Wayne. The best there is at passing on life's little details."

"I was wondering if I could ask you something."

Eilene glanced at Victoria and said, "About angels."

Jerry snorted. Wayne looked over. His dark friend kept his eyes on his food. "That's right," Wayne said.

Eilene reached into the briefcase at her feet. She came up with a worn Bible. "Here's the deal. I can walk you through the pages. But it won't do you any good unless you're willing to listen to more than just me."

"So you think this guy I saw could be, well . . ."

"I don't know the answer to that. And neither will you, long as you let the past stand between you and what's inside this Book."

He worked through a couple of bites, chewing on more than the food. "Okay."

"Okay, what?"

"I'm hearing what you're saying."

She clearly had not been expecting anything as easy as that. "Will you pray with me?"

Wayne let the words hang there between them while he finished his breakfast. Long enough to go through all the times he had avoided that issue with his father. As in, slipping into his seat after the blessing had been said. Refusing to say the words himself, turning his father's request into an argument about eighteenth century tribal missionaries in Hawaii and South America. Sparking the sort of standoffs that had ruled his homelife. Enduring his father's frigid disapproval. Responding with a pretense of not caring at all.

Finally Wayne set his plate on the coffee table, wiped his hands, and asked, "Will you say the words?"

Eilene blinked at him, but could not speak.

"Here. Let me." Victoria perched at the edge of her chair. "Let's all bow our heads."

Wayne heard the voice more than the words themselves, a gentle wash asking for wisdom and healing and a lot of other things he rarely named, much less figured he deserved. When Victoria was done, no one else met his eye. Not Jerry, nor Julio, and certainly not his sister.

"Three miracles in one morning. I don't know how much more I can take." Eilene fumbled in her briefcase and came up with a sheet of paper. She passed it over without looking at him directly. "These are some verses you may want to take a look at."

"Thanks, sis."

"Do you have a Bible?"

Victoria offered, "I can loan him one."

"Okay. Fine." She was breathing in little puffs of shock as she rose from her chair and stuffed her Bible back in her briefcase. She patted Wayne on the shoulder as she passed, then hesitated in the doorway, turned back, and leaned down to kiss him on the cheek. The arm not holding her briefcase wrapped tightly around his neck. She kissed him a second time, then turned and walked from the home.

Wayne didn't know what to expect as he returned down the path. He didn't walk on air, he didn't feel like he'd made some major breakthrough, he didn't feel much of anything. Julio walked beside him in silence until Wayne said, "You know what's strange? You say you don't like the quiet, but when we're together, you don't have much to say."

Julio shrugged. "I guess when I'm around you, I don't feel like I need to."

"I like that. I don't know why, but I do. Thanks."

"You know, I never prayed before. I guess I didn't pray really then. Miss Victoria, she said the words and all. But it felt sorta like I was there with her."

Wayne was going to say something back. Something about how he'd spent a lifetime avoiding what he'd just done. For reasons that right now didn't mean much at all. How maybe what had happened was he had outgrown the reasons, or something.

But that was the moment the waterfront came into view, and what he said was, "Run get Jerry."

"Where's Foster?"

The signs were all too clear. A boat had dug a channel into the bank. A jumble of footprints marked a scuffle. The broken pole was half in and half out of the water. The line hung limp. The water was as empty as the bank. A loon cried a mournful warning.

Wayne turned and said, "Hurry."

TWENTY-SIX

John's Island security chief Officer Coltrane showed up about two hours later, in response to a call Wayne had placed. Wayne felt an illogical wash of relief at the sight of the big-bellied officer. The chief had given Wayne no reason to believe he might be an ally. Nor did he show anything in his expression. Even so, Wayne hurried over and said, "Thanks for coming. A lot."

He nodded a hello to the lone Vero Beach cop standing at the waterfront. "What've we got here?"

"Possible abduction," the cop answered. "But nobody saw anything."

"Who's the possible vic?"

"One Foster Oates, aged seventy-four, resident of the Hattie Blount Community for seven years and nine months." Wayne guessed the Vero cop had to be in his late twenties but looked even younger. "Mild diabetic. Pacemaker. Widower. I'm thinking he might have wandered off."

"He was kidnapped," Wayne said. "The signs are clear enough. Or were, until you walked over them."

Coltrane studied the waterfront a while, his gaze sweeping further and further until it came to rest where Jerry stood by Holly. "You folks live here too?"

"Six years," Jerry replied.

"You been here a while too, ma'am?"

"Yes," Holly replied. "Coming up on forever."

Just beyond them, Eilene stood holding Victoria's hand. Coltrane asked, "And you, miss?"

"Eilene Belote. I serve as occasional pastor."

Victoria said nothing. Something about the way she continued to stare out over the water, her face lined with far more than age, kept the officer from asking about her. Beyond them stretched a semicircle that had gradually grown until it included almost everyone else in the community.

Jerry said, "Foster Oates is not the wandering kind."

Holly added, "Foster has been on the community board for two years. He is extremely capable and very alert."

The young cop shook his head and kicked at the narrow strip of sand lining the bank. He was hot, he was bored, and he showed a rising irritation over being surrounded by old people.

Jerry's voice hardened. "That's a crime scene you're messing up there."

The cop glanced over, his expression lost behind his shades. He kept kicking the earth.

Coltrane asked Jerry, "You a cop?"

"Thirty years. Orlando. Retired from Homicide."

Coltrane turned to the young cop and said, "Why don't you take a step or so back there, son."

The young officer bristled. "Whose jurisdiction is this?"

"Yours. Which means if it does turn out to be a kidnapping, and there's been a transport of the vic across state lines, you're gonna have yourself a time explaining to the fibbies why you dug a furrow in their evidence."

The cop did his best to stomp across the pine-cushioned ground. "I need to go call this in."

"You do that." Coltrane waited until the cop was out of range to say, "Tell me what you think happened here."

"This is tied to the surveillance on Easton Grey," Wayne said. "We messed up their operation. This is payback."

"That why you called?"

"Partly. You see how the local cop is treating this. They're going to shut us out. We can help here. Jerry's got more time on the force than that punk's been alive."

"And you?" Coltrane stripped off his aviator shades. His eyes were tight and hard and pink-rimmed. "You good at what you do?"

"The best."

He used both hands to slip the shades back behind his ears and settle them tight against his forehead. "We found bugs in almost every room of the Grey home. Four in his office. And cameras. Ultra high-tech stuff. Sent one off to the lab in Miami, got a call from the FBI agent in charge. Bottom line, this ain't your basic beachside surveillance."

Wayne asked, "Can you help us here?"

In response, the officer reached into his shirt pocket and

pulled out a cell phone. He hit a couple of buttons, waited, then said, "This is Coltrane. Our patrol boat back in the water? Okay, here's what I want you to do. Swing on across the bay and pick up two fellers from the Hattie Blount Community. They'll be waiting for you by the shore. They'll tell you what they need." He listened a second, then hung up. "Most likely this won't do anybody any good. But we ought to just check out the local marinas and boats fishing off the island, see if they spotted anything."

"Thanks," Wayne said. "A lot."

"I called that Mehan feller over in Naples. The detective said you were either a good man to have on your side or a felony waiting to happen. He couldn't tell which." The chief tilted his chin so that Wayne could see his distorted reflection in Coltrane's sunglasses. "Guess we'll just have to wait and see how this dance turns out."

The John's Island patrol boat was a twenty-one-foot center-console with twin one-fifty Evinrudes. They covered the local marinas and all the boats within a five-mile radius in less than two hours. Jerry carried a photo of him and Foster on a boat from happier times. No one had seen him, or noticed any sign of a struggle on another boat. Fishermen were a private group who kept to themselves. Wayne had expected nothing less. Even so, he felt hollowed out and defeated when they returned. He thanked the patrol officers the best he could, but he knew they also felt they had wasted half a day on sunshine and empty waters.

Many of the community gathered at their return. Wayne held back while Jerry gave them the news, or lack of any. He waited until everyone had dispersed except for Holly, Victoria, and Eilene. He walked over to where they stood, flanked on one side by Julio and the other by Jerry.

Jerry said, "Still no call."

Eilene said, "We've got volunteers manning the phone around the clock. Both Foster's home and the community."

Wayne directed his gaze at Holly. "I can leave if you want."

"Leave?" Victoria sounded bereaved. "Leave and go where?"

"It's your call," Wayne said. "Whatever you decide, I understand."

Eilene said, "This is not your fault, Wayne."

"If what Jerry says is true about these things being connected, it might be. Or what I did yesterday trying to help Tatyana could have stirred them up."

Holly bit her lip and did not speak.

"You can't leave," Victoria said. Her unsteady voice turned it into an abject plea. "Who would look after us?"

Wayne felt hundreds of eyes, as though even the folks who had returned to their homes were still watching. "There's a chance if I leave, they'll let Foster go."

"Not much of one," Jerry said. "More likely, you go and they think this is a lever they can keep using till they're done."

Victoria said, "Holly, tell him." When the community chief did not respond fast enough, Victoria's voice rose higher still. "Daughter, do it *now*."

Holly blinked. Her voice was very weak. "Stay."

Wayne nodded. It was hardly a resounding vote of confidence, but it was probably all he deserved. He said to Jerry, "We have to move."

"I'm coming," Julio said, and when Jerry looked over, he added, "He's my friend too."

"Let him help," Victoria said. "But first we have to pray. Everybody, hold hands. Eilene, you say the words."

The second time around was easier, though the feel of Jerry's huge mitt in his own was odd. Not bad. Just odd. Wayne could not recall ever having touched a man that way. The sound of his sister praying for him brought up images of him waking in the Santa Fe park, watching a sunrise and feeling like her prayers were the only reason he made it back. Only this time he heard her words more closely and felt the impact more intensely, such that the feel of Jerry's dry skin brought comfort. Standing alone, the moment would have been too weighed down with a lifetime of wrong moves.

❧

Wayne rammed his truck through the afternoon I-95 traffic like the other vehicles were nothing but stationary obstacles. Jerry glanced over a couple of times, leaning across Julio to take in the quivering speedometer, but he said nothing. When they pulled up in front of Julio's apartment house, Jerry said, "You don't have to do this, Julio."

"I told you, man. I want to help."

"The first sign of trouble, you get out. Don't play a hero."

Jerry squinted into the midafternoon glare. "Nothing worse than a partner who won't call for backup."

Julio shifted in the seat next to him. The word Jerry had used hung in the air between them. Partner. Wayne said, "Let's hear you tell us the plan."

"I already told you twice."

"So tell us again," Jerry said.

"I ask around. I don't talk to nobody but friends. I see if anybody knows anything about somebody holding an old man. This ain't rocket science."

"And what are you gonna do if you hear something?"

He held up the phone and showed them how fast he could get her number up on the screen. "Call Tatyana's cell."

Jerry said, "The first breath you feel on the back of your neck, you phone in. We'll pull you out. If we're out of town, you call my buddy on the force. I already spoke to him." Jerry's eyes looked translucent in the sunlight. "Give me his name, Julio."

"Clarence." Making a big deal of the repetition. "Detective Clarence Hattley."

"You got his number. He knows you're out here and he's looking too."

"I heard you the first time. Now let me outta the car."

When Jerry didn't move, Wayne opened his door and slid out. Julio was back into his barrio gear—floppy jeans and unlaced sneakers and a big silver-plated chain banging on his neck. Julio offered Wayne his fist. "Later, *jefe*."

Wayne slipped back behind the wheel and said, "I was going to take him to Disney today."

Jerry watched the kid slip around the first line of buildings and said, "There's nothing the kid can find that my buddies won't turn up first."

"You're probably right." Wayne restarted the truck. "But if he does find our man, think of the world of apologies you're gonna have to make."

Tatyana came through the Arrivals portal and took aim straight at Wayne. "Do you have any word?"

"Not yet." A time like this, he should be focused as tight as a laser. But his throat became clogged by the look of her, standing there in a suit that shimmered softly, grey with a hint of something the airport's muted light almost masked, maybe blue. All the people who passed glanced her way.

Jerry asked, "Who told you about Foster?"

"Easton phoned just as we were taking off." She looked like she wanted to weep. "I'm so sorry."

"It's not your fault, Tatyana."

"I got you involved. All of you." She took a breath and said the inevitable. "Maybe you should resign."

"No."

"But Foster—"

From behind them, a man barked, "Can we get a move on here?"

The pressure that had been building behind Wayne's eyes all day long tightened another notch. "Hello, Jim."

The bullish man Wayne had last seen retreating from the conference room snarled, "Try any of your tricks on me today and I'll have you locked up."

Wayne asked Tatyana, "What's he doing here anyway?"

"He's working on the Teledyne project."

"Which means I've got a lot bigger problems to worry about than one missing geriatric." Jim Berkind snapped his fingers. "Let's *move*, Kuchik."

Wayne said, "I need to ask you something."

The guy actually laughed. "Not a hope."

One minute Jerry was standing on Tatyana's other side. The next he was directly in front of Berkind. "That old guy who's gone missing is my friend. You, I don't even *want* to know."

Berkind tried to step around Jerry and failed. He pushed uselessly at Jerry's solid bulk. "Get out of my way."

Travelers split and spread like a school of disturbed fish. Jerry held his ground. "The badge in my back pocket says I served with Orlando's finest for thirty years. We yell for security, who do you think they're gonna believe?"

Tatyana said, "Jerry, please."

Jerry held his ground. "I'm giving you one more chance to answer the man's question."

Wayne said, "I need to know who sent you to harass me in the conference room."

Berkind rubbed his neck. "You're all insane."

Jerry stepped in closer still. "Else you want to see what rough really means, you *answer* the man."

"Who sent you?" Wayne repeated.

"I'm not telling you a thing." His eyes were red-rimmed and almost teary with rage. "What is *with* you, Kuchik?"

"Easton told you to help us, Jim."

"Easton Grey is hunkered down in his house like it was

a cave." The guy huffed his breath now, like a bull ready to charge. "I checked up on you. Mister Special Forces, the man who won't be stopped, the big warrior hero who's going to make everything safe for our fearless leader to come crawling out of his hole."

"Jim."

"No, Kuchik. You're on *their* side. I'm the one who's trying to keep this deal together. And I know an enemy when I see one."

"Who is trying to kill the deal, Jim?"

Berkind swiveled around the former cop and stalked away. This time Jerry did not try to stop him.

Tatyana said, "He's been like this all day."

Jerry asked, "Easton told you to travel with him?"

"It was supposed to be somebody else. But when I got to the airport, he was here waiting for me."

Wayne said, "The data I found online says Teledyne is made up of three different groups. Hotels, private clinics, and condominiums. Is he working on the whole deal, or just one part?"

"Jim Berkind has been working with Teledyne's hotel group for almost three years. We partner with them on hotels in Colorado resorts. That's how we came to know they were interested in being acquired."

Jerry said, "I don't see the connection."

Tatyana gave her face a weary swipe. "Can we leave, please? It's been a very long day."

Wayne took the briefcase from her limp fingers, then slipped the overnight bag off her shoulder. "Who was supposed to be coming with you?"

"Another of our legal team. He is genuinely sick. I checked."

"I need to get back inside your company, Tatyana."

"I thought the books wouldn't tell you anything."

"Not Grey's. Teledyne's. I need to go deeper."

She nodded slowly. "Our company keeps a suite at the Peabody. I'll make a call. If it's free, you can stay there tonight."

"I'm not talking about tomorrow," Wayne replied. "I need to do this now."

Jerry checked his watch and said, "We need to make one stop on the way."

Tatyana looked from one face to the other, then decided. "Do you remember where I live?"

"Sure."

"I'll take a taxi home. Make your stop and come meet me at my condominium. I have a dedicated line to Grey's mainframe with unlimited access to Teledyne data. You can check it out and nobody needs to know."

TWENTY-SEVEN

The area around the projects where Julio and his grand-mother lived looked a lot worse at sunset than it had in the middle of the day. The sky was not completely dark yet, but already the shadows held big-city nightmares. A cluster of kids passed by. All of them slowed to inspect the faces inside Wayne's truck.

"Five gets you twenty, every one of them is packing." Jerry checked his watch. "Try your sister's number."

Wayne drew Tatyana's cell phone from his pocket. He punched up Eilene's number. Julio answered on the first ring with, "What."

"Where are you?"

Jerry said, "Give me that." He took the phone from Wayne and said, "You're late. Which means we're sitting here in a free-fire zone and you're out shooting hoops or whatever—"

Jerry stopped talking. He listened intently, shot a glance at Wayne, then said, "You shoulda called this in."

"What is it?" Wayne asked.

Jerry raised one finger. Wait. "That's good thinking, kid. But you shoulda let us know what you were doing. Yeah. Okay. You stay safe, you hear?"

Jerry slapped the phone shut. "Let's roll."

"He scored?"

"Hard to say. Julio hit the evening service at Eilene's church. Then he's going over to the late mass at the Catholics. He's asking all the maids to keep an eye out. He'll bunk at Eilene's. Let's go, okay? I seen back streets of Da Nang that felt safer than this place."

Tatyana's home held the same muted elegance as the woman herself. Twelve-foot ceilings, recessed lighting, marble tiled floors, a couple of nice oil paintings. She ushered Wayne and Jerry into her home office. Twin twenty-one inch screens flanked a wireless keyboard and Bluetooth mouse.

As she switched on the computer and tagged in her ID, Jerry said, "Mind if I make a few more calls on your cell? I'd like to check in with the cops here and down around Vero."

Tatyana did not look up from the screens. "Keep the cell phone, it's my personal line. I can use the company's. Okay, here is the accountant's summary on Teledyne. You scroll down and touch the blue script and it will flash you over to the raw data."

"I can handle this."

"Good, because I'm exhausted." She patted his shoulder—nothing intimate, just two colleagues pushing hard on a deadline. "Help yourself to anything you need in the kitchen. Call me if there's an emergency."

Wayne soon lost himself in the books. The story was a far more complicated one than Grey's, and it held him. He heard things in his periphery. Wayne registered on some vague level that Jerry spoke to his buddies on the Orlando force. Then Jerry called Coltrane and the Vero Beach Police. He called his Orlando buddies again. Jerry then set a cup of coffee by Wayne's hand and repeated what he had said earlier, how there were basically four clearinghouses for Florida crime. Jacksonville was focused mainly north, handling things south of Atlanta. Miami's gangs covered the glades, Lauderdale, and the Keys. Tampa controlled the panhandle to where the reach of New Orleans began. And Orlando handled the rest—most of central Florida, most of the East Coast. Jerry's pals on the force might hear if a local syndicate or gang was involved. If. Wayne heard all these things. He even glanced up several times while drinking from his mug. But nothing registered below the surface, down where the numbers churned and the Teledyne tale spun itself out.

The phone rang sometime after midnight. First the home phone, then the cell. Wayne heard it chirruping from the living room. Jerry did not pick up. Ten minutes later the home phone started again. Wayne picked up the receiver on the desk. "Kuchik residence."

"Mr. Grusza? Easton Grey."

"Tatyana's asleep."

"Good. I was hoping to speak with you. How are things?"

"Still no word about Foster."

"I'm so sorry about your friend." The company chief did not need volume to express his genuine regret. "I just spoke with Officer Coltrane. He's set a surveillance team on our home."

"Mind if I ask you some questions?"

"Of course not."

"I've been going through the Teledyne books."

"And?"

"I haven't found a thing. I don't know what I was hoping for, but it isn't here."

Easton Grey waited a moment. "But something causes you to want to know more."

"I'm probably chasing smoke here." Wayne rose from his chair. "But my friend is missing and it's hard to see much else."

"Sometimes any movement at all can be seen as progress. Any action is better than standing still."

The words connected at some visceral level, down below conscious thought. Two men struggling against the night and forces they could neither identify nor attack. "Teledyne lists three official lines of profit. Hotels, clinics, condos." He grabbed his mug and opened the office door. He didn't want more coffee. But the office felt claustrophobic and going for a refill gave him an excuse to move. "Everything is pretty clear, not totally, but nothing that'd throw up a serious red flag. At least, nothing I found."

"Nothing anyone has found. And my staffer looked carefully. Let's go back to that earlier word of yours. Official."

"A lot of their profit comes from partnerships. They're listed, but I don't have access to the books."

"How long have you been studying these accounts?"

"All night."

"I am impressed. Well, the answer is, they concern me too. We are interested in acquiring Teledyne because one of their divisions meshes well with us, while the others cover markets we currently do not. But Teledyne holds minority shares in nine partnerships. All but one are with the same group. A privately held company."

"And because it's a minority share, you can't demand an inspection of the private company's books." Wayne passed through the living room. Jerry was conked out on the sofa, snoring softly. He waited until he entered the kitchen to ask, "Who's the majority partner?"

"A group called Triton."

"Never heard of them."

"That is no surprise. Triton is very closely held."

"I'd like to have a look at whatever you have."

"It's very little, but I will instruct the team to make that available. Anything else?"

Wayne pulled the coffee pot from the burner, held it poised over his mug, then put it back in place and turned the machine off. "Probably. But I can't think of it right now."

"I can't tell you how sorry I am about Foster Oates. I feel as though this is all my fault."

"Get in line."

"All because of a warning from an extremely black gentle-man who might have been . . ."

239

"You might as well say it, since we're both thinking the very same thing."

Easton Grey might have huffed a laugh. "I've spent my life trying hard to follow God's edicts. And it has led me to a place where I'm trapped inside my own home, my wife is upstairs lying awake alone in our bed, my daughter has cried herself to sleep, and a helpless old man has vanished."

"I can go one better." Wayne leaned on the polished granite countertop. The stone was rose colored and cold to the touch. He faced a central island with a stove framed by more granite. Above it hung a variety of copper utensils and pots. Everything perfectly in order. Mocking the haphazard disarray of his life. "By the time I hit sixteen, I figured if God was in the market for people like my dad, I didn't want to have anything to do with either of them. I used a fake ID to lie my way into the army. I discovered a vocation. If you can call small arms, high explosives, and hand-to-hand a trade."

"But you liked it."

"I thought I did. Until I let my mind wander on patrol one day and got two of my best buddies killed."

There it was. The deed never mentioned, hanging there like greasy smoke in the polished kitchen. Wayne breathed a couple of times, feeling his way through the shock of having let it out. He was tempted to blame it on the hour and the strain. But he refused to mock the moment with a lie.

Easton Grey's voice was as lean and dry as the man himself. "Is that what the visitor referred to when he said the deaths were not your fault?"

Wayne liked that term. The visitor. "He didn't say. But that was what I thought."

"He could have obtained that information from any number of sources, I suppose."

"Sure. The patrol is in the division records. We went out. We took incoming fire. They carried me and my buddies out. Several of us got awarded bronze stars." Wayne rubbed his hand along the counter, streaking the granite with sweat. He started over at the beginning. "I was on point. We were following a goat trail along a ridgeline. Maybe we were inside Afghanistan, maybe Pakistan—up there it's impossible to tell. We were so high, man, the clouds were a couple of miles *below* us. Then I heard an eagle. Just amazing, the sound. I dream about it. If the mountains had a voice, it would sound like that bird."

The refrigerator clicked on. Wayne listened to the hum. He heard the man's breathing on the other end of the phone line. He knew he should stop talking. There was no reason to go on and four years of reasons to stop.

"The bird hovered about twenty yards off to my right, out where the world just dropped away to nothing. I watched the bird instead of the trail. Then I caught something, maybe out of the corner of my eye, maybe a sound, just enough to shout, 'Incoming!' I yelled it before I really saw them clearly. The RPGs flew at us like oversized bullets. Two of them. Coming slow and fast at the same time."

"Your shout saved the lives of the other men."

"No. That was the official line. But it's not right. Watching that bird got my two buddies smoked."

"The visitor says you're wrong to think so."

"Yeah, well, the visitor wasn't . . ."

Easton Grey let the unfinished thought hang for a moment, then said, "I find great comfort in speaking with you, Wayne."

The usage of his first name came and went naturally. "Lessons from a life gone all wrong."

"No. Not that at all. I'm glad you're on our side." He could hear Easton shifting the phone. "Wait one second."

Wayne felt the silence settle in around him. Like a blanket scented with some kitchen cleanser and the vague presence of something beyond his vision. Not the people sleeping in other rooms. Something unnamed, yet comforting.

Easton Grey returned. "I thought I heard my daughter. She's been in such a state, I can't tell you how hard it is to live with a teenager sometimes, even one you love more than your own life. She's started going on about moving to Africa. She's downloaded maps of every country on the continent and pinned them to her walls, along with drawings of native dress. I tell my wife at least it's not some punk band with body piercings and misspelled tattoos."

"I have a friend who lived there for, I don't know how long. Years. She's . . ." Wayne tried to decide how to describe Victoria. "There's something special about this woman. If anybody can help your daughter, it's her. And with Foster missing, this might help my friend a lot."

"Will you speak with her?"

"Sure."

"Thanks." A pause, then, "If you will go lay down and try to rest, so will I."

"Deal."

"Could we have a moment of prayer before we close shop?"

Three times in one day. *Definitely* a record. "Say the words."

TWENTY-EIGHT

Wayne heard the knock on the office door from a very great distance. A gentle rumble of a voice said, "This dude is out for the count."

"Is he decent?"

"Can't answer that one. But he slept with his clothes on."

"Wayne?"

The tendrils of his last dream reluctantly let go. But the instant he opened his eyes, he could not remember what he had been dreaming.

Tatyana wore dark leggings and a loose-fitting top knit from clouds that hung almost to her knees. She wore no makeup. Her hair was caught in a silver clasp. Her face was oval with cheekbones slanted like her eyes. He had never noticed that before.

"It's just gone eight."

He pushed himself upright and rubbed his face. He could not think of anything to say. His entire world had room for just one thing.

Tatyana seated herself beside him and handed him a mug. "Jerry said you took your coffee black."

He mouthed thanks but could not give it enough air. His breath caught a hint of her fragrance, clean skin and soap and flowers. He felt his heart catch at her seated there beside him, while he sipped from the mug and struggled to knit his barriers back into place.

He slipped his feet back into his shoes and took another sip. "I was dreaming."

"What about?"

"I can't remember." He sipped again. "Given the state of some of my dreams, that's probably a good thing."

"I always told people I never dreamed. But it was a lie. I dream all the time. Mostly about things I wish I could leave behind forever."

"I just have one bad dream. But I have it a lot."

She used one finger to trace her hairline along her forehead and down behind her left ear. With the blinds closed and one lamp burning, her eyes were one shade off slate. The flecks were soft bronze buried deep inside. "I don't know which would be worse."

"Aren't you going to work?"

"Not until this is over. I spoke with Easton and he agrees. Foster's disappearance changes everything."

He had so much he wanted to say to her, the words became clogged in his throat. He sipped from the mug, but the obstacle would not dislodge.

Jerry stepped through the office's open door. "There's a razor on the bathroom sink, you don't mind using it after me."

Tatyana rose with him. "Easton called. The data you requested is online."

"You stay and work," Jerry said. "I can go pick up Julio on my own."

Wayne handed him the keys. "Any word?"

"Not a peep." Jerry looked from one of them to the other. Then he smiled. Jerry was not a smiler and the gesture surprised Wayne. His entire face reshaped itself, creases vanished, his forehead cleared, his eyes grew brighter.

Jerry said, "It does my old heart good."

Wayne stood there in the doorway as Jerry turned and left. He heard the former cop's footfalls across the front hall. Wayne walked into the bathroom and shut the door. He turned on the water, then just stood there, listening to the water drown out whatever noise Tatyana might be making. His eyes stared back out of a face that might have been handsome. He had heard that from people, but he couldn't tell. His eyes said it all—what a shame it was that his one remaining friend could read the moment so wrong.

*

When he came out of the bathroom, Tatyana stood in the living room with the phone to her ear. "He's here now. Yes. I'll put him on. All right. We'll be waiting."

She walked over and handed him the phone. "It's Easton for you."

"Good morning."

The company president asked, "Did you sleep?"

"Some."

"Me too. Miracles do happen. Have you looked at the files yet?"

Tatyana motioned with his empty mug. Wayne nodded yes. He said, "I was just going to get started."

"I went over them again. Like I said, there's not much. The one thing that jumps out at me is Trace."

"The guy on the disciplinary board."

"He's also on the board of the Triton partnerships. All of them."

Wayne walked over to the computer and sat down. "Trace Neally, your friend for twenty years."

"I called him this morning. He's working from home today. I said you wanted to speak with him. He wanted to wait and meet you tomorrow in Orlando. I said this was urgent. I hope that's all right."

"No. This is good."

"He lives just south of Naples, someplace called Lantern Island." He rattled off the address. "Hello?"

Wayne watched Tatyana walk over and deposit the cup on her desk. "Lantern Island. I know it."

"Call me as soon as you leave his place, will you? The walls are closing in over here." Easton paused, then added, "It meant a lot talking to you last night. I pray for patience, but my mind keeps racing like a hamster on its little wheel. I've never been good at being still. I worry about Foster, about my daughter . . . I wonder if I left the house if it would all just go away."

"You sit tight. I'll call you soon as we know something."

When he clicked off, Tatyana asked, "What's the matter?"

Wayne handed her the phone. "More and more."

Jerry Barnes pulled into the parking lot of Eilene's church and had to search for a free spot. Eight-thirty on a weekday morning and the place was packed. He saw a flood of school-aged kids headed to a building beside the basketball court. A larger tide of women headed into the main building. He followed them, slightly uncomfortable being the only man in sight.

He found Julio standing in the doorway talking with Eilene. The pastor hugged the overgrown kid who was as tall as she, and was rewarded with a bashful grin. Julio became more embarrassed when he spotted Jerry approaching, but Eilene refused to let him go. Instead, she said, "The kid here hit a home run with the bases loaded."

"I didn't know you played baseball."

"We're talking about the only game that matters." She hugged him harder. "Right, brother?"

Jerry asked, "You got saved last night?"

Julio muttered to the floor at his feet, "Miss Victoria, she's been talking to me."

"Yeah, that lady's got a place on God's front line, I'm sure of that," Eilene agreed. "But this is about you, right? You're the one who found the courage to step forward and commit. How cool is that?"

"Loosen up there," Jerry said. "Let the kid breathe on his own, why don't you."

Eilene let him go. "Way to rock, Julio."

"I left my stuff in the hall."

"I'll wait for you right here." When the kid trotted off, Jerry said, "I've never seen you this happy."

"Hey. My brother, the guy who made a profession of skipping town, is not just back and helping me out, he's *committed*. He *prayed* with me. I handed him the worst kid we got, a case so tough I was this close to barring Julio from ever coming back on church property. And what happens, but the kid turns around."

"Like Julio said, Victoria was the one who twisted the screws."

"You think a barrio kid would've listened to some old white-bread lady on his own?" She pointed at the world beyond the sun-splashed exit. "Wayne is everything this kid dreams of becoming, if he can manage to live that long. A true-blue warrior. A strong stand-up guy who *cares*. Julio listened to Victoria because Wayne listened first."

She dropped her arm. "What about you, Jerry? You ready to make the long walk home?"

He held both hands protectively in front of him. "Quit while you're ahead, sister."

"No way. I'm aiming for a clean sweep here." She turned serious, which meant going softer. "I was watching you when we started praying. Dropping those barriers you think nobody sees. What's *with* you?"

He scouted the empty hall for his excuse. "I got to go."

"One question, one answer. Is that so hard?"

Matter of fact. "My wife was into the church thing full-time."

"The *church* thing." Eilene was no longer smiling.

"She got sick. We went through all the regular stuff. Nothing helped. We started trying other things, treatments that weren't covered by our insurance. Went through our savings in nothing flat. Mortgaged the house. Spent that too."

"Then she died," Eilene said softly. "Leaving you broke and alone and stuck in a place with nothing to do but serve your time."

Jerry shrugged like it didn't matter. "Seems kinda strange, us standing here talking about things that don't matter while Foster's still gone."

"It matters," Eilene replied. "It matters a lot."

Julio came pounding around the corner. He stopped and looked at one face, then the other. "What's happened?"

"You big, sweet, gentle bear." Eilene closed the impossible distance and hugged Jerry. "I'll be praying for you. Hard as I know how."

❦

The sunlight and the humidity turned the asphalt silver-white. Wayne rode with Tatyana in her rented car. Jerry drove Julio in Wayne's truck. When Tatyana had suggested they take two cars to Lantern Island, Jerry had smiled and said simply, "Sure." Julio had remained caught up in something beneath the surface of his opaque stare and did not speak.

Tatyana said, "I need to ask you something."

She had printed out all the pages on Triton. Wayne had finished going over them before Jerry had returned with Julio in tow. He had them spread out in his lap now, sifting through the data a second time. He had forgotten to get his sunglasses out of the truck before they left Orlando. But that was not why he refused to lift his gaze. "Fire away."

"All yesterday and now today I feel like you are angry with me."

"It's not you." He hated how the strain caused her accent to thicken. "It's nothing."

"Don't tell me that. I know it's something. You won't even look at me. How can it be nothing?"

"Tatyana, please."

"Please what? Tell me what I've done."

The childlike tone of this woman beside him melted the stone he had carried in his chest since forever. "It's me, Tatyana. It's us."

"Us?"

"Yes."

"You don't like me?"

"I shouldn't."

"Why shouldn't you like me, Wayne? Am I such a horrible person you can't like me?"

He raised his eyes because he had to. Beyond the window was flat Florida wilderness. The Florida of cattle ranches and horse farms and black-water rivers. "You know that's not it."

"You said we were always friends, yes? Do friends not talk in your world?"

"They talk."

"That's all I'm asking."

"You will heal. You will go back into your world of rich people with classy jobs and flashy cars. You'll talk about smart things with other successful types." His breath fogged the side window. "I don't belong there. I'm me. Sergeant Wayne Grusza. One of life's born losers."

"Stop."

"What would you say to those people in the boardroom? How this guy you know, he slept rough for almost two years?"

"Wayne, listen to me. I hate those things."

"No, Tatyana. No. You *belong* there."

"I will *never* belong."

His smile felt false even on the inside. "Sure thing."

"Sometime soon I will tell you just how wrong you are. But not now. Because I can't speak of these things without weeping. Me. Tatyana Kuchik. Belonging." Her voice did not alter. But her neck was locked taut in her determined battle for control, and the skin of her wrists and hands were chalk-white where she gripped the wheel. "I will tell you how I felt as a child. I will explain just how horrible it was in that orphanage, and what my beauty cost me. I will describe how I returned to those exact same feelings when my husband cheated on me. How I tried to belong to that world for him, and how I failed. How it was all a lie."

"You're beautiful. You're intelligent. You've got a killer job. You'll pick yourself up—"

"Yes. All this is true. All right. I agree. But answer me this, Wayne Grusza. Why was I so miserable all the time I tried my best to belong? Why do I feel happy *now*, when I am with you?"

"You can't be happy. You're crying."

She released the grip of one hand so she could pound the wheel. "*Answer* me."

He started to reach over and touch her cheek because he had never seen anything so beautiful in his entire life as that tear.

The only thing he could think to say was how he had a knack for making women cry. But no way was he going to ruin the moment with anything that sounded so stupid in his head.

Maybe he could learn a little impulse control after all.

Then it struck him.

"Wait a minute. Wait a minute."

"What?"

"Stop here for a second. Just pull over. I need to check something."

Tatyana put on her blinker with one hand and used the other to clear her face. She sniffed loudly and slowed. "What is it?"

"I'm not sure." He flipped through the papers. Back and forth. Searching.

"Wayne?"

"Hold that thought." He heard a vehicle pull up behind them and doors open and close. He kept turning the pages, ignoring the sound of approaching footsteps.

Someone knocked on his window. He flipped another page.

Tatyana sniffed and wiped her face again, then used the driver's controls to lower Wayne's window. Jerry asked, "What's going on here?"

"Wayne thinks—"

"Here it is!" Wayne held the sheet over where Tatyana could read. He felt a current surge through his fingers. "Okay. Tell me what you see."

Tatyana blinked hard and rubbed her cheek a third time. "A list of minority partners for one of the Teledyne partnerships."

"Right." He lifted the second sheet. The charge emanating from the page only grew stronger. "Now here."

"You okay, Tatyana?" Jerry asked.

"Yes." She struggled hard to reknit the professional veil. "The same thing again. Another project run by Teledyne, another group of minority shareholders."

"The one name that's the same in both places. It mean anything to you?"

"Cloister." She thought hard. "No. Why?"

Jerry said, "I heard that name before."

"Sure you have." This from Julio. "They're building that swanky development down from the community. We ran there."

Jerry snapped his fingers. "The new mini-town. Sure."

"Call the office," Wayne said to Tatyana. "See who owns them."

Instead, Tatyana reached to the back seat and pulled her laptop from her briefcase. She keyed in and waited for the satellite link to search and hook up. She typed for a moment, then raised her eyebrows. She turned the computer so Wayne could read from the screen.

Jerry said, "You want to clue us in here?"

Wayne interpreted what the data was telling him. "Triton lists Cloister as a wholly owned subsidiary. Cloister is based on Grand Cayman Island. The Caymans are one of the world's most notorious centers for money laundering and crime-backed financing. Three months back, Cloister set up a US subsidiary. Probably required to handle their new development. And guess who is listed as their joint venture partner."

Jerry shrugged. "I give up."

Tatyana said, "Triton."

Jerry said, "Triton is partnering with itself? That makes no sense at all."

"Sure it does. If the guys putting it together are in the business of hiding profits and manufacturing scams."

Jerry tapped his marine ring on the window frame. "I'm not following this tune and I'm still ready to boogie."

Wayne asked Tatyana, "Can you find out the names of Cloister's corporate officers?"

"I'll check."

Time was marked by the swoosh of passing cars and the low of cattle. The day's heat flooded through the open window. No one complained. Finally Tatyana breathed, "I don't believe it."

"Show me."

She watched his face as she angled the laptop so both he and Jerry could read together. "Trace Neally."

Jerry fisted Wayne's shoulder. "Lock and load, bro."

TWENTY-NINE

They stopped for gas on the outskirts of Naples. The day and the traffic swirled around them. Tatyana used the time to call her office, then had to step away and argue with chopping hand motions for emphasis. Jerry watched her for a time, then said, "I wouldn't trade places with that lady for a truckload of gold."

Julio said, "Like that's a big worry, the execs gonna come looking for a retired cop."

"Look at this. The kid finds religion and grows a lip."

"Hey, just telling it like I see it, bro."

Wayne asked, "You know Victoria's phone number?"

Jerry took Tatyana's phone, keyed in a number, waited, and asked, "How you doing, sister. Yeah? That's real good. There's a man here wants to have a word."

Julio asked, "When you're done, mind if I say something?"

Wayne took the phone and asked, "Have you heard anything?"

"Not from the kidnappers. But I have from God."

Wayne turned away from the watching men. "Say again."

"He spoke to me in my morning prayers. Clear as daylight. He said it was all going to work out fine. Thanks to you."

Wayne worked on that for a moment, his thoughts keeping pace with the highway traffic. "He give you any details? As in, how we're supposed to pull this off?"

"I expect He's waiting for you to ask Him that yourself."

Wayne allowed himself to confess what had been weighing on him for days. He pitched his voice low enough for the thundering traffic to mask it from the others. "I'm so tired. And worried."

"Well, of course you are." Victoria's smile was as clear as a song. "I'll tell you something that comes from my own heart, Wayne Grusza. You're a warrior. You're made to slay dragons. But even warriors need strength from beyond themselves. Not muscular strength. You have that in abundance. The wisdom of right choices and correct directions. The wisdom to know where the dragons lie in wait. Even Solomon needed the Lord's wisdom."

He tasted the words long before he actually said them. "Will you pray for me?"

"Son, I've been doing little else. I'd say it's time you tried that for yourself, wouldn't you?"

"All right." He stepped further from the others. He stared into the daylight and pushed the words out in tight little puffing breaths. When he was done, he had to hold himself apart like that a little longer, waiting for his world to unlock.

"Amen," the quiet old woman said. "I say, amen."

He collected himself a moment longer, then said, "The reason I called, Easton Grey's daughter is having a hard time with all this. She's dreaming of escape to Africa and it's getting to her folks. I was wondering if maybe you could call her."

"I'll do that soon as we hang up." Her quiet song rang above the traffic's din. "But son, that's not why you phoned."

"No. Maybe not." He returned to the two men. "Here's Julio."

Julio grabbed the phone and did his own two-step across the parking lot.

Jerry observed, "Looks to me like the lady gave your tree a good shake."

"She said God told her everything was going to be all right."

"First time she gave me one of those God messages, I laughed in her face. Then it turned out she was totally on target and I had to eat my words. Victoria told us God said we shouldn't give the scammer a job." Jerry shook his head. "No telling where we'd be if we'd listened to her on that one."

Tatyana clicked her phone shut and stalked back to where they stood. "My two allies in the company, the ones who have searched for what might be going on, they've both been fired." She was more than tight. She was furious. "Because they tried to help me. I've cost them their jobs."

Wayne touched her arm. Felt the anger and the steel.

Said what he thought she needed to hear. "The fight is not over yet."

"There you go," Jerry said. "How you want to handle this?"

Wayne kept his arm and his gaze on Tatyana. "We go in there and we take back what's ours."

THIRTY

The bridge to Lantern Island shone like polished coral in the sunlight. Wayne felt his mouth turning dry. There was no reason for it. But he could not control his response. He watched Tatyana lower her window and give her name to the security guard, then point to the truck pulling in behind her and saying they were with her also. The guard picked up his phone and dialed, leaning over as he did so and glancing into the car. Wayne's gut tightened.

Tatyana accepted the day pass, rolled up her window, then noticed his reaction. "What's the matter?"

He was about to say, Nothing. He had never thought of it as his normal response before, but that's what it was. Offering the outside world a standard denial. Pretending he wasn't touched by a thing.

"Wayne?"

He touched his lips with his tongue. No longer. Not with her. Not as long as she let him. He said, "This is the first time I've ever done this legit."

A car behind the truck popped his horn. Tatyana put the car into gear and moved forward. "Done what?"

"Come to Lantern Island." He pointed to his right. "There's your turn."

"I don't understand. You've been here before?"

"Too many times. My ex-wife lives down at the island's other end. She married a doctor." The place looked remarkably different in the light of day. Besides which, he had not been to the island's north end. Until now, he had had no reason. The lots were even bigger here than in the south, the homes almost completely hidden behind banks of blooming oleander and walls given over to ivy and wisteria.

Wayne felt her eyes and faced her. Waiting for the question. But whatever she saw was enough for her to turn back to the road.

The Neally residence was what Wayne had come to think of as typical Florida rich. Stucco exterior painted off-gold. Oversized windows. Clay-tile roof. Pillars around the front entrance and side porch. More pillars visible through the front door's etched glass.

Tatyana rang the doorbell. The house interior echoed with four big chimes. Jerry glanced back to where Julio sat in the truck, watching them. "This here is some serious strangeness."

Tatyana said, "You know about Wayne having been here before?"

"Done one trip with him. Came in to extract the scam artist and his cash." Jerry examined Wayne more closely. "You okay with this?"

Wayne touched his lips again. Wondering the same thing himself.

"Why didn't you say something before we got here?" Tatyana asked. "We could've handled this one on our own."

Wayne heard footsteps echo toward them. "Foster's still out there."

A maid in a monochrome uniform and a face trained to show nothing answered the door. Tatyana spoke to her in Spanish. Wayne recognized only Tatyana's last name. He made a mental note to ask how many other languages the lady spoke.

The maid stepped back with the door. Her stare was blank. She did not speak. She merely pointed toward the rear of the house, shut the door after them, and departed. Wayne tasted the air.

Jerry noticed it too. "This place don't smell right."

The maid's footsteps pattered softly into the tiled distance. The house had an empty feel.

Tatyana looked from one man to the other. "What's the matter?"

Wayne said, "Go find the maid, see if she'll tell you anything."

Jerry motioned with his chin. "Take a look at our guy."

At the rear of the house, glass doors opened onto a large pool area. A man was seated partly protected from the sunlight by a big square umbrella. A glass of something that sweated sat by his hand. The sun had shifted while he sat, so that the man now rested half in and half out of the sunlight. Neither the sunlight nor the doorbell had shifted him. Jerry said, "Something is seriously wrong here."

"Try the maid," Wayne repeated.

He and Jerry started toward the rear of the house. The living room was basically an extension of the front hall, given a mock separation by a large frame around the entryway and three marble steps down to a divider of some expensive looking wood, maybe cherry. The fireplace to Wayne's right was carved from the same wood and rose in inlaid waves the entire twenty feet or so to the ceiling. The rear of the house was one long series of glass French doors. The furniture outside was an all-weather match to the same ivory tones used for the living room. Everything very tasteful and feminine.

Jerry said, "You know the good-cop, bad-cop thing?"

Wayne pointed at the living room's coffee table. A *Cosmo* magazine and a *People* sat next to an empty vase. "The magazines are from last month."

"Pay attention here."

"That's exactly what I'm doing. This place is shouting feminine, and there's not a woman in sight."

"Yeah, so listen to what I'm telling you. I won't say a thing out here unless you give me the signal. Just pull on your ear and I'll be all over the guy."

Wayne opened the middle French doors. "Mr. Neally?"

The man did not rise. "I was told to expect Grey's attorney," he said. "What's her name. Kuchik."

Wayne crossed the blinding white pool deck. "We're her associates."

"There's nothing I can tell you."

He was in his midfifties and had enough paunch to hide his belt. But he still looked like a little boy. Inflated cheeks, rosy lips, wispy moustache. The legs emerging from his shorts showed no definition whatsoever and were red in the manner of someone who did not tan easily. He wore a tan knit shirt with crossed golf clubs and the island's name on the crest. Wayne took it slow, picking up a chair and drawing it to where he could sit sheltered beneath the umbrella. "The sun's so hot, Mr. Neally. Why don't you scoot over a bit."

"I was just going inside."

"Sure. Listen. We have just a couple of questions and—"

"Why is your buddy standing up like that?"

"We've been sitting all the way from Orlando. We made the trip just so we—"

"Tell him to move over where I can see him. I don't like people hovering."

Jerry stepped across to where an overhang protected an outdoor grill and steel-fronted fridge. He moved deeper into the shadows and effectively vanished. Wayne said, "I need to ask you—"

"There's nothing I can say that will be of any help. I told Easton the same thing. I received an unsigned memo requesting my attendance at a disciplinary board hearing. I did not know it was about Kuchik until I got there. End of story."

To his left, the pool glistened a perfect blue. A motorized vacuum robot scoured the pool floor, snaking a long accordion hose out behind. A hummingbird flitted down in a lightning stroke of rose and gold, drank from the pool, and vanished. The air held an edgy metallic flavor only a real-time combatant ever tasted. Wayne felt the entire day was etched with acidic clarity.

The man was not speaking to him.

He did not know why he felt that. But his gut was working overtime. All he knew for certain was he needed to keep the guy talking.

"We're way beyond that, Mr. Neally. We wanted to talk with you about Cloister."

The man had been still before. Now he froze. "What?"

The paper in his lap was the *Wall Street Journal*. Wayne read the date upside down. The paper was from the previous weekend. Only three or four of the crossword's spaces had been filled in. "Cloister. You're a member of their new US subsidiary's board of directors, aren't you?"

"I can't talk about that."

"We can wait until Tatyana comes out if you like."

"Bring whoever you like. It won't make any difference." The guy's voice was very loud for carrying to someone seated next to him. Each word came out separated, as though he were reading a speech to an oversized crowd. "Cloister is involved in a wide variety of confidential projects."

"We're only interested in the partnerships with Triton."

"I don't care what you're interested in." The pudgy fingers deliberately tore off a strip from the corner of the newspaper. "I am unable to answer any questions about Cloister or Triton or anything else."

"Where is your family, Mr. Neally?"

"That's none of your concern." Trace Neally balled up the slip of paper, then used both arms of the chair to push himself to his feet. The rest of the newspaper slid unnoticed onto the deck. "I told Easton this was a mistake. Now you really must leave."

Jerry emerged from the shadows. But before Jerry could give voice to the bellow building in his face, Wayne jerked his head. Back and forth very swiftly. Jerry subsided.

Wayne followed Neally back across the blinding deck and into the living room's cool shadows. There Neally offered Wayne his hand. "I'm sorry you made this trip for nothing."

Tatyana emerged from the back of the house. Again Wayne shook his head before her question could be fully formed. They gathered at the front door and let themselves out. Wayne led them back down the sidewalk. Jerry signaled to Julio that he would be just a minute and the three climbed into Tatyana's car. She started the motor and turned the AC on high.

Tatyana said, "The maid is terrified. She said the family is on vacation. And claimed that everything was fine. But all the while, she kept making these little gestures, like she was pointing at the ceiling with her eyes."

"Like she was being watched," Jerry said.

Wayne unfolded the balled slip of newspaper. He showed it to Tatyana, then Jerry.

On it were written two words.

Help me.

THIRTY-ONE

The homicide detective from the Naples Police, Mehan, met them where the entrance to Lantern Island joined the main five-lane drag. He didn't like doing it, but he showed up. "Explain to me why we're standing out here in hundred and ten degree heat, hundred and ten percent humidity, when we got a nice cool interview room—crank the AC up high, even buy you a Coke, you ever think of that?"

Jerry just gave him stone. "We have something we think you ought to see. And we can't leave this spot."

Mehan glanced over to where Julio sat slightly hunched over inside Wayne's truck. Julio might have started communicating with God, but it didn't make him pals with strange cops. "You're gonna tell me the reason, I hope."

Jerry nodded to Wayne. Tell the man.

Wayne set it up. Showed him the pages from those Tatyana had printed out. Explained the connection between Triton and Cloister. "There's no reason why they would enter into a partnership with themselves unless they were hiding something. As in, sweeping profits under the carpet."

"We're back to this scam thing of yours, am I right?"

Jerry said, "Let him finish."

Mehan sighed heavily. He used two fingers to pluck the shirt off his chest.

Wayne described their meeting with Neally. Then he showed Mehan the strip of newspaper.

Mehan tried hard to hold onto his skepticism. "He gave you this how?"

"When he shook my hand."

"After he told you he couldn't help you."

Jerry said, "Now tell him the good part."

"There's more? You got to be kidding me. What, he gave you a map with a skull and crossbones?"

Tatyana said, "This is serious, Detective. We have an elderly gentleman who's been abducted and the possibility of a serious statewide scam."

"I am still waiting for the first bit of evidence on that scam deal." But Mehan was no longer sneering.

Wayne described what had happened at Easton Grey's on Saturday. The false gardeners, the surveillance amp, the cameras. And Foster being kidnapped the next morning.

Mehan looked from one to the other. "You got somebody official who'll back you on all this?"

Jerry opened Tatyana's phone, keyed in a number, said, "Jerry Barnes for Officer Coltrane. Yeah, I'll wait."

Mehan accepted the phone. "Officer Coltrane? Detective Mehan, Naples Homicide. We spoke yesterday."

Jerry waited until the detective stepped away to say, "I believe we finally got the man's attention."

A Lexus SUV turned off the highway and pulled past them. Wayne glimpsed an all-too-familiar face wearing a startled flash of recognition. The car continued another hundred feet or so before the brake lights came on.

The young woman emerged stiffly from the car. It was Patricia, but different. Four years older. Slightly fuller around the middle. Far better dressed. Her hair was cut stylishly short and the ends frosted. Perfect makeup.

But her rigid anger was exactly the same as he had seen, and caused, all too often.

"Wayne?"

"Hello, Patricia."

"What are you *doing* here?"

Wayne was still sorting through various responses when he felt another person step up beside him and declare, "He is with me."

"And you are?"

"Tatyana Kuchik." She offered a business card. "Counsel to the Grey Corporation."

The restyled Patricia took her time over the card, using it as a focal point while she reknit her day. "You're a lawyer."

"That is correct."

Memories flooded back at the sight of her face pinching up tight, compressing her lips and her eyes. Wayne ached with the ability to name the reason for every line that extended almost to her hairline.

Patricia asked Tatyana, "What's he done now?"

"Wayne is aiding us in an important investigation."

Patricia took in the unmarked cop car with the flasher on the dash. Mehan stood two steps away from Jerry, listening to the phone and watching the drama with a faint smirk.

Patricia said, "I'm a little out of practice. Is that cop talk for he's not been arrested yet?"

"Wayne is not in trouble, ma'am. He's a consultant—"

"Whatever. I do *not* want to hear."

She stomped back to her car, then turned back for a parting shot. The line might have been different, but the song was one he recalled all too clearly. "You stay *away* from my family!"

Mehan slapped the phone shut and walked back over. "Charming lady. She's got to meet my ex. They can have coffee, trade arsenic recipes." He handed Jerry back the phone. "Okay. Coltrane confirms what you've told me. Everything except the abduction, which they still have on the books as a missing person."

Wayne stared at the space where Patricia's car had been. The air still shivered from the heat.

Jerry said, "Foster Oates was abducted."

"No note, no ransom, no call. Guy's got no assets to speak of." Mehan raised his hand to stifle Jerry's protest. "I hear what you're telling me, and it don't matter. Where I'm standing, there's nothing to substantiate your claims. And nothing to tie what we got here into this surveillance deal clear on the other side of the state."

Tatyana's ire raised the day's temperature another notch. "You're dismissing everything we have just shown you?"

"Absolutely. This has waste of time written all over it."

Jerry stabbed at the strip of newspaper dangling from Mehan's hand. "What about that?"

"Come on, man. You're a cop. You know chain-of-evidence rules same as me."

"My friend's been abducted and this is the first clear indication—"

"Correction. Your friend is *missing.* And for all I know you got that homeboy hiding in your truck to write this up."

"Julio is clean."

"Sure he is. That's why he's plastered to the floorboards." Mehan handed Tatyana the strip of newspaper. "Soon as you got some *real* evidence, you be sure and give us a call."

THIRTY-TWO

After the detective left, Jerry explained he and Julio were going to try and find an ally within the local force, then swing by some of the churches with big Hispanic populations. Wayne had no intention of leaving the terrain unguarded. It both surprised and warmed him, though, how Tatyana insisted on staying with him.

He couldn't tell her how often he'd been there on his own before. "It's fine," he told her.

Tatyana saw Jerry's smirk and asked, "You think I am funny?"

Jerry said, "No, sister. Wayne is one lucky dude, is what I'm thinking."

"This is a serious issue," Tatyana said. "This is a safety issue."

"You've been calling the man a warrior, right? I'm guessing our hero will be just fine on his own."

Tatyana made him wait at the entrance while she walked across the street and bought them sandwiches from a deli-grocery. When she returned, she drove them back to the north point and parked just past the Neally entrance. A pair of giant live oaks formed a living canopy over the road. The street was completely empty.

They unwrapped the sandwiches, pastrami for him and tuna for her. There was a tension in the silent car. A pressure Wayne found he did not mind in the least.

She waited until they had both finished their meal to ask, "What do you hope will happen?"

Wayne glanced at the clock set in the dash. It had taken her forty-three minutes to ask the question. He liked that about her. This sort of patience was not normal in Americans. He had seen it overseas, where television and film and games and life's rush meant nothing. He liked it a lot.

Wayne replied, "We won't know until we see it."

She nodded. Accepting both his answer and his lack of certainty. She gave the silence another fifteen minutes. Then she asked what he had been waiting for.

She said, "Do you want to tell me about her?"

A simple no would shut that door. Wayne knew she would never ask him again. And he was tempted. He had, after all, been storing away his secrets for years. This was not something the military had taught him. He had been working on that trait a long, long time.

Even so, he replied, "My whole life feels like one giant mistake just rolling into the next one."

He expected her to deflect. That had been his experience with women. Tell them the raw truth, even when they'd asked for it, and they'd change the subject.

Instead, Tatyana turned in the passenger seat so she was half facing him, and said, "Tell me the worst."

"There are a lot of those too."

"Pick one."

That was the trouble with memories. Lift the lid looking for one, and all sorts of beasties started crawling out of the pot. "When I was fourteen I got arrested for the second time. Maybe the third. A buddy lifted a car and I went along for the ride. When my dad came down to get me, we had to sit with a police counselor while they decided whether to book me or not. The counselor asked my father if this was typical behavior for me or if this was something new. Pop told the lady, 'The boy's been looking for trouble since the day he discovered long pants.' They booked me as a juvenile accessory and gave me ninety days, suspended."

"So you never had anybody stand up for you."

"Eilene did."

"She is what, three years older than you?"

"Two."

"She was a child then too. I meant someone who mattered when you were young and most vulnerable. Someone who could shield you from harm and offer you a way out." She started to reach for him, but stopped herself. "We have more in common than you realize."

"I bet you didn't make a profession of learning all the wrong moves."

Her gaze was not so much open as bruised. He glanced over and found himself unable to look away.

She did not demand so much as softly remind. "We were talking about you."

A pair of white egrets stalked insects by the side of the road. Their impossibly slender legs took ballet steps through the trimmed grass. "Patricia and I were just kids when we got married. She was eighteen and I was a year older. By then I'd aced my basic training, advanced infantry, long range surveillance, whatever they threw at me. For the first time in my life I'd found something I was good at."

"What about accounting?"

"That came next." The army's logic defied explanation. How they managed to tie him into the office corps was anyone's guess. But they did. Him with the two stripes and a whole truckload of gung ho, getting strapped to a desk. The lieutenant in charge knew there had been a mistake the instant Wayne opened his jacket. He promised to do what he could, if Wayne would give him his best until things got sorted out. What neither of them had expected was how much Wayne enjoyed the work. Wayne told Tatyana about the class work, the simple pleasure he found in making numbers talk. "The instructor and the lieutenant said I was one in a million. Words I'd never heard before. I was almost sorry when they pulled me into Ops."

But not for long. The training and the high-wire tension molded the recruits into the first real family he'd ever known. Which was true for a lot of the grunts. Misfits with a lot of reasons to rage, learning how to turn their fury into the edge to stay alive.

He realized he'd gone quiet. "Sorry."

She gave him that smile that remained buried down so deep he wondered if he was the first who had ever seen it. "For what?"

What she said next caught him totally off guard. "I used

to think getting the worst over early had its advantages. After that, life would just get better. That kept the pressure on me. Made me work harder for what I wanted to achieve. There must be worse things in the world. I know that now. But back then, I only knew my life. Being beautiful, becoming a woman, and locked up in a Siberian orphanage. That is what I have tried to run away from. And failed."

The bruises in her gaze had grown deeper still. Wayne stared at her face and wondered if, in fact, the conversation had ever really been about him at all. "I'm so sorry, Tatyana."

"I was married to Eric six months before I ever mentioned this. When I did, he acted like I had something wrong in me, not being able to walk away from my memories. I used to think that was why he cheated on me with those women. I learned later that there had been many of them. I thought maybe he did it because I couldn't let the past go."

"Listen to me. I don't know him and I don't know what happened. But I know this. He never deserved your trust."

Then the car appeared.

Tatyana said, "It's the maid."

Wayne opened his door and slid out. He leaned back in and spoke hurriedly. "When she stops, try to see if she'll tell you anything more. I'll be around. You won't see me but it doesn't matter. Call me when you can."

She started the car. "I'll be back as soon as possible."

He did not shut the door. "Promise me we'll finish this talk later, okay?"

She looked at him but did not speak. She did not need to.

THIRTY-THREE

Jerry answered the phone with, "Yo."

"Where's Julio?"

"Working the crowd outside this church, place used to be a warehouse. You oughtta see him. Got the ladies all cackling, crowding around like he's giving away candy. What's up with you?"

"I'm sitting in a tree watching the Neally house. Tatyana just left, following the maid. She took off in a brand-new canary-yellow Escalade."

"Must be the wife's car."

"That's what I'm thinking. I'm hoping she'll stop at the market or someplace and let Tatyana in on what's happening."

"I don't like you sitting surveillance with no backup. You keep your phone on. We'll get back over to you soon as we can."

Wayne cut the connection, then checked to ensure the cell phone's ringer was set on silent buzz. He slapped the lid shut, stowed it in his pocket, and lifted his head just in time to watch a limo pull into the Neally drive.

The stretch Lincoln had all its windows down. There was just the driver and one man in back. Wayne knew it was a man because of the jacket sleeve and the edge of starched white French cuffs and flash of gold cuff links. The man was hidden behind a newspaper. Another day, another deal. Wayne's perch was a live oak whose branches grew out and over and dug back into the earth again, following the wall that fronted the Neally estate. Unless someone looked straight up, Wayne was invisible.

Wayne waited until the limo purred up the long drive and disappeared around the side of the house. He waited until the silence took charge once more. The street was empty save for the wavy heat rising off the asphalt and the golden rivulets of afternoon sunlight lancing through the higher limbs.

Wayne rose from his crouch and climbed up one level. A bough thicker than his waist extended a full thirty feet into the Neally front yard. Wayne scampered out to where the limb began rocking under his weight. He crouched and readied himself to drop to the ground. The house was just visible through the foliage, about seventy yards to his left.

He stopped.

The sprinkler system for the house next door switched on. Wayne listened to the metallic rush and smelled the wet. He swiveled slightly and studied the Neally house. The yard and the home looked utterly empty. A squirrel leapt from the ground onto the tree about fifteen feet from where he crouched.

Wayne listened to the squirrel's claws scramble across the bark and felt a rising sense of dread.

He crawled back along the tree limb to his lair. Far more than the surrounding leaves blocked his vision. Wayne pulled out his phone. He stopped in the process of opening it. He did not bow his head so much as curl his entire body around the apparatus. What was it Victoria had said he needed? His chest quivered with a laugh that was far more irony than humor. If gut-level truth counted for anything, he had prayed more in the past twenty-four hours than in the past two dozen years.

When he dialed, Jerry answered with, "You missing me?"

"Where are you now?"

"Ten minutes out. Less. Why?"

"Something's happened. A limo just pulled in the drive."

"Who was it?"

"Couldn't tell you." Wayne realized then what had been bothering him. "What kind of guy rides in the back of a smoked glass limo with all the windows down?"

"Is this a trick question?"

"Think about it."

"So the dude's a fresh air freak." But more serious now.

"The driver too?" Wayne said. "Both of them in suits? On a day this hot and muggy? The newspaper he's holding rattling in the wet wind?"

Jerry took his time, came back with what was already rocking Wayne's brain. "They wanted you to see inside."

Wayne nodded enough to make the limb creak. "One man and his driver."

"Which means they got a welcome committee waiting for

us." Jerry was talking to himself as much as to Wayne. "How'd they do that? The place is one way in, one . . ."

Wayne supplied what Jerry had already realized. "They came by boat."

"Worked for us."

Wayne was very pleased he had a sudden reason to grin. "I've got an idea."

❦

Jerry stayed trapped inside his thoughts as they drove toward Lantern Island. He had to hand it to the kid. While Jerry had remained in the truck, the kid had glad-handed his way through three churches, trading jokes with the ladies, coming out with everything he could possibly hope for. Call it fifteen minutes for each, start to finish. The kid would make a good undercover cop. Which was not why Jerry was glum. He felt let down by his own side, Mehan giving him "chain of evidence." Jerry knew exactly what had been going down and he didn't like it. Mehan was resisting a handover to the Naples white-collar crime unit. Maybe he was worried the white-collar crew would ridicule his lack of solid evidence. But Jerry had started case files with less to go on. He was thinking either Mehan feared losing control of the case or he was just plain lazy. And neither of these was a good response to a request from another cop.

But that wasn't the real reason Jerry burned inside his own skin.

As they approached the final stoplight before the turn to Lantern Island, Julio shifted in his seat and said, "What about you, bro?"

"Don't call me bro."

"You been around Miss Victoria for years, right? How come you're not saved?"

Jerry stopped at the light and looked over. It was the exact sort of conversation he'd be having with a long-time partner. The two of them easy in silence until one gave voice to a thought, usually starting midway through the concept. Like they were so in tune with one another they could assume the other would understand everything that went before.

Only this was with a barrio kid, him of the low-rider pants and the juvie sheet sixteen pages long.

Even so, Jerry hated how Mehan had treated Julio. The sneer, the suspicion, his ready attitude to slap on the cuffs first and search out the reason after.

Which was exactly how Jerry had acted.

That was what burned his craw.

Jerry said, "Who says I'm not saved?"

The kid shrugged. "The smell of this pizza is killing me. Okay if I have some?"

"Wait till we're through the gate. The guard sees you chomping down and smeared with tomato sauce, he's gonna know something ain't kosher."

"What, you think I can't eat and stay clean?"

"Just hang on a sec, we're almost there."

"I know how to eat, man. I ain't no animal." Julio turned glum. "I know some, though. Animals."

"So how come you're not a banger? Last I checked, the Churos still had your area locked up tight."

"Them and the Black Hands, yeah."

"So you never joined?"

"They started on me. I talked to Eilene."

"And?"

"She never said. But I think she phoned my old man."

It made sense. "That was smart."

"Or my brother. One or the other. I think. They never said. All I know is, one day they were on my case, the next and I had this bubble around me—they see me coming, they cross the street."

Jerry made the turn. He glanced over, saw how the kid had gone morose on him. Amazing how the simplest question could rake across old wounds. "I asked for a miracle once. God said no. I got mad. End of story."

"You don't believe in miracles?"

"I didn't say that." He slowed for the guard station. The guard checked their day pass and opened the gate. Jerry waved his thanks and said, "But no. Matter of fact. I don't."

Julio grinned. "We're sitting here, talking like two normal people. That's a miracle in my book, man."

Jerry rolled his window back up. "You got me there."

⟐

The first thing Jerry said when Wayne opened the truck door was, "How'd you do that?"

"Move over." When Julio shifted Wayne climbed in. "Did the guard call through?"

"Checked our day pass and license number is all. Now answer the question. I was watching all the angles, I glide the street, I park a block away, then poof, up you come."

Julio said, "Man don't need no cape to be super bad. But if you got one of them Bat-cars, I'm claiming shotgun."

"Dude don't need a black car with fire out the back end. Man's already got hisself a Ferrari. That ride and that lady, I'd say the combo's good for a shiver."

Wayne took note of the change in the truck's atmosphere, the easy grin the two men shared, but decided there was nothing to be gained by asking about it. "Where's the pizza? I can smell it but I don't see it."

"What Julio didn't scarf is behind the seat."

"Right. Like you didn't hose down five slices."

"Two. I ate two."

"Whatever. Man looks at me holding the box—don't touch that, don't touch, then whoosh. The box is empty."

Wayne asked, "You ate all the pizza?"

"We got two more, don't worry."

"And a Coke, you get thirsty eating yours." Julio twisted around, came up with a pungent box and a can. "The driver there, he can talk your head off, going on 'bout how hungry you get on stakeouts. Like sitting in a hot car watching an empty street is something I need to know about."

Wayne ate a slice, drank, asked Julio, "Tell me what you're going to do."

"Man, there you go with the rocket science again. Jerry already melted my brain with all his orders. You want a blueprint, call NASA."

"Got to admit, the kid has a point," Jerry said. "Julio carries the pizza boxes to the door and rings the bell. How hard is that?"

Wayne selected another slice. "You're taking his side now?"

"Whatever gets this show on the road."

"You've got your gun, right?"

Jerry lifted his shirt. A snub-nosed revolver was attached to his belt. "Haven't taken it off since they nabbed Foster." He watched Wayne eat, and asked, "You phone the lady and tell her what you've cooked up?"

Wayne took another bite, shook his head.

"No, best not. She'd probably go all lawyerly on you, want you to sign some release or something."

Wayne finished his slice and the Coke, then slid from the truck. He stood holding the door and said to Julio, "Just don't go scouting the terrain looking for me or Jerry."

Jerry opened his door. "And don't go inside the house, whatever they tell you."

Julio looked from one to the other. "I been thinking. Miss Victoria, I know she'd like it if we prayed first."

Jerry's eye found Wayne's across the truck. His eyebrows were high enough to dig furrows across his forehead. "That a fact."

Julio nodded, said to the former cop, "You want, you can say the words."

"I told you already. God don't pay any attention to me."

"You don't know that."

"Kid." But the heat wasn't there. "You started this motor. You drive the car."

The men got back in the truck. When Julio was done praying, Jerry gave Wayne another look, as in, You believing this?

He climbed out, watched Julio slide behind the wheel, and said, "Tell me you've driven a truck before."

"Man, who you talking to?" Julio fired the engine. "I been boosting cars for years."

"Of course. Silly me." When the kid drove off, Jerry said, "Having a barrio kid talk to God on a cop's behalf, this day is already beyond strange."

Wayne doubted many pizza delivery drivers bounced the curb hard enough to lift all four wheels. But as far as he could tell, no one in the house took notice.

Wayne used the truck for cover until it was midway down the drive and passing a stand of pink oleander. He dove and rolled and crawled in a training ground sprint. By the time Julio pulled up at the front door, Wayne was on the house's other side between the bougainvillea and the concrete side wall. The bougainvillea had thorns like a cactus that sliced through his shirt. But he couldn't pull away. Because right then he spotted the first shooter.

The man was inside the house and moving fast. Wayne tracked him past three windows.

Wayne still wasn't sure how the game was going to play out. But he knew he had to do something. Standing there with a thorn in his rib and the heat pounding his head and shoulders, the clearest sound was of the clock ticking.

Julio whistled his way up the walk. The chains he wore for

a belt jangled with each step. His jeans flopped over his shoes. He rang the front door bell.

Wayne waited until he was certain the man was not going to answer the door. He searched the front lawn once more. Saw nothing.

He stepped out far enough to spot Jerry standing exactly where they had agreed, back where the road met the drive, hidden by the live oak where Wayne had crouched. Wayne waved his hand.

Jerry nodded back. He slipped behind the tree and disappeared. Across the street from his hideaway was the telephone pole connecting the house to the island grid.

Julio hammered on the front door. "Domino's delivery!"

There was a moment's silence, then a sharp *pow* down at the roadside, followed by a *crack*. The sparks flying off the transformer were less visible in the afternoon sunlight than at midnight, but impressive just the same.

Julio started to look back, but caught himself and pounded harder still. "I got the pizzas you ordered!"

The shadow inside the house moved to the doorway leading to the front hall and stopped.

Julio gave a shrug that could only be called theatrical, and started back down the stairs. He jangled and whistled his way down the walk and disappeared around the corner of the house.

The shadow followed.

Wayne ripped his shirt pulling free of the bushes. He sped across the front lawn, his back itching from the sniper's scope he feared might be tracking him. But he made the distance and took the portico's railing like a chest-high hurdle. He applied his forward momentum to the front door, punched the lock clear out of the doorframe. He stumbled slightly on the polished marble floor but kept his speed high enough to catch the shooter in the process of raising his gun.

The shooter had one finger pressed to his earpiece and his back to the front entrance. His arm was across his chest and blocked his shooting arm. He spun around and gaped at Wayne's charge and did his best to aim. But Wayne was faster, covering the distance in three giant strides. He hammered the shooter with an elbow to the throat and a fist to his chest. He gripped the shooting arm and wrenched the pistol free. He kept spinning around and applied the pistol butt to the same point where his elbow had struck.

The shooter flew backwards and crashed into the stools lining the half wall separating the dining area from the kitchen. He went down hard.

Wayne stripped the mike control box off the shooter's belt and fitted the unit into his own left ear. Still at a full sprint, he sped past the glass doors opening onto the pool area. He saw two men seated by the pool, or part of them, because the umbrella had been moved to where their faces were blocked from the house. Wayne moved to his right, the shooter's pistol in one hand and the communicator in the other. He heard two voices, both hissing for Paulie to reconnect. Another voice, one that crackled slightly, complained that they had lost all the leads to the house.

The house was shaped in a stucco U surrounding the rear pool with the Gulf sparkling in the distance. The right-hand room behind the dining area held a massive flat screen TV, entertainment center, and leather cinema seats. Wayne checked the rear doors again, saw just the legs of two men seated at the pool. A second umbrella had been dragged over and positioned so they were effectively protected from all sides. The suited visitor had slung his jacket and tie over a side chair. Wayne had time for an instant's wonder over the home's soundproofing, that a man crashing over a trio of wooden stools wouldn't even cause them to uncross their legs. Then he spotted the second shooter.

Julio came around the side of the house and raised his three pizza boxes in greeting. The shooter was half hidden in the shadows of the outdoor kitchen's roof overhang. Wayne opened the French doors and used Julio's loud approach as the only cover he was going to have.

This shooter was faster. He spun and got off his shot without trying to either crouch or aim. A half second more and Wayne would have been breathing through a new chest hole. But the bullet *whacked* as it passed him. The doors he had just passed through shattered. Wayne slapped the gun aside and chopped the guy in the throat. The shooter dropped his chin, but not fast enough. His eyes widened with the sudden effort it took to breathe and he gave a tight "Ack." He made his mistake then, trying to bring his gun around rather than protecting himself from Wayne's next blow, which was to hammer the shooter's left ear with the fist holding the communicator. The shooter's eyes fluttered. Wayne hit him again, this time with the hand holding the gun.

The shooter collapsed.

"*Down*, Julio! Get *down*!" Wayne did not take aim so much as let his gut direct him, taking him back and to the side. The third shooter rounded the house at the same moment. Wayne was one giant stride away. He leapt and caught the gun that came into view and wrapped both hands around it, dropping his own gun in the process.

The shooter got off two random blasts, blowing out something made of glass. Wayne was too busy to inspect for damage. He wrestle-danced his way across the pool deck, the guy using his free hand to land a trio of close punches. Wayne protected his head best he could with his near shoulder, kept a two-fisted clench on the gun hand, and raced for the blue.

They took their deadly tango into the pool.

Wayne came up for a single breath. Then he rolled and let the guy's struggling weight take him back under. Making sure to keep himself between the shooter and the surface. Focusing his strength upon the gun in his double grip. The shooter tried for Wayne's eyes, then his throat, missing both times. Then his roaring bubbles and his struggle slackened somewhat. Wayne pushed harder until the guy scraped against the bottom.

The gun hand released. Wayne wrested the pistol free. He swung around behind the guy, gripped his throat from behind, and kicked off the bottom. Headed for light and air.

The shooter came up choking and floundering for the poolside. Wayne let him dog paddle for them both. When the shooter made the side, Wayne swung onto the ladder. He shifted his grip on the pistol and came out of the water aimed for the pair still seated under the umbrellas.

"Do us all a favor and point that thing somewhere else, won't you."

Wayne stripped the water from his face. Saw Julio rise slowly to his feet.

"Excellent. Now the gang's all here. How convenient."

Wayne squinted hard, working to bring the man into focus. Try as he might, the guy seated beside Trace Neally remained Eric Stroud. Tatyana's ex.

THIRTY-FIVE

Wayne said, "Keep your hands where I can see them."
"By all means." Eric Stroud was far too relaxed.
"How's this?"

Wayne was still doing a one-handed wipe of his face and getting used to the fact that Tatyana's ex-husband sat at the poolside when Jerry came around the side of the house. The former cop looked very glum and held his hands higher than the lawyer.

Which was hardly a surprise, since he had a pistol jammed between his shoulder blades.

"Who woulda thought," Jerry said. "Thirty years' practice and I still get blindsided by a limo guy hiding in the shrubs."

Wayne said to the lawyer, "This is your one and only chance."

He knew something was seriously awry when Eric leaned back in his chair and laughed. "Excellent line, Mr. Grusza. But it happens to belong to me."

Wayne motioned with the pistol at the two approaching shooters. "Call off your dogs."

"By all means." Eric asked the driver covering Jerry, "Did you show him?"

Jerry answered for the driver. "They got Tatyana, man. In the trunk."

⁌

"Bind their hands."

Wayne knew they expected him to resist. He saw the glimmer of metal as the second shooter stepped to a firing angle, one that would let him get off a shot without risk of hitting his mate. Wayne held himself perfectly still. The man behind him dripped on his arms as he fitted the plastic tie and drew it tight enough to pretty much halt the flow of blood.

When they tied up Julio, he yelped. "Ow, man, not so tight."

"Take it easy on the kid," Jerry said.

A voice replied, "I'll give you easy."

The man turning out Wayne's pockets used the process to get in a few quick punches. The limo driver searching Jerry said, "Hey, Mr. S., this guy's packing a badge."

"Let me see that."

"That's right," Wayne said. "You're actually ready to kidnap an Orlando police officer?"

"Retired." Eric slipped the leather wallet into the pocket of his jacket. "If they were the least bit interested in what this grandfather had to say, they'd have paid more attention at the gate."

"Who says they didn't," Wayne retorted, and heard how lame it sounded before the words were even formed.

Gold fever. Wayne recognized the glitter in Eric's eyes. He had seen it often enough before. Guys trained in every conceivable form of violence, facing the terror of a tomorrow when their only skills became outlawed. They could dump it all in a carryall and hide it under floorboards in a closet, or they could pretend it was all just over and done. Or they could turn rogue. A lot of Wayne's former buddies had talked the dream. Joining the mercs and taking on a major score. Nighttimes in the desert had been good places for such tales. Wayne had seen a lot of other eyes show that same feverish gleam, as the ultimate questions were finally asked. How much would it take? And what would they do to get it?

No question. Eric's number had come up on the screen. And his response was locked in the trunk of his limo.

Eric turned to the shooter still covering Wayne and said, "Go get Tommy."

The guy Wayne had laid out still wore grass stains on his face. "He's just coming to."

"I didn't ask how he was. I said get him." He turned to Neally. "Up."

The board member had observed the entire scene with a look of helpless tragedy. Wayne said, "They nabbed your family?"

"Borrowed," Eric corrected. "I'm an attorney. I prize proper syntax. We borrowed them. Temporarily."

Wayne asked the silent, defeated man, "You believe that?"

Eric said, "I could gag you if you want."

Wayne asked, "What is it you're after?"

"That is no longer your concern. Not that it ever was." Eric picked up Wayne's phone from the glass-topped table and dialed a number. "You have two choices. You can tell the man what has happened, or I will have the gentleman you dunked shoot you in the knee. I will hold the phone while you scream. Then I will say the words. It hardly matters."

Wayne knew before the phone was pressed to his ear that Easton Grey would be on the other end. He said, "They have us."

"Wayne?" The man sounded weak with confusion. "Triton has just made a ridiculously low offer to buy my company."

He felt the pistol barrel drill into the point where his jaw met his ear. "Me, Jerry, Julio, Tatyana. They have—"

Eric took the phone away. "Do what is required, Easton. And all this will go away."

He tossed Wayne's phone into the pool and said to the driver, "Put all three of them in the trunk."

"It'll be a tight fit."

"Good. Fit this one in close to my ex. They were so chummy at the club. I wouldn't dream of keeping them apart for an instant longer than necessary." He did not smile at Wayne so much as reveal what lay beneath the surface. "If this one gives you any trouble, break something."

THIRTY-SIX

Wayne knew he was going to have one chance. Not even that. A fragment of a chance. Maybe less. Maybe the only way he could do it was take a hit. One thing for certain, though. Wayne was not going inside that trunk.

What did they call those people, the ones that got stuck with arrows or boiled in oil, and got their agony frozen in colored glass for their troubles? Martyrs. Right. That was him. Wayne Grusza. A martyr for broken promises and impulse control.

Just like now.

"Move."

Wayne wanted Eric talking. A talking guy meant part of the brain was occupied with something other than watching. "Why, Eric?"

The shooter behind him said, "No questions."

"Why did you—"

Wayne stopped because the guy he'd dropped in the pool whacked the back of his skull with the pistol. "Shut up."

But Eric took the bait. "Why does anyone do anything? Profit and personal gain."

"Triton?"

The space between the house and the property's side wall was constricted by the limo and the shrub border. Tall blooming oleander in shades of ivory and coral framed the drive and hid the cement wall. The ground underneath Wayne's feet smelled of the cedar chips bordering the trees. Wayne's every sense was on full alert.

Jerry was directly in front of him. The cop shuffled with shoulders slumped and wrists bound behind his back. Julio was in front of Jerry. One shooter stood by the open trunk. Another, the guy from inside the house, was out back somewhere readying the boat they used to get here. The limo driver stood on the car's other side, watching it all with a sardonic smirk. The other shooter followed directly behind Wayne, his wet pants flapping with each step. Wayne slowed slightly, as though uncertain where to go. The shooter stepped in close enough to prod the pistol into his spine. "Step it up."

Eric said, "I had always considered the islands too restrictive a place to live. But that was before Triton introduced me to the pleasure of flying by Lear."

"Talk about flying." Wayne saw Julio glance into the limo's trunk and blanch. "Sorry about what happened to your Ferrari."

The pistol jammed Wayne's skull this time.

"No. Wait." Wayne heard the approaching footsteps. "What's the matter with my—"

Wayne used the limo's fender as a launching pad. He

climbed straight up, the last thing in the world they expected. He knew that because of how they all stared as he tightroped two steps alongside the open trunk lid, pausing only to spin and toe-kick the wet shooter in the temple, sending him flying into Eric. The limo driver had his gun raised but was clearly worried about hitting his boss. The guy behind the limo was blocked by the open trunk. Or so Wayne hoped.

He pounded across the limo's roof and sprang impossibly high. He crested the oleanders and the wall, but barely. He did not so much step across the wall as try and keep himself erect for the landing.

The wall's opposite side was laced with gravel bordered with rail ties. His hands were bound behind him, so he just rolled and rolled until his face met grass. A rock or rail tie or something had jabbed him hard. The way it hurt when he pushed himself to his knees, using his chin for balance, Wayne feared he might have cracked a rib. He stumbled away from the muffled shouts coming from the wall's other side. He jackrabbited over the low hedges lining the front walk and raced around this home of stone and mock coral.

Wayne was spurred on by his one glimpse into the limo's trunk. When his climbing had rocked the lid, the opening between the lid and the car had sliced across a vision of dark hair, taped mouth, and terrified grey eyes.

The boundary walls were faced in stone like the house. Shouts and curses bounced at Wayne from every side. He could not tell where they were, but he knew they were coming.

For once, he hoped for motion sensors in the lawn. But he couldn't count on them. Tatyana's survival depended upon his getting the one chance not just right, but solid. So when he rounded the neighboring home's rear corner, instead of peeling for the water like he should, Wayne raced midway back across the lawn.

Then he turned around and took aim for the home's rear glass doors.

Fast as he could.

Head down and legs pumping almost to his chest.

Not even thinking how much it was going to hurt when he hit.

Wayne's catapulting leap took out not just the glass but one entire door panel. He slid on the interior tiles and heard the broken shards beneath his body. He knew he was going to pay for that one. But right then he didn't feel any pain, not even from his rib. Because out front was the sweetest melody, a constant *whoop-whoop* of the house alarm.

"Come and get me!" He actually yelled it out loud.

THIRTY-SEVEN

The evening shadows were long enough to drape across the entire street. Wayne limped from palm to shrub to telephone pole. Lantern Island was one of the oldest developments on Florida's Gulf Coast, which was why the lots were so deep. Nowadays waterfront lots were cut so skimpy and the houses built so big, a sneeze was enough to break the boundaries.

Those were his thoughts while hustling along in pain and solitude. A meandering assortment of nonsense that kept him from focusing on the *other* thoughts. As in, the state of his body.

He could have waited for security. Should have, most likely. But he then risked meeting some ambitious kid who saw Wayne as his chance to break into real copdom. Do the interrogation himself, lock Wayne in a back room until he figured how to best work the whole deal. Wayne had no idea how real the risk was. He only knew he couldn't afford the threat of more lost time.

He walked.

The island was so quiet Wayne had no trouble hearing a car

long before it appeared. He crouched behind whatever cover was closest while one security car after another cruised by. They might always be so diligent, but Wayne didn't think so.

The limo with its overstuffed trunk had taken off soon after the house alarm had sounded. One of the shooters had come over for a quick scout, but Wayne had remained safely hidden in a pantry off the living room, far from the broken back window. He had heard an outboard motor roar into life and then someone shout a name. Tommy. Twice. The shooter had cursed and fired two rounds into the kitchen wall before taking off. Wayne had stayed where he was long enough to be sure they were truly gone. He had used the time to work on his plastic band with a paring knife he had picked up off the kitchen counter. But he had been unable to saw through the band. The plastic seemed as strong as steel. Or perhaps it was his urgent need to scoot before the security arrived.

He had slipped the knife into his rear pocket and headed out, making it to the shrubs on the opposite side of the street just as the first patrol car had flashed into view.

His hands were still bound but they didn't bother him anymore, which Wayne took as a bad sign. His rib hurt and blood from a slice across his forehead wouldn't stop dripping into his vision. He felt something dig into his right thigh with each step. Wayne assumed it was glass. He kept to the grass so he wouldn't leave a telltale trail on the asphalt for any vigilant patrol.

He half walked, half trotted past the scam accountant's house. Police tape fluttered in the breeze, blocking the drive and the front portico. Wayne kept looking over, wondering why he felt as though he was missing something. But Dorsett's house was empty and so silent he could hear the plastic tape flap in the wind.

Up ahead at the next house, the lights glowed rich against the backdrop of blue and gold water and green and golden lawn. The setting was a tropical version of paradise, far too fine for this troubled earth. Too nice as well for the man scurrying along the drive, doing his best to keep to the long shadows.

At the edge of the porch, Wayne froze.

Up to that point, all the way across the island, the clearest sound Wayne had heard was the ticking clock. Now even this was almost drowned out by something completely different.

Inside the house, a child laughed.

Wayne stood at the porch stairs and willed himself forward. But he could not take that first step.

He could not risk frightening the child. The little boy lucky enough to live in this place. Nurtured and kept safe and loved by his parents.

Wayne stayed like that, frozen between his need and his inability to reveal the world's underbelly to the child inside that house.

He had nowhere else to go. But he could not take the risk.

He turned away.

He was midway down the drive when headlights appeared at the road's far turn. Wayne trotted around the back of the garage and waited.

A car purred down the drive. The garage doors ground up. Wayne hustled back around and stepped inside just as the engine died. He waited.

The passenger window powered down. A man yelled, "I'm calling the police!"

Wayne's relief was so great he had to choke out the words. "Ask for Detective Mehan in Homicide! Tell him it's an emergency!"

From beyond the garage's perimeter, a small voice called, "Daddy!"

Wayne flinched so hard he stumbled over a child's toy and went down hard. He rolled under the other car. "Don't let him see me!"

"Stay out, Roger!"

"Daddy's home!"

"Daddy's still working. See the phone? Go back in the house. Tell Mommy I said not to come out."

"But—"

"Do what I say, Roger!"

"Okay."

Wayne remained on the cold smooth concrete. His rib throbbed from the latest fall. He watched the approach of polished loafers attached to legs in fashionable trouser legs. "Is he gone?"

"You're tied up."

"Your son. Is he gone?"

"Yes."

"Did you call the police?"

"You want me to?"

"Yes. Hurry. Detective Mehan. Homicide. Tell him it's—"

"An emergency." The man spoke into his phone. "They want to know who's calling."

"Wayne Grusza."

There was a longer pause. "Wayne?"

"Tell him."

"All right. He's coming."

"There's a knife in my back pocket. My hands, I can't feel them anymore."

"Are you dangerous?"

Wayne found it good to chuckle. Even when it hurt. "Not to you."

THIRTY-EIGHT

R obert was his name. Roberto, actually. Roberto Pavet. Mother Nicaraguan, father Cajun French. He was a small-ish man, neat and concise with his movements as he led Wayne around the house and into the bathroom connected to the pool. "Can you undress yourself?"

Coming from a doctor, it felt less like an insult. "There's something in my leg."

He bent over. "Hold very still."

The pain was almost cleansing. "I'm sorry about this. I had nowhere—"

"Clean yourself off and I'll have a look at your wounds. How are your hands?"

"They hurt a lot."

"That's a good sign." He shut the door.

Wayne let the shower run as hot as he could stand. The water at his feet pooled pinkish. Robert returned with a ratty towel, his doctor's bag, and clothes. He dumped Wayne's tat-tered garments into a plastic waste can.

Wayne cut off the water. "I'm going to bleed on your towel."

"This one doesn't matter. Slip into the shorts. No, leave the shirt off for now."

Wayne did as he was instructed. Robert then turned and said, "You can come in now." To Wayne, "No, stay in the shower. All right, your head first."

Wayne gripped the shower stall and leaned forward. Patricia slipped in the door and leaned against it. She said nothing. Just watched him.

The doctor's hands were deft, his motions swift. "What happened?"

"We are investigating a scam involving people who live on the island. It turned bad."

Patricia asked, "Our neighbor?"

"He was one of them."

"I'm going to need to stitch this. Do you want something—"

"I can't. They've kidnapped my friends."

Patricia asked, "That lady?"

"Yes. And three others."

Patricia crossed her arms. Wayne winced, not at the needle in his skin, but the memory. It was so familiar, that gesture. He had watched it so often. The trigger was cocked and she was about to fire. Like so many times before.

Patricia said, "I have something I want to tell you."

Robert glanced around, then went back to his stitching. He was a handsome man with a polished Latino edge.

Standing so close only accented the difference between himself and Wayne.

Patricia took a breath. A big one. "I need to tell you how sorry I am."

Wayne rocked back. Robert warned him with his eyes. Stay still.

"I had no business talking to you the way I did there on the bridge. But seeing you there . . ."

Wayne waited until Robert had snipped the dangling thread to say, "It must have been a major shock."

She held up her hand. Not in the angry manner of before, pushing hard against the distance between them. Just asking for patience. "I've told myself a hundred thousand times, I needed to find you. Speak to you about, well, everything."

The words seemed to take shape of their own accord. "It's not just you. I should have called, told you I was coming. But I couldn't either."

This time she nodded agreement. "Then there you were, with a police car and those tense men and that woman. I wasn't ready. I should have been. I've prayed about this for *years*. But all I could think was, you're back and you're going to destroy what I've built for myself and my family."

"I don't want that, Patricia."

"I just wish . . ." She fought against the tremble that struck her chin. When she could not hold back the tears, she fumbled for the door and slipped out.

Robert sighed. A quiet professional sound. "Okay. Turn around."

Wayne emerged from the bathroom to hear, "Daddy, why is the man wearing your clothes?"

The boy had his mother's blond hair and a pure Florida tan. He was an impossibly beautiful child. And immensely happy.

Wayne made a process of looking over the room, keeping his gestures slow and steady. "You have a beautiful home."

"Come sit down. You must be hungry. Roger, this is Mr. Grusza. Say hello."

"The man wearing Daddy's clothes?"

"He got his clothes dirty."

"He fell down?"

"Twice," Wayne replied. He slipped into the stool at the kitchen counter next to the young child. "At least."

"I fall down too."

"Finish your supper, son."

There was a cross between the pair of sliding doors that formed the kitchen's rear wall. The child was watching cartoons on a television tucked into an alcove at the end of the counter. The sunset splashed upon the entire setting, the water's motion sparkling the walls and the faces with a beauty so strong it almost masked the adults' strain. Wayne saw how the two of them would not meet his eye, and felt bulky and threatening. "Could I use your phone?"

Robert set the handset on the counter in front of Wayne without meeting his eye. Wayne dialed information and asked for Easton Grey's residence on John's Island.

"I'm sorry, sir. That number is restricted."

He pressed the phone to his chest. Only one other name came to mind. He asked for the number, then when he realized he did not have anything to write with, he asked the operator to put him through.

In his weakened state, it seemed as though age had distilled the woman's sweetness to a point where she could soothe his spirit merely by saying hello.

"It's Wayne, Victoria. I need to contact Easton Grey and I was hoping—"

"He's here."

". . . What?"

"He came with his family. He got word of some mess—I didn't ask and he didn't say. But I was there at the house and I could see he was worried. So I invited him home. He's been trying to call you and the others but no one has answered. Where are you?"

"Easton is there?"

"I just said that. What is the matter, son?"

He tasted every different response, then finally turned away from the boy and said softly, "I'm with my ex-wife and her family."

The two adults glanced over, then away.

Victoria said, "Your ex-wife."

"Yes."

He expected his father's style of criticism. As in, stern disapproval over having let the faithful side down. Instead, he got a soft, "Life is so very complicated sometimes."

It felt so good to smile. "You can say that again."

"How are things, son?"

He touched the bandage on his forehead and murmured, "Difficult, but better than I deserve."

"May I have a word with her?"

He did not hesitate. The fact that he did not understand changed nothing, given who did the asking. "Patricia."

"Yes?"

"A friend would like to speak with you."

She looked at her husband, then doubtfully accepted the phone and stared at him as she said, "Hello?"

She listened a moment, then said, "We are. Yes."

Whatever she heard caused her to turn away from both men. She traced one finger around the corner of her son's finger painting attached to the refrigerator door. She did not speak until she finally said, "All right."

Patricia handed back the phone, her expression directed inward.

Victoria said, "We're all praying for you, son. Here's Easton."

Wayne rose from his stool and moved stiffly to the rear doors. When the man came on, Wayne said, "They've got them. Jerry, Trace Neally, Julio, Tatyana." The last name cost him dearly.

"They are messengering over the documents. I'm to sell my company for shares in Cloister."

"A wholly owned subsidiary of Triton," Wayne said. "Nothing more than a brass plaque on a wall outside a Cayman bank."

Easton gave it a minute, then, "I want to come help you. I can't just sit here and wait for them to steal my entire life's work."

Wayne knew the man was ready for any argument. Instead, he said, "Ask Victoria what she thinks."

Another pause, then, "You want me to ask this lady's permission."

"If she says it's okay, call me back here." He heard the front bell. "I've got to go. The police are here."

Wayne held back, and Patricia understood. "Go see to them, Robert."

"They're here about him."

"Please."

The doctor didn't like leaving Wayne alone with his wife and son. But he did as Patricia asked.

Wayne handed back the phone and said, "I'm the one who has to apologize."

Patricia looked at him. He could understand her shocked expression all too well. He never apologized. It was one of his defining traits. The tough guy whose life depended upon getting it right the first time, every time. Or so his excuse had always gone.

Not anymore.

"Everything you said, everything you ever accused me of. It was all at least partly true. I just want to say I'm sorry. I wish I could have been a better—"

"Mr. Grusza?"

Wayne recognized the detective's voice. He finished, "I'm sorry I wasn't the man you deserved."

THIRTY-NINE

D etective Mehan arrived with an officer from their white-collar division, a young woman with an old face named Karen Watanabe. The two officers listened in silence as Robert described how he had discovered Wayne, bound and bleeding, then as Wayne described what had happened at the Neally residence.

The woman said, "You're suggesting they've taken these actions to force Easton Grey to sell his company."

"They've made no other demands," Wayne replied.

Mehan said, "On the surface the whole deal is beginning to look like we should be involved."

But the woman was not convinced. "Why doesn't Triton just up their bid?"

"Up to now," Wayne pointed out, "Grey's firm was buying Teledyne."

"Teledyne is part of Triton?"

"Not that I can determine. They're in a couple of partnerships together."

Watanabe looked at Mehan. "Can we get back to the office? I've got a ton of stuff on my plate."

"What about the kidnappings?"

"Sir, excuse me," Karen Watanabe said. "What was your name again?"

"Wayne Grusza."

"Right. For all I know, you folks have a scam of your own going here."

The homicide detective protested, "Come on, Karen."

"No, Mehan. They've got nothing to suggest this was more than a response they cooked up to a hostile takeover."

"I've checked him out. Grusza was full-on Special Ops. Afghanistan, medals, the works. You heard how he arrived here."

"That's a sign that a criminal act has taken place. Sure. But nothing to tie it to what he's suggesting."

"What about the dead guy next door?"

"You were there the same as me. We got nothing out of that. Place was totally clean."

Wayne asked, "What about the money inside his safe?"

Mehan looked at Wayne. Then the cop actually smiled. "There's a safe?"

❦

Wayne's conversation with Easton Grey caused them to delay leaving the house. Victoria did not think Easton should risk travel. In a moment of inspiration, Wayne asked for someone else to come represent the company. Wayne used the time to eat his first meal since the slice of pizza, which by then felt like a dozen years ago. Patricia reheated a black bean soup, then prepared more for the two detectives. Wayne tried to thank the homicide detective for taking his side, but the cop shrugged it away as no big deal.

When they left the house an hour later, the sky was a raucous assortment of blues and copper. The earth sought to expunge its load of heat bulked up during the long summer day. The air stayed humid, a cloying mixture of blossoms and bay water. Thunder rumbled in the distance, but the storm remained well beyond the horizon.

Watanabe was still unconvinced as they left the house. "I still haven't heard back from the lieutenant as to what our role should be here."

"We're rolling, Karen. You want to hang in the car, be my guest."

"We got no warrant, Mehan."

"This is still a crime scene, remember?"

She looked at Wayne. "How did you know about the safe anyway?"

Wayne caught Mehan's warning glance and replied, "Long story."

She swatted at the bugs flitting around her face. "That's your answer?"

Mehan said, "Works for me."

Wayne did not mind the argument or the pace. He walked the street and reveled in the night. Even the humid seaweed-laden air tasted sweet. Something had definitely altered his internal universe. He had sat with Patricia and they had talked. More than that. She had voiced regrets and fed him. He had apologized. Such simple acts when viewed from the side of it all done and gone. A few short moments an eternity in the making.

Mehan's phone rang. He pulled it from the belt, listened, then said to Wayne, "A company rep is at the front gate."

The female cop said, "You're inviting more unauthorized personnel into a crime scene?"

Mehan crossed the lawn and climbed the front steps. "In case you hadn't noticed, Karen, we got a murder that's growing colder by the minute and no suspects."

Mehan was peeling back the crime scene tape when headlights pulled into the drive. Wayne said, "I'll get him."

The engine died. A door slammed. The all-too familiar voice of Jim Berkind barked, "Of all the people in the world, why do you have to bother me?"

FORTY

The interior of Zachary Dorsett's home was in total disarray. Furniture was ripped open, tables overturned, paintings torn apart and their frames shattered. Cushion foam littered the floor. Watanabe pointed at the fingerprint powder staining the walls and doorframes. "Think we'd find a match here, Grusza?"

Jim Berkind, the bullish executive, groused his way inside. "What is this, your twisted idea of payback? So I got a little aggressive in the conference room that day. Sometimes aggressive is the only way to get the job done."

"Through here," Wayne said.

"I don't appreciate this. Being dragged away from vital work and ordered to drive halfway across the state."

The kitchen floor was littered with smashed plates and the debris from upended drawers. "Triton has put in a bid to take over Grey."

Berkind froze in midcomplaint. "That's insane."

"Actually, the offer came from Cloister. Which is basically

323

the same thing." Wayne watched the blood gradually drain from Berkind's features. "Easton Grey didn't tell you anything?"

"I've spoken to Mr. Grey maybe three times in my life. Tonight he phoned and ordered me out here." Berkind's voice had gone reedy. "I said I wouldn't do it. He offered to send up security to help clear out my desk. He said you'd asked for me."

"That's right."

Berkind took a slow look around the wrecked room. "What's going on here?"

"Tatyana's been kidnapped. And Trace Neally's entire family."

Watanabe snorted and kicked a wall. But she was listening. Wayne could tell.

"Wait. You're saying they're gone?"

"Tatyana and Trace were snatched this afternoon. And the big former cop you met at the airport."

A hint of color returned to his features. "I didn't *meet* him. He *attacked* me."

"Focus, Jim. They're *gone.*"

Watanabe shook her head. Snorted quietly. But kept listening.

Berkind said, "Grey's been hit with a takeover bid?"

Wayne laid it out for him. The evidence he'd uncovered, the linked companies, the scam that had brought them there. It wasn't his best job, but with everything piling in, he had every reason to get the pieces a little jumbled.

Berkind asked, "Why isn't Easton here himself?"

Because a frail old woman said God told her the CEO

should stay with his family. Wayne said, "Call him. He'll confirm everything I've told you."

Berkind wore his thinning dark hair plastered carefully across his bald spot. He mashed it flat with a hand that trembled badly. "This doesn't make sense. Why would Triton move on us?"

Wayne saw how Mehan was watching Berkind. Giving him a cop's look. One that sparked Wayne at gut level. "What's the matter, Jim?"

"Matter? This changes everything."

"You were getting a payoff for making this work," Wayne realized. "Who was paying you?"

Jim turned and faced a cabinet with the doors ripped off.

"Come over here and sit down, Jim." The man had gone so limp Wayne could shift him with two fingers. "The payee. Is it the same guy who ordered you to confront me in the conference room?" When Berkind remained silent, Wayne pressed, "Tell me who that was, Jim."

"You don't know him."

Wayne heard Mehan start for the guy and raised his hand. *Wait.* "I don't need to know him. Was it a board member?"

Berkind's swallow was audible. "Not Grey's board."

"It was one of Cloister's board, wasn't it, Jim."

"How did you . . ."

"I told you. Cloister is owned by Triton. They want the Grey Corporation so bad it's got our friends kidnapped and Easton's home bugged."

"Oh. So he's Easton to you now."

This time it was Watanabe who said, "Focus, Mr. Berkind."

"They're working a scam," Wayne said. "The guy who lived here is part of it too. Or he was. He's dead."

The sheen of moisture had spread from Berkind's forehead to cover his face and stain his shirt collar. "What?"

"He was popped." This from Mehan. "Two to the heart when he opened his front door. A professional hit."

Berkind gestured weakly at the surrounding destruction. "This is tied to Triton?"

"Maybe." Wayne took the executive's arm. "Let's go see."

FORTY-ONE

The safe still contained two shelves of cash. The cops got seriously excited about that. Watanabe phoned for a forensics team and started photographing and labeling the find. Wayne didn't care. He searched everywhere and came up dry. The money didn't help him, except that the cops were behind him now. But the cops didn't have any more answers than he did.

Jim remained blanked out, staring only at the inner desolation. He gave no resistance as Wayne pulled him back into the living room. "Do you have your computer with you?"

Berkind wiped his face. "I'm seriously in debt."

"Jim, this is not about you anymore." When the guy only glazed over more, Wayne said, "Look. You help me, I'll talk with Easton. He can try and arrange something."

A glimmer of something came back into his eyes. "Yeah. Sure. I can do that."

"Great. I need a computer with a hookup to the Grey mainframe."

The thread of hope had Berkind's entire body nodding. "It's in the car."

⟨⟩

Darkness webbed the living room windows. Berkind was both there and not there. He responded to Wayne's questions in a robotic drone. Otherwise he stared into his own private abyss. Mehan was long gone, called to another crime scene. Watanabe had come and gone from the room several times. She was back now and Wayne knew she wanted to ask what he'd found. But he was glad she kept quiet. Even staying silent like she did, her presence severely spooked Berkind.

Berkind had asked Wayne, "Am I going to jail?"

Pressure stabbed behind his eyeballs, making it difficult to keep hold of his calm. "I've already told you. This isn't about you anymore. This is about clearing up a mess you helped cause. This is about saving innocent lives."

Berkind mashed the strands hiding his bald spot. As though the scalp marked a point where his turmoil threatened to erupt. "They called it a consulting fee."

"Your contact with Cloister." They had been all through this before. But the computer was giving him nothing.

"Yes."

"Did you ever meet with Eric Stroud?"

"Who?"

"Tatyana's ex-husband."

The hand froze in midpat. "Kuchik was married?"

Wayne eased the strain in his neck muscles. The mantel clock with the shattered face lay upended on the tiles. It read nine o'clock or a quarter to midnight, depending upon the angle. Wayne decided it was the perfect timepiece for this night. "Let's go back to the data on your computer."

"I never worked with Kuchik before this deal came up."

"Fine. I need your help here, Jim."

Watanabe was a compact woman in her midthirties. Her hands were stubby, her motions quick and economical. She gave Wayne the impression of someone who put in serious gym time. She spoke to Wayne like Berkind was not there. Which was at least partly the case. "Can you give me the lowdown on this guy?"

"Berkind is one of the execs responsible for the hotel division. How many hotels does Grey operate, Jim?"

"Thirty-seven in nineteen states."

Someone called Watanabe's name from inside the safe. She said to Wayne, "Which gives us nothing, right?"

Wayne felt the pressure build, like Watanabe's question was pushing him in a direction. One where he should be finding answers. He resisted the desire to stand up and add his own furious search to the room's chaos. "Not that I can see."

She headed back toward the kitchen. "We're almost done here. I'll need to lock up."

Wayne watched her leave, then asked Berkind, "Can I use your phone?"

He passed it over. "Are we finished?"

"Soon." Wayne punched in a number and moved to the rear of the room.

Easton Grey answered. "This time of night, I figured it had to be you."

"I feel like it's right here in front of me. But I can't—"

"Pull it together. Happens to me all the time." He spoke in the quiet voice of being surrounded by sleepers. "Has Berkind been helpful?"

Wayne glanced over. Berkind had once been a powerful man. Now he sprawled on the sofa, so slack if Wayne had torn off the man's suit he might ooze into a puddle on the tiles. "Yes and no. He's drowning in debt and has visions of doing hard time."

"I'm still trying to get used to the concept that one of my senior executives had anything to do with this."

Wayne turned back to the window. Florida houses were built to let in the light. But when the light went, the house became rimmed with night-stained mirrors. "I don't know what to do."

"There's nothing harder for a strong man to accept than helplessness."

His inky reflection revealed far more than his physical form. A man who had made a profession of needing no one. A man whose greatest pride was in handling life on solitary terms. Even when it cost him his marriage. Sharing his utter helplessness now with a man he had only days ago called a stranger. "My gut tells me it's right here."

"Well, this time of night, the only thing I can suggest is for us to—"

"Pray," Wayne said. Filling in not just the word, but the

bond between them. He took a long breath. "I want to say the words."

"Go for it."

There came that pause. A moment beyond time. Wayne did not let his head drop so much as remove his focus from the window and toward the unseen.

Then a thought hit him square between the eyes. "Hold on."

"Yes."

"What did Berkind do before?"

"You mean before his current position?" Grey thought a moment. "I should know. But I have forty-seven vice-presidents, and it's well past midnight."

"Hang on." Wayne turned around. "Jim."

The man blinked slowly, like he was coming back from another space entirely. One lined by concrete and steel bars.

Wayne raised his voice. "Yo, Jim."

Watanabe appeared in the kitchen doorway. Wayne asked, "What positions did you hold before this one?"

Even before the man answered, Wayne knew he had scored. Watanabe pushed herself off the doorjamb. Both of them brought to full alert as Jim Berkind straightened with the stiff tenseness of a puppet.

"I've been with the Grey Corporation for eighteen years."

Wayne lowered the phone to his side and walked over. "Tell me what I want to know, Jim. Your last job. What was it?"

Berkind had the expression of a trapped and exhausted weasel. "I ran the land bank."

Watanabe said, "What?"

The phone in Wayne's hand squawked. Wayne felt all the pieces fall into place. "That's what this is all about, isn't it, Jim."

Watanabe said, "Is that your phone?"

Wayne clipped it shut without taking his eyes off Berkind. "You fed them the list." But his gut told him, "There's more than just that, isn't there, Jim."

"I want a lawyer."

Wayne heard Watanabe's footsteps scrunch over the debris and kept his voice calm. "Sure, Jim. Sure. The cops will be happy to get you lawyered up. But you're not under arrest, right, Detective?"

"Absolutely not."

"See, Jim, right now we're only talking about a misuse of your corporate position. You bring in a lawyer, they could take you downtown as an accessory to an abduction. Several of them."

Wayne felt the sofa dip as Watanabe seated herself beside him. The detective said, "Not us. If there's any indication they crossed state or national borders—"

Wayne said, "Cloister is based in the Caymans."

"There you go. So we're talking a federal offense. Maybe I should phone the feds now."

Berkind's face had gone so slick it might as well have been oiled. "I don't know anything about that stuff!"

Wayne leaned closer. The man gave off a tinny odor. "You

fed them the list, and you showed them which properties were seriously undervalued."

Berkind's hand on his face made a squishing noise. "It wasn't supposed to be like this."

Wayne slid over the computer. "Show me the list."

FORTY-TWO

The car drilled through a Florida downpour. Watanabe drove like a cop, which meant she held to a speed that bordered on reckless. She punched through turns and steered with one hand, even after the car twice slammed into troughs of rushing water. "I sure hope you know where we're going."

"This is right." Wayne gripped the door handle and held Berkind's computer wedged open between his knees. He tracked their progress on the laptop's GPS linkup. Outside he could see nothing save the flash of falling rain in their headlights, slick streets, and the empty wetness of central Florida.

"What you were working on with the guy back there. The company's property. What did you call it?"

"A land bank. Companies like Grey keep most of their capital in something other than cash. Cash doesn't pay dividends, cash doesn't build jobs or extend the company's reach, and too much cash can attract the wrong kind of buyers. Grey is a developer. Their bank was real estate."

"And this list you were working on there at the end?"

"Berkind did several things. My guess is, he convinced himself that none of them were totally illegal. But all of them were very wrong. He valued the land bank's assets at the prices they were originally bought at. But Florida land values have skyrocketed. So if a buyer acquired the Grey Corporation at book value, they'd be looking at huge profits."

Watanabe's free hand reached for the coffee mug in the cup holder. "This is why I love working fraud."

"It gets better. Berkind then took this list of undervalued assets and linked them with land that Cloister and Triton held through partnerships. He pushed them into other partnerships that would build more linkages."

"These links are important?"

"The hardest asset for a developer to locate these days is prime waterfront property. The larger the site, the bigger the project. The bigger the project, the greater the profit. Not just total, but per square foot. It's called economies of scale. The bigger the deal, the less it costs them to build each segment. Which is why Triton went after the property owned by the retirement community where I live. They are building a development just north of there. They wanted to expand, but the retirement community wasn't selling. So they brought in a scam artist to drive the community into bankruptcy."

Watanabe slipped the mug back into her cup holder. "We're talking major buckaroos, right?"

"The developments would be worth hundreds of millions of dollars."

She glanced over. "I was totally out of line with you earlier."

"That's okay."

"Is it true what Mehan said about you being Special Ops?"

"Yes. I did two tours in Afghanistan."

"And here you are now, a CPA. Man, that's a trip."

Wayne rubbed his face. The numbers and the names behind his eyes jerked and danced. He had to be right about this. "I really appreciate your taking me out here."

"Least I could do."

"I might be totally wrong about this."

"Hey. Won't be the first time I've chased down a ghost. Or the last."

"This is your turn up ahead. Highway 120."

"I was watching you in there with the man. You're good. I mean, this is obviously tough and you're still holding it together. You handled Berkind like a pro." She jammed them through a slewing left. "You ever thought of joining the force?"

Wayne stopped rubbing his face. "No."

"Maybe you should. Your background, the accounting angle, that's some combo. White collar is always on the lookout for fresh meat."

Wayne studied her. "Thanks, Detective. I appreciate that."

"The name is Karen." She met his gaze for an instant. "The lady up ahead, she's special to you, right?"

Wayne turned his eyes back to the night and felt his gut clench. "If she's there at all."

FORTY-THREE

They pulled up in front of new metal gates that glinted silver and wet in the headlights. A massive chain clenched the gates shut. A *No Trespassing* sign banged a strident beat in the wind.

Watanabe squinted into the rain. Other than the gate and the rattling sign, the night was utterly empty. The first faint light of a grey wet dawn revealed scrubland and stumpy palms and not another soul. "Explain it to me again how come you're so sure."

"First back away from here, in case somebody is watching."

Watanabe reversed them back onto the main road and down another fifty meters to where a ranch trail opened on the highway's other side. "This do?"

"I went through all the sites they're putting together. This place is perfect."

"How so?"

He pointed to a massive dirt hill in the distance. "Behind that dike is Lake Okeechobee, the largest inland body of water in the southeast US. Forty miles across. Nine miles north of here is Port Mayaca, the point where the Inland Waterway enters off the Saint Lucie Canal. Boats can cross the lake, connect with the Caloosahatchee River, and follow that all the way to Cape Coral, Fort Myers, and Sanibel Island. And from there on into the Gulf of Mexico. It's a perfect inland development, Detective."

"I told you to call me Karen."

"They own seven square miles here. It's a small city just waiting to be built. You got Palm Beach forty miles to the east, some of the most expensive real estate in the world—"

"Okay, so it's perfect for building. So why are we here?"

Wayne pointed to the north. "Three-quarters of a mile up there is a small tributary. And on that tributary is a motel. My guess is it used to be a fishing camp."

"Used to be."

"This was the only name on the land bank list that was described as derelict. There was no mention of structures on any of the others."

She tapped her stubby fingers on the steering wheel. "I call the local sheriff at this hour and request an emergency warrant, you know what they're gonna tell me."

Wayne opened his door. "I'm not waiting."

She sighed but did not object. "You keep your phone on the whole time, you got me?"

⟨℞⟩

The actions were so ingrained he would never lose them. Wayne melded with the grey fractional light, with the rain, with the rising wind. It was all cover. He moved with the ease of a man who was born to slip in and vanish, like the trace of wind that slid under a door or through a crack in the shutter. A tiny little rattle was all the sign he gave of his passage. A splash of water, a shiver of motion. Less than the rain falling off a rattling palm frond. Less substantial than the dawn.

He covered the three-quarters of a mile in about seven or eight minutes. He waited until he was within sight of the roofline to turn on Berkind's phone. He called the number Watanabe had given him. "I'm thirty yards out."

She hissed, "I told you to keep that sucker *on*."

"There's no outside sentry. I'm moving closer."

"Wait, Grusza, *wait*."

He put the phone back to his ear. "I'm here."

"Let me call this in."

"Do whatever you want, Karen. But I'm going in." He clipped the phone shut.

The tributary was the size of a large creek and heavily overgrown. Wayne slipped into the water and used mangrove branches to pull himself hand-over-hand, keeping a close watch for snakes and gators. Rain dimpled the creek's green waters. Up ahead he heard the faint sound of a radio or television. Coming from what was supposed to be an abandoned motel. The sound amped his heart rate to where he could scarcely breathe.

The fishing camp's side of the tributary was marked by rotting timbers and the remnants of a marina. He crawled out of the water and took cover behind a pair of rusting gas pumps. The rain swept in hard, then subsided. But the wind grew with the grey light, making it impossible to see more than a dozen or so yards ahead. Wayne readied himself for a sprint across the cracked concrete ground, the open and coverless terrain between himself and the first building.

Then he froze.

A figure came around the corner of the building. He was covered in a grey poncho with the hood pulled far down. His shoulders were hunched and he was far more concerned with keeping dry than watching for someone coming out of the dawn.

Wayne checked in both directions. Saw no one. He leapt forward.

His feet scrabbled over loose rock. The man jerked around. Through the rain dripping off the poncho's hood, Wayne caught sight of two startled eyes. He recognized the same guy as he had taken down inside the Neally house. Tommy.

Tommy got a shot off at the concrete to Wayne's left just as Wayne's fist hammered his jaw. Tommy's eyes rolled back and he went down hard.

Wayne's ears rang from the gunshot and his nostrils were filled with the stench of damp cordite. Off to his right came a banging door and the cry, "Tommy!"

Another voice yelled, "Back over there!"

He thought he heard footsteps running from two different directions. He couldn't be sure.

He fired a round through the window directly in front of him and leapt inside.

The shouts were shriller now. Wayne rolled and came up with the gun extended. The room was empty. Rain swept through the open door, the door through which the guy must have just run. He ran after him. Speed was everything now.

Two bullets whapped the doorjamb as he exited. Wayne dove low and rolled. He felt the heat of passing lead and kept rolling until he came up against the corner of the next building. Two more bullets struck the wall beside his head.

Wayne scrambled to his feet and raced away. The motel was shaped in a U with the parking area in the center. Three trucks and a limo were pulled into the area. Wayne took the angle around the first truck too close and whacked his leg. He felt the stitches in his thigh tear. He heard more gunfire and the hammer of bullets striking metal. He ran around the next truck. Three shooters, he figured. The only good thing he could say about the odds was the men were all behind him. Wayne crawled under the limo and sprinted around the building's far eastern corner. Headed for the almost invisible dawn. Just trying to draw the shooters away from the people trapped inside those rooms.

Then he heard it. A motor far beyond redline. Screaming toward them, the engine bellowing in time to the siren.

Karen Watanabe's Crown Victoria slid on the wet road and skidded into the pillars fronting the motel office. The sign connected to the roof gave a rusty creak and came down on the hood. Watanabe burned rubber reversing back far enough to free up her door. She spilled out and screamed, *"Police! Put down your weapons and come out with your hands up!"*

Wayne raced through a ninety-degree change of course, heading back around the buildings now, pumping as fast as the sedan through the final corner.

The three of them were clustered there, looking through the opening between the side and rear units, clearly uncertain how to handle the sudden appearance of the cop. A cop that was now between them and escaping with one of their vehicles.

Wayne took them down like human bowling pins.

He pounded the nearest with the butt of his pistol. Kicked at another. Punched a third. Shouting half-shaped words and feeling his chest and gut impossibly tight, waiting for the strike that didn't come.

Instead, Watanabe said, "Okay, sport, ease up there. I got them covered. You three, spread-eagle on the ground. You're under arrest."

Wayne pulled out of his next punch, jammed the pistol into his belt, and raced off. Behind him, Watanabe yelled something about waiting, and evidence. He was too focused on what was ahead to pay any attention.

He did not bother with either locks or knobs. Doors were simply another foe to destroy. "Tatyana!"

He rammed his way into one room, then another. Empty. Then he found Neally huddled with a woman and two young children in the third room. In the fourth, Foster was on his knees by one bed, hands tied behind his back, with Julio and Jerry bound back to back on the other. Wayne was in serious conflict about whether to stop.

A voice called to him. Her voice. He ran back outside. *"Tatyana!"*

The voice came from the room behind the office. He demolished the door and the frame both.

She was tied but had managed to slip into the space between

the bed and the wall. Wayne lifted her back onto the bed, then made a mess of untying the knots. He knew she was saying something, but his heart was pounding so loud and his trembling was so bad he couldn't make out what she was saying.

But he knew how her mouth felt. He could feel the heat of her lips like a branding iron on his face.

FORTY-FOUR

Two days later, they were back home again. The police had not wanted to let them go. The cases kept opening up, more law enforcement types came and went—FBI, Treasury, IRS, state and federal prosecutors. But there came a point when all the questions had been answered at least once. So they shrugged off the demands and the complaints and they left. Tatyana slept over at Easton's that night. The Greys had a guest apartment that they said Tatyana could call home for a while. Easton wanted to have his legal representative close at hand while all the questions continued.

The next morning, Wayne went for a run with Julio. The kid stayed the distance, especially as Wayne had to take it easier with his restitched thigh. They stopped in front of the Cloister development and stared at the silent bulldozers and the empty half-finished structures. Then they turned and ran home.

When they got back and finished stretching, Jerry walked down from the porch to hand Wayne his coffee. All without breaking stride in his argument with Foster. "Nothing beat Sid Caesar for funny."

"Oh. Like you actually know what you're talking about."

"I know what I know, all right. Victoria, help me out here."

"You gentlemen are doing fine without me." She looked up long enough to smile at them. "Hello, boys. Have a nice run?"

"Julio pounded me into the dust."

"Oh, right. Like I suddenly got ready for the navy."

"Don't have anything to do with them pansies," Jerry said. "They got them pretty white uniforms, they might as well sashay around in a skirt. You want macho, you go marine."

Julio snorted but said nothing. Wayne pressed his grin into his knee. The kid was definitely learning.

Foster went on, "Ed Gardner, now, he was the king of funny. You ever see *Duffy's Tavern*? They had everybody on that show. Edward G. Robinson, May Whitty, Bob Hope, Fred Allen, John Garfield, Jack Benny, Tallulah Bankhead. Anybody who was somebody fought for a chance to get on *Duffy's Tavern*."

"Huh. You want talent, you don't got to look no further than Sid Caesar's radio show. They had Neil Simon writing with Larry Gelbart. Not to mention Mel Tolkin. Howard Morris. Mel Brooks. And what's his name. Max Liebman."

Julio asked Wayne, "You know what they're talking about?"

"I think you've got to be a hundred and nineteen to understand."

Jerry called over the porch railing, "You want, I can toss your breakfast out in the street."

Julio rose to his feet and pointed at where the Ferrari had sat under a live oak for four days. Long enough to become richly coated in leaves, pollen, and other donations. One of Detective Mehan's buddies had driven it back to the community. "The lady in the parking lot, she's crying for a bath."

Victoria said, "What about breakfast?" But the kid was already moving.

Wayne went in for a shower. He heard the voices through the bathroom wall. Then they stopped. He dressed and came out, pretty certain what he would find.

Tatyana was seated in his living room. She was dressed in what for her was very casual—white shorts and a rose-colored top that fell off one shoulder in a manner that was both modest and revealing. She had on no makeup and looked about nineteen years old. "I didn't ask them to leave."

Wayne stood in the doorway to his bedroom. "You're too fine looking for this place."

"This is your home, Wayne. I am very comfortable here, thank you."

He pulled a chair over. Glad now that no one else was there. "I need to finish telling you something."

"No, Wayne." She pulled up her legs and sat cross-legged on the couch. "Not unless you really want to."

"I want." And amazingly enough, he truly did.

"You are talking to a girl born in a place of ice and dark and cold. A small girl without family or friends. I grew up and tried to build order and protection into my life. Then a man hurt

349

me. Then another man. I vowed to wall myself up and never let anyone close. But inside I always yearned for someone to come for me. Someone good and caring. Someone..." She swallowed hard and clenched her features against the emotions, and she never took her eyes from his face. When she could, she finished, "You're not the only one carrying ghosts."

The simple acceptance made him want to reach over and kiss that incredible face. Like he had permission. Which, in fact, maybe he did. But the memories were pushing out now. He did not need logic to know it was time. "Patricia and I met, dated, and married. All in nine weeks and one day. The army is a lot of things, but flexible in its timing it ain't. I already knew we were headed out. Southern Afghanistan. Patrol duty. I had no idea what the words meant. I couldn't have found the Paki border on a map. But I was going, and she was willing, so we found a justice of the peace and got married."

He turned so the memories could scroll across the sunlight outside his front door. More than the trees' shadows cut the day's light without diminishing the heat. "Every time I got a leave, we fought. It wasn't working out and we didn't know what to do about it. She was in noncom housing outside Fayetteville, North Carolina, a tough place for a lady who'd never lived away from home before. Her folks were so upset over what she'd done, eloping with a guy they had met just one time, they basically just shut her out."

Strange how he could sit there in the shadows and see things so clearly. Far clearer than he ever had before. Distanced by the day and the woman listening so intently beside him. "I loved her and I'd like to think she loved me. But I just don't..."

"She loved you," Tatyana said softly. "Accept it for a fact and let it go."

He nodded without taking his eyes off the spooling memories. "I was totally conflicted. I wasn't ready to be a husband, much less a family man. But I loved her. I came back after my tour was over and had the two roughest months of my entire life. Duty upcountry was nothing compared to that. And it was my fault."

"Partly."

"No." He looked at her then. Ready to accept the word *guilty*. For the very first time. "I'd signed on again before I came home. They asked me to go back for another tour and I was ready. I loved her, but I knew I wouldn't be able to settle down. So I came back, but only halfway."

She started to say something, but stopped. Just rocked back and forth with her body, as though keeping the words inside forced her to do something. But her gaze never left his face.

"The month after I got back to Kabul, she wrote me this letter, blamed me for everything. I felt like I'd taken a mortar round straight to the heart. I tried to call, she wouldn't speak to me. I wrote, she sent the letters back unopened. The next communication I got from her was a request from her lawyer for a no-fault divorce. She got remarried as soon as it was final.

"The week before I was discharged, the guys in my platoon, they put together this going-away present, a duffel full of semi-stolen gear. Topped it off with instructions on how to take the guy out."

He had to look away. "I found out where they'd gone and I basically started stalking them. Her new husband was a doctor she'd met on base. When he went civvy they moved down here. Bought their place on the island about two years ago."

He wanted to stop. The shame ate away at his core. But the memories, now released, refused to stop. "She was a different woman. She had all the things I'd never given her. Happiness. A husband who came home at night. A real home." He took a very hard breath. "A son."

She reached over then. Just rested the tips of three fingers on his hand. Not saying a word. Just there.

Somehow the touch was enough to stifle the need to confess more. About how he admitted defeat and ran away. Again. This time running so far and so well he almost didn't make it back. Even now, wondering if he ever really could.

She rubbed his shoulder through the shirt. Back and forth. A gentle motion. Kneading away the ache.

If only she could do something about the memories.

Then again, maybe she could.

In time.

FORTY-FIVE

They sat there throughout the afternoon, sometimes talking, sometimes not, until Foster stumped up the front steps and called through the screen, "You folks about done in there?"

Tatyana smiled at Wayne. "No."

"Well, you got to come anyway."

They did not hold hands leaving the cottage. But there was considerable brushing against one another. Foster moved more slowly than usual. Wayne sensed something was behind the movement, something serious. He waved Tatyana forward and held back to match the old man's pace. "Where are we going?"

"You'll see." The old man gave Tatyana a small two-fingered wave. Go on. He said to Wayne, "I hear they been working their religion under your skin."

Wayne recalled something his sister had said. It seemed like years ago. Another lifetime. "Their faith."

Foster didn't limp so much as test each step in careful turn.

"When my wife got sick and then passed on, I pretty much fell apart. Not just emotionally either. Suffered a heart attack three months to the day after we put her in the ground. When I got back on my feet, nine months had passed and my nephew was running my company. Mine. Me and my wife, we sweated blood to make that thing work, and now it was gone. All of it. I hired a lawyer and I fought 'em and I lost. Not just money, either. When it was over, my family wouldn't have anything to do with me. Barely had enough left to buy this place. And no place else to go. Or anybody who wanted to ever lay eyes on me again."

Wayne saw the gathering up ahead, and understood when Foster stopped and took a step off the walk. He kicked at the pine needles spread on the ground and said, "Victoria won't have anything to do with me unless I get with the game plan."

"Not much of a surprise, given who she is."

"After I was kidnapped, the whole time I was left alone there in that room, the only thing I thought about was seeing how my hard heart and my stubborn ways kept me from her. Different place, same old man." Foster huffed a shaky breath. "I never thought I'd ever love another woman."

"She's as fine a lady as I've ever known," Wayne agreed.

Foster pulled off his glasses and pressed hard on his eyeballs. "You think maybe you could help me find what it is she's going on about?"

Wayne settled a hand on his bony shoulder. "What say we find it together."

FORTY-SIX

With Foster on one side and Victoria on the other, they led him back down past Jerry's house. On to the waterfront.

The strip of green was wall-to-wall food.

Every member of the community was there. Or so close to everyone that the few absentees weren't missed. Certainly not by Wayne. He had never seen so much food, not even coming into base from duty out in the boonies, when the cafeteria staff went all out to make them feel welcome. Nothing compared to this spread. The food smothered a half-dozen trestle tables covered with flimsy paper that flapped noisily in the late afternoon breeze. And that was the only sound.

Nobody made a big deal about his arrival. But he could see they had all been waiting for him. His voice sounded as loud as a megaphone when he asked, "What is this?"

Victoria replied, "Just a crowd of old people saying thanks."

A retired pastor said grace. They then made Wayne go

first through the line. Ladies stepped forward and explained with quiet pride what they'd made. He tried to take a tiny bit of everything and still wound up with too much. They made him take a nice seat there by the dessert table and left him pretty much alone after that, stopping by now and then to ask him how he liked the food or see if he needed another drink or just say how grand the weather was. The soft voices almost shy, the smiles when he responded as warm as the setting sun.

Harry, the guy with the faulty hearing aid, seated himself next to Wayne and declared, "Always did like my grub. Got bits and pieces falling off every whichaway. But I managed to keep hold of my appetite. Leastwise, I have so far."

His wife came over. "That chair is reserved for Wayne's young lady."

"She's down yonder flirting with Jerry. And this young man needs some company." Harry waved his fork. "Tell her, son, else she'll make me move."

"He's fine where he is."

"Hmph. I don't know what the world's coming to, a handsome young man doesn't have enough sense to go tell a beauty like that to join him."

Wayne waited until she had departed to say, "Any lady that pretty can pick and choose where she wants to sit."

Harry harumphed what might have been a laugh. "Seeing what she drives, I figure she's a prizewinner at the fast getaway."

Wayne ate until his belly needed a break, and set his plate on the grass next to his cup. The sun was about five degrees above the horizon, a huge orange globe that had lost enough of its heat to give the day a guise of easy comfort. The water was molten and gold. The breeze gradually diminished to a final consoling breath. A flock of migrating waterfowl, so numerous they resembled a cloud with a million wings, circled the bay once, twice, then came in for a landing. The grass and the trees and the weather-beaten cottages all melded into one sunset hue.

Harry set his own plate aside. "I was a schoolteacher back before the last ice age. Taught Greek and Latin and French. You know what my favorite lecture was? The hero. I looked forward to that year in and year out. The question of what makes a hero occupied Greek art and literature for over two thousand years. But not us. Today, we're *modern*. We've summed it all up in one flash-bang two-hour film. We say it's simple. A hero is a guy who *wins*. You know what I say to that? Rubbish!"

"Harry," his wife called over. "Pipe down."

"Rubbish," he repeated, only slightly softer. "A hero is somebody willing to risk all to gain all. It doesn't *matter* whether he wins or not. What matters is he tries. What matters is what he tries *for*." Harry pried himself free of the chair. "You want more lemonade, son?"

"I'm good, thanks."

Easton Grey slipped into the chair Harry vacated and asked, "Did Tatyana tell you what security discovered?"

"We sort of got sidetracked."

"Before we get into that, I need to tell you one other thing.

357

The two senior partners in Eric's firm, that is, the firm where he used to work. They are executors of my estate."

Wayne felt the familiar tightening of his gut. "So if you'd been killed, they'd have taken total control."

"They would have been responsible for the disposition of my corporate shares." Easton's smile was very tight. "They have spent hours trying to convince me they knew nothing of what Eric had been doing. Which brings us to point number two."

"The angel."

"It seems there has been an exchange student working in Eric's firm the past month. From Nigeria. Son of a chief, who also happens to be a pastor. A brilliant young man, on a full scholarship to Harvard Law. He's back in Boston now. I have not yet tracked down a photograph. But his description bears a remarkable resemblance to the man you and I confronted."

Wayne had to struggle to fit what he was hearing inside his brain. "He worked for Eric, probably signed a confidentiality agreement that legally bound him not to divulge what he knew."

"So he warned us without giving away anything," Easton agreed.

"He ordered you to hide and find yourself a human shield," Wayne said.

The company chief let that sink in a moment, then said, "Something else. Eric Stroud accessed your military file."

"Which explains what the African said to me about my past."

"If it was him."

"You still think it might have been an angel?"

Grey smiled and gave a general's shrug, one that could be easily missed. "I'm not so sure it matters anymore."

Wayne tasted that thought for a time, then slowly drew out his words. "What do you know. . . ."

"The truth is, I don't know much of anything at all." Easton fished in his pocket. "Except that I owe you an enormous debt."

Wayne saw what he was offering and said, "No way."

"It was Tatyana's idea. She knew you wouldn't accept money. So I bought this from her and now I'm offering it to you." When Wayne refused to take it, Easton set the gold-plated Ferrari key in his lap. "Along with a job, if you're interested."

"I'll give it some thought." Wayne found himself unable to stay where he was. He struggled out of the folding chair and meandered down the line of people. Smiling people. People who made him feel he belonged. Down the line beside the waterfront to where Jerry sat with Tatyana on one side and Julio on the other. Victoria and Foster were an arm's length away. Easton's daughter was seated on the ground between Tatyana and Victoria.

Wayne said, "I was thinking."

At that point, he found it necessary to stop and catch his breath. He tried again. "I was thinking maybe we should all take a run up to Disney World. Show Julio the sights."

The kid went round-eyed. "No way."

Clara, Easton's daughter, hugged her coltish legs up tight

to her chest and turned to Victoria. "Say you'll come with us, Maliaka!"

Jerry asked, "What did you call her, girl?"

"Maliaka. It's what the village children called her back before. In Africa." Clara beamed at the older woman. "It's Swahili for angel."

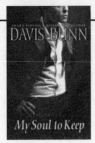
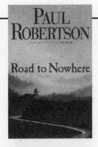

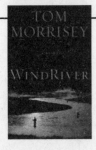

Looking for More Good Books to Read?

You can find out what is new and exciting with previews, descriptions, and reviews by signing up for Bethany House newsletters at

www.bethanynewsletters.com

We will send you updates for as many authors or categories as you desire so you get only the information you really want.

Sign up today!